# THE ALEUTIAN PORTAL

## A SAM REILLY NOVEL

Christopher Cartwright

*To my good friend Mike Riley,*
*whose sense of humor and love of the outlandish*
*were the basis for this novel.*

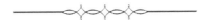

# CHAPTER ONE

*Bering Strait — Present Day*

THE PASSENGER STUDIED the face in the old American passport. He bit his lower lip as his eyes locked onto the photo. It looked distant, almost forgotten, yet familiar too. Like a relative he'd once known well, who had passed away when he was just a child. He'd been living a lie so long he'd almost forgotten how to distinguish it from the truth. He read the name along the bottom line out loud, *Ryan Balmain.* That too, seemed familiar to him, yet somehow aberrant and grotesque — because for nearly twenty years he'd lived in Russia under the name of Sergei Orlov.

Hearing the sound of his real name brought back a flood of memories. Some good, some not so much, and one in particular he'd spent that entire time trying to forget. He sat on the portside observation deck looking out as though he was a passenger on a cruise ship without a care in the world. But like everything else about him, that too was a deception. He was neither a paying passenger, nor was he on a cruise ship, and despite his outwardly calm appearance, he was terrified. He was on board the Russian owned, *Gordoye Dostizheniye* — a five-hundred-and-sixty-foot cargo ship.

The captain of the vessel had been heavily bribed so his name was not entered into the ship's registry. Nor was there any financial or other way to make a connection between him and the customized shipping container, numbered 404. The owner of the large container was registered to a Rare Arts and Antiquities House in Seattle. The captain made it abundantly clear to him that the onus would be on Balmain to enter the USA on his own, and that if he was caught, the captain would cast him off as a stowaway.

Balmain felt his chest tighten as he imagined the ramifications of getting caught. No, he needed to illegally enter his own country of birth. Balmain had once been an undercover operative for the CIA, but that was a long time ago. His parents died when he was still in basic training. He had no siblings and few friends—certainly none who would notice if he disappeared—and as a consequence a recruiter from the CIA contacted him for an undercover mission.

He thought about the recruiter, too. Had they sent anyone else, he might have rejected the idea at the outset. But they had sent Margaret—a young, attractive woman, with dark red hair and olive-green eyes, which he recalled were as inviting and tempting as the Devil. She was to be his mentor, and despite a nagging uncertainty, he was never able to reject her offer. Like a beguiled teenager, he'd accepted what she proposed—and as a consequence had spent the last two decades living a lie in isolation in a foreign country.

*Reminiscences!*

Balmain snapped the passport shut, as though by doing so he could erase the image of her face from his memory. Margaret had unwittingly been the greatest source of his happiness, regret, and profound remorse over the course of his life.

He thought about the fateful night when everything changed. To save her life, he had to maintain a secret so dangerous, that it might just destroy the current structure of modern civilization.

Balmain forced himself to smile with the practiced expertise of a spy. It had been long enough that he doubted he still had anything to fear. He'd done some terrible things in those days. But that part of his life had been over for a long time—nearly twenty years to be exact. He'd stayed away from that past, living and working as a fisherman in the coastal port of Pavek, Russia, on the edge of the Siberian Sea.

Not many days went by without thinking about that night all those years ago. His crime had remained buried for nearly two decades. He had doubted that anyone would ever ask about it in his lifetime. And then all that had changed two weeks ago— when he received a call from a girlfriend from long ago, and his crime came crashing down upon him. After all this time Margaret needed the truth to be brought to the surface. No, he would pay for that crime. It would be a sacrifice he was only too willing to make. But the question remained, would he still be able to protect her? Could he protect any of them?

He glanced upward. The sky was a crisp, empty cerulean blue. Even though the time was only 2:45 a.m. the permanent sun of the arctic summer shined with an obtuse glare on the north-eastern horizon. The air this close to the Arctic Circle was just shy of freezing. He wore a heavy woolen jacket, which he'd pulled upward until it covered the lower half of his face. On his balding head, he wore a thick beanie pulled down until the only visible aspect of his face was his eyes—dark brown, nearly black with specks of gold that had once made him highly attractive as a young man.

Even that much betrayed the physical harshness of the life he'd led. The skin around his eyes bore tiny creases and damaged blood vessels, the give-away marks of an alcoholic. His eyes were intense and the pupils heavily dilated. The U.S. Navy, Coast Guard, and Russian Warships were all out there— anything, even a small aircraft could mean trouble. The approach of a US Navy vessel, Coast Guard, Russian Warship, or even any fixed or rotary wing aircraft. He found nothing. The sea was a glassy millpond devoid of any other vessels.

It was a relief. Not that he expected any trouble. His crimes were committed long ago. His eyes darted across the coast, taking note of the tiny island of Little Diomede, with its big brother behind it. Balmain waited a few minutes and then stood up, ready to take refuge in the dark confines of container 404 once more.

He reached for the door, but stopped short of opening it. Balmain's eyes were fixed on the little island to the portside. It looked impossibly familiar. *No, it couldn't be!* He remained transfixed, as the *Gordoye Dostizheniye* passed what appeared to be the same bit of land for the second time in the past few minutes. He'd been lost in thought, watching the sea from the portside observation area below the amidships deckhouse. But the tiny island of Little Diomede, with Big Diomede on the horizon it was distinctive. He could swear they'd passed by them only a couple minutes ago.

The tower of containers on the deck behind him prevented a visual from the opposite side of the cargo ship. From the deckhouse itself, situated high above him between the stacks of containers and straddling the ship from port to starboard, he'd be able to command a 360-degree view. With no sense of movement aboard the heavy vessel, he couldn't be sure the ship was circling, which was the only explanation he could come up with. It was immediately followed by the conclusion that there was only one reason for the *Gordoye Dostizheniye* to circle back around in the middle of the Bering Strait—someone wanted to board the ship.

It meant someone knew he was on board. And that person almost certainly knew the contents of the specialized shipping container numbered 404.

*How could THEY possibly know that it had survived all these years?*

Balmain opened the door and started to climb the steps. He could hear the pounding of blood in the back of his ears as he climbed the series of steel steps to the bridge that stood nearly a hundred feet above the waterline. Balmain had expected to face the consequences of his past actions. But not here and not now, where it served no purpose whatsoever. When he reached the top, he burst open the door and entered the bridge.

Inside he found a very different chaos than the one he feared. Officers barked observations and commands at each other, while the captain stood at the port side of the deckhouse, focusing on something in the distance.

Balmain approached quietly. He felt the pace of his heart slow and his breathing settle. If there had been a boarding party, the captain and his crew would have simply slowed down and allowed the routine boarding of either the Russian or the US Navy to occur. The pandemonium he saw in front of him spelled a far more significant disaster. Perhaps there had been a collision with a smaller vessel, and they were going back to help? Or maybe there was damage to the hull and the ship was taking on water.

Either way, it meant there wasn't a boarding party and that he was safe. Hell, if the ship was mortally wounded he didn't even care. Port Clarence was less than fifteen miles away to the southeast. He was sure the *Gordoye Dostizheniye* could limp that far.

Balmain crossed his arms and set his jaw firm in an overt display of concern to override any chance of the crew noticing his starkly contrasting appearance of relief over the unfolding disaster, whatever it might be.

His eyes swept the sea, following the direction of the captain's fixed gaze. He cast his own farther and farther out until he spotted it—a maelstrom created an unnatural shape in the water like a giant eye, with a deep, abyssal black that left no doubt that its steep, churning sides led to a deadly fate in deep water.

"What in holy hell is that?" he whispered, more to himself than to the captain.

"Our death!" Shaking himself, the captain turned to his only passenger. "We must abandon ship. Go find yourself a lifejacket and go to your assigned lifeboat."

"Lifeboat?" Balmain was certain he'd misheard the captain. "Surely we're more likely to survive in a ship this size than a tiny lifeboat."

The captain ignored his question and instead strode away from the observation windows, calling out the order to his senior officers to be relayed to the crew. He ordered the radio operator to broadcast a mayday and then get to safety, before heading below himself to make sure his crew was all accounted for.

Balmain watched the crew increase their already wild pace. Incredulous, he listened to the communications officer give out a distress signal. He took a moment to digest the news, his gaze rapt upon the unbelievable sight.

In that moment, the ship inched perceptibly closer to the turmoiled water. It was clear she was circling closer and closer, and would be swallowed with ease sooner than he could fathom. The turbulence looked to be half a mile in diameter, far larger than the ship's five hundred and sixty feet could possibly overcome. She was circling faster now, and Balmain finally understood the implications. The circle was getting tighter. The ship was in the grip of an irrevocable tug toward the void in the center of the vortex.

His thoughts flew to the item stored in the shipping container. He'd sworn to protect it with his life—a statement he was only just now realizing he would have to commit to. In one giant gulp, the sea was going to swallow the ship whole, along with the specialized container. It would drown the hopes of the only woman he'd ever truly loved and those of the human race.

The profound knowledge triggered something primal in his brain to become active. Adrenaline surged throughout his body. Hopes and fears were sidelined while all of this attention and focus concentrated on what must be done. The only thing that could be done. He saw it with perfect clarity.

He needed to reach container 404!

Balmain opened the door and began his descent to the lower cargo hold. Six flights to the main deck and then five more to the lowest level of the internal cargo hold. His feet made a metallic clunking sound as he made a steady descent. He planted each step confidently as though reaching the container was far more important than the time it took. He knew there wasn't a lot of time before the *Gordoye Dostizheniye* went under, but there was enough time for what he needed to do.

Three levels off the bottom deck he was stopped by the captain, who appeared to be making a final search for any other crew who were still down below. The man was coming up from below and stepped in front of him, forcing him to stop. "You must abandon ship! There is no time! Where is your life jacket? Go, go! Save yourself!"

Balmain stared at the captain. His lips fixed in a sardonic grin. "Don't you see? No one can save us."

The captain moved forward to block his passage, and gripped him by his shoulders. "Good God man! Get control of yourself. You have to put a lifejacket on and find a lifeboat!"

Balmain struggled to push past. "Let go. I need to get to the container!"

The captain's eyes narrowed. "There's no time to retrieve personal effects! Surely you can see that!"

He didn't have time to argue with the captain. Instead he relaxed his shoulders. Took a step backward and then jabbed his right arm upward in one sharp movement. Despite his moderate stature, the punch had an immense and surprising amount of force behind it. His fist connected with the captain's nose. He heard the crunch of cartilage and bone being crushed.

The captain stood upright in a daze. Blood dripped from his

nose. He touched the blood with his hand and shook his head. He fixed his horror filled eyes at Balmain. "What the hell is wrong with you?"

"We can't save ourselves..." Balmain sighed as he met the captain's eyes with conviction. "But there might still be time to save the rest of them!"

He walked past the captain, who stepped to the side without saying a word. Balmain continued down the series of steel steps into the main cargo hold a farther three decks below without looking back at the captain.

Balmain stepped onto the steel passageway that ran the length of the ship. The hull creaked loudly in protest of the pressure being exerted by the ocean. It was a horrific sound. The metal was slowly becoming distorted, twisted and eventually would be torn apart as the behemoth vortex attempted to drag the cargo ship down by her stern.

The ship went quiet for a moment, as though its hull had somehow made some sort of gain in the battle to survive. Balmain continued moving toward the container. He knew better. The ship wasn't winning. It was merely in the midst of its death throes.

As though to confirm his suspicion, the silence was shattered by a series of loud popping sounds, as the glass portholes toward the stern finally gave way to the intense pressure being exerted on them. Seawater gushed in. He heard the roar of the automatic diesel motors kick into life as the bilge pumps attempted the impossible task of overcoming the incoming tide of seawater. The shallow wall of seawater lapped his ankles along the passageway. He moved quickly, but didn't rush. He had time. All he had to do was reach it. The water was at his ankles, gushing toward the *Gordoye Dostizheniye's* stern.

He followed the steel corridor eighty-five feet until he reached the container. The stainless steel specialized shipping container stood in a stark contrast to the other weathered containers nearby. It had a digital keypad on its side, perpendicular to the main door. Balmain calmly typed in the code and the door unlocked.

The door opened automatically and he stepped up into the dry water-proof container. Inside it looked more like something out of a spacecraft than a cargo container. It had been purpose built to protect and conceal the item. A small writing desk was mounted to the sidewall on his right. He quickly withdrew a black permanent marker from it, stepped outside and scribbled something next to the security keypad.

Balmain then stepped inside the container, switched on the internal lights, and closed the door. He listened as a series of hydraulic bolts moved to seal the container once more. He took a deep breath in, feeling more confident now that he'd reached it.

He could hear the rumblings of water now filling around the sides of the water-tight shipping container and made a silent prayer in gratitude that he'd reached it in time. He quickly scribbled a note to the salvage crew who he knew she would certainly send. He had no doubt she would. The only question was — would they be the first to reach it? When he finished the note, he read it again.

Now that he'd done all that he could, Balmain felt a sudden wave of relief. It was time now, and he would gladly pay for the crimes of his past. He felt the shipping container tilt downward, reaching an almost ninety-degree angle.

Balmain gripped the metallic hold on the side and felt the floor slip out from under him. A moment later his entire world was falling, like he'd just dropped off the end of a rollercoaster ride. Only this time his heart didn't race. For once, there was no doubt where this ride would end. There was no chance of survival. Instead of racing, his heart seemed to slow. As though it was simply biding its time, and counting the seconds until the very end.

A moment later, he felt the vibrations of the ship breaking apart around him and wondered if the purpose-built shipping container could possibly withstand the pressure.

There was no way to tell how far the *Gordoye Dostizheniye* had sunk. He mentally recalled the maritime maps of the Bering Strait. The depth was meant to be as little as fifty feet, yet somehow, he felt like he'd dropped hundreds of feet.

Slowly, the ship finally came to rest and the container settled at a forty-five-degree angle on its side. He glanced at his wristwatch. A handmade Russian mechanical chronometer. Unlike its quartz counterparts that required batteries, this worked on a complex series of springs and components that ingeniously self-wound to maintain time. He'd bought it when he first arrived in the coastal village of Pavek. He smiled curiously. In all that time, this was the first he could remember where the arm had finally stopped turning.

It now permanently read 3:10 a.m.

He looked up and stared at the stone—the cause of all his problems in the past twenty years—a lie against humanity. Standing four feet high and shaped like the letter T was the ancient megalithic stone structure. He looked at it once more— his eyes fixed on the image carved into its ancient surface—the tail end of a comet blazing through the earth's sky.

It was the last thing he ever saw, before the lights, damaged by the recent jarring movements, began to flicker and finally went out—leaving him entombed in pure darkness to await the death he now welcomed.

# Chapter Two

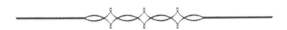

*Chukchi Sea, South of the Arctic Ocean — 3:15 a.m.*

S AM REILLY SAT up in his bed with a jolt. His heart raced as he felt a surge of adrenalin flow through his muscles, but for the life of him he couldn't remember why. He switched on a sidelight. He'd been in a deep sleep. It was meant to be another twelve hours before they reached the Queen Elizabeth Islands of the Arctic Archipelago.

*What happened?*

The sea gave little credence to the passage of time above the Arctic Circle where the summer's sun never fully disappeared. Instead, it required of those who navigated these waters to become attuned to every little change in the action of the sea. The thought triggered a memory. For a moment Sam found it difficult to distinguish between his dreams and reality. *Had he felt the Maria Helena shift direction?* They were approaching the open ocean of the Arctic, on their way to Nunavut, Canada, to study the depth of the polar ice cap. There had been a prolonged centrifugal pull toward the port-side of his bed. He glanced at the compass at the end of his bed. It showed a southwesterly heading.

*Why have we turned around?*

Sam climbed out of his bunk. He slipped into a pair of thick working pants, a shirt and sweatshirt. He slid his boots on and tightened the laces. He glanced at the clock fixed to the side of his bed — it read 3:18 a.m.

*So much for twelve hours of R and R…*

He closed the door to his cabin and ran up the three flights of stairs to the bridge. Inside, he found the heater set to maximum and Tom Bower at the helm. Wearing cargo pants and a Hawaiian shirt that made the bold statement of saying, "So what if I'm above the Arctic Circle, no reason why I shouldn't treat this like any other vacation." But Tom's eyes weren't as cheery as his shirt.

Sam said, "What's going on, Tom?"

"We've been appropriated by the U.S. Coast Guard for a rescue mission. I've already taken the *Maria Helena* up to her maximum speed. We'll be there in two hours."

"Where?"

"Middle of the Bering Strait." Tom kept his eyes fixed on the sea ahead. The hull of the *Maria Helena* was rated for ice, but any collision at the speeds they were travelling now would be fatal for her hull. "The *Gordoye Dostizheniye*, a Russian cargo ship — she's gone under…"

Sam looked at the ocean, it was glassy and almost perfectly still in the night. "In this weather? What did she collide with?"

"I don't know."

"Great. How big was the cargo ship? Any idea how many lives we're chasing here?"

"No idea…"

Sam nodded. He understood the situation. It was all happening at once. No one had information yet. Tom had turned around upon hearing the mayday call on the radio. The U.S. Coast Guard was sending their nearest resources. The Russian Navy would be trying to get there, too. In the meantime, men and women, right this instant, were most likely trying to stay alive in the near freezing waters.

He took a breath in and asked, "What do we know?"

"Nothing. I think you're up to date with all we have. Matthew's speaking with the Coast Guard now, trying to find more information. We'll know more in a minute."

Matthew stepped onto the bridge with a few loose pieces of fax paper in his hands. His eyes met Tom's and he spoke with gentle accusation. "I leave you in charge for an hour and a cargo ship sinks!"

Tom shrugged. "You can hardly hold me responsible for maritime events taking place nearly two hours away?"

"Just watch me."

"All right. Enough of that." Sam looked at Matthew, who was still wearing what he'd presumably gone to bed in—a pair of shorts and tee-shirt. *Does no one around here realize we're sailing through sub-freezing waters?* He asked, "What have we got, Matthew?"

"Morning, Sam. Have a read of this." Matthew handed him the faxed report to him.

Sam took the full transcript of the radio transmissions from the previous half-hour and quickly read the two-page brief. He wore an incredulous and wry smile, as though it had to be some kind of sick joke. His eyes swept to the end of the report, where it confirmed the ship had fifteen crew on board when she went under. His smile instantly disappeared.

He turned to Matthew. "How does a modern cargo ship of over a hundred twenty thousand tons get into trouble in calm seas, and sink within minutes?"

Matthew shook his head. "Beats the hell out of me."

# Chapter Three

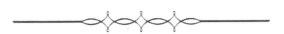

AT 5:06 A.M. THE *Maria Helena* slowed to an idle and coasted into the site of the *Gordoye Dostizheniye's* sinking. The sea was already flooded with daylight, allowing Sam a good visual of the entire location. It was as calm and still as any harbor. The seas were rarely this settled near the entrance to the Bering Strait. Tom steered in a slow, wide, clockwise direction.

Sam turned to face Tom and Matthew. "Either of you see any flotsam or debris?"

"Not a thing," Tom answered.

Matthew's eyes swept out toward the horizon. "It makes a perfect postcard picture, but I find it hard to believe a cargo ship's gone down within a hundred miles of here."

Sam turned his focus to Elise, who was tapping away at the keys of her laptop. "Do you have those satellite images yet?"

"Got them, but from what I can see, all they show are the crystal-clear waters of the Bering Strait." Elise wore an expression Sam had seen before. It said, someone got something wrong, but it wasn't from my end. "I'll get Laura to run a search of the images to see if anything correlates to any suspected debris from a sinking ship."

"Laura?"

"That's your newest member of the crew."

"Really?" Sam was incredulous.

"It's what I've named my new Artificial Intelligence system I've designed to run complex tasks autonomously."

"All right." Sam said, indifferent to Elise's creation. He spoke to Tom, "Have you got any visual of the *Gordoye Dostizheniye* on the depth sounder?"

"Not a thing." Tom shrugged, glancing at the computer screen behind the helm that depicted the outline of the seafloor. "The seabed's flat as the surface and just as remarkably clean, too. The National Parks and Wildlife people would be proud of the state of it."

Sam stepped beside Tom. "There's no debris at all?"

"I don't know what to tell you, the seafloor's completely clean." Tom increased the angle of the multibeam sonar transducers in order to increase the range of the surveying range.

Sam asked, "What about the image quality?"

"The quality's good. I'm telling you, there's nothing down there but sand."

Sam shook his head in dismay as he stared at the depth sounder's visual screen. The *Maria Helena* used state of the art multibeam bathymetry. Unlike traditional, one-dimensional depth sounders, which used just one transducer pointing downward, the system used an array of a hundred and twenty 12 kHz transducers to develop precise geometric patterns of the seafloor. It could send out the swath of sounds to cover a distance on either side of the ship that is equal to about two times the water depth. The sound then bounces off the seafloor at different angles and is received by the ship at slightly different times. All the signals are then processed by computers on board the ship, converted into water depths, and automatically plotted as a bathymetric map—also known as submarine topography — with an accuracy of about five feet.

Sam crossed his arms and stepped back. His eyes staring at the calm waters. "Does it strike anyone as odd that the sea is not just completely devoid of any debris from the cargo ship, but also of any sea life?"

"Good question..." Tom thought about it for a minute. "All I can think of is that whatever did happen nearby certainly got the local marine life rattled."

"Matthew," Sam said. "Can you please get the Coast Guard back on the satellite phone? See if they can confirm the location."

Matthew nodded. "I'm onto it."

Tom decreased the angle of the multibeam swath, which increased the range of its sonar image, while decreasing its quality. He watched the results and smiled. "Hey, Sam, I think I've got something."

Sam stared at the bathymetric display. "What is that?"

Tom threw the twin propellers into reverse and straightened the helm until the *Maria Helena* was directly facing their discovery. "I think it's a giant mound of sand."

Sam ran the palm of his hand through his thick brown hair. "So, the seabed is completely flat and devoid of marine life, there's no sign of the *Gordoye Dostizheniye* while a strange mound of sand is waiting in the middle here?"

"Yeah, I think that's just about the gist of it," Tom confirmed.

"Any chance that strange mound of sand is large enough to cover the cargo ship?"

"Not a chance."

"All right, let's set up a wide grid search pattern. See if we can come across anything." Sam turned to Matthew. "Any luck with the Coast Guard?"

Matthew shook his head. "They're saying the GPS coordinates are correct."

Sam walked over to Matthew. "Let me speak to them."

Matthew handed the satellite phone over.

"Good morning. My name's Sam Reilly. I'm in charge of the *Maria Helena,* currently at the site of the *Gordoye Dostizheniye's* sinking. There's nothing here," he reported. "Can you please verify the location?"

"You're right over the top of it." The man spoke quickly and with certainty. "We've got your ship on satellite tracking. You're definitely right over the top of it now. You should see the wrecked hull of the *Gordoye Dostizheniye* right now."

"Negative. We've searched the area, we're not picking up any sign of the ship. Maybe you got the GPS coordinates wrong?"

"We didn't."

"Maybe whoever sent the mayday call did then?" Sam breathed in. "It would be easy to do under the circumstances."

"Not possible. We had a spotter plane in the air within minutes of the mayday call."

"And? No sign of the ship?" Sam mentally urged the man to answer in more detail, but said nothing.

"No, sir. What they did see was an area of disturbed water, and what looked like a small vortex in the middle of it. The vortex disappeared as the pilot observed it."

"And it didn't occur to anyone that the vortex could have sucked the ship down?" Sam asked, allowing a hint of sarcasm to enter his tone.

"We did, sir. But what the spotter saw would have been too small and too weak to sink a vessel of the size of the *Gordoye Dostizheniye.*" He pronounced the Russian name with fewer syllables than required, but Sam didn't hold that against him. Few Americans could navigate the double vowels of the Russian language.

"So, you're pretty sure of the coordinates," Sam repeated.

"No, sir. I'm certain of them."

Sam ended the call. "Tom, let's get a close up of that mound of sand."

Tom increased the resolution on the bathymetric map. "It's a big mound of sand. It looks unstable. You can already see where parts of it have fallen in upon itself."

"What do you think the possibility is that the Russian ship was pulled into a submarine sinkhole?"

"It's possible, but pretty unlikely. You think the entire ship was pulled into a sinkhole and that forty-foot pile of sand is covering its bridge tower?"

Sam shook his head. "No. But right now, I can't think of anything else it could be."

"What do you want to do?"

"Not much we can do. It looks like we're going to have to take *Sea Witch II* down for a closer look."

# Chapter Four

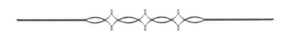

SAM STEPPED DOWN the stairs onto the main deck. Veyron already had the *Maria Helena's* runabout winched into the water and tied up along the starboard side of the hull. The engine was in the process of warming up on the slim chance they would still find any survivors. The smell of thick beef stew wafted up from the kitchen. On the helipad, Genevieve was in the process of taking off with the Sea King to start an aerial survey for survivors.

The downward thrust from the helicopter sent a gust of sea-spray over the deck. Sam ducked to cover his face. A few seconds later Genevieve dropped the nose, and the Sea King quickly headed off toward the south.

Veyron switched the runabout's engine off and climbed back on board the *Maria Helena*. "Any news of survivors, Sam?"

"No. Right now, we're still trying to locate the *Gordoye Dostizheniye*."

Veyron glanced at the clear seas. You could only just make out the flat seabed below. "Are you sure we've been given the right coordinates?"

"I don't know." Sam looked at the clear water below. He shared the same thoughts. It seemed impossible you could hide a massive cargo ship in these waters without some sort of hint of its destruction. "The Coast Guard tells me they're a hundred percent certain we're in the right place. They even said they had a spotter plane overhead when the last of the cargo ship disappeared inside a vortex. The pilot took a GPS reading at the time."

"Sure. What do you want to do?"

"There's a giant mound of sand right below our keel. Tom and I going to take the *Sea Witch II* down there, and cast our eyes over it."

Veyron's eyes narrowed. "You think it's the remnants of the *Gordoye Dostizheniye's* bridge tower buried?"

"I doubt it, but it's the only thing we have to go on at the moment. So, I'm going to take it."

Veyron nodded, like it was the only reasonable possibility in a series of impossible events. "I'll come down and give you a hand putting her in the water."

Sam headed down the next set of steel steps until he reached the dive center, housed in the heart of the *Maria Helena,* between her massive twin hulls. The *Sea Witch II,* the bright yellow Triton 36 000/3 submarine stood next to the moon pool, perched on a frame to protect its twin hulls. Its borosilicate glass dome in the middle could house up to three divers, but that wasn't on the agenda for this trip. The two pilot seats at the front of the bubble waited for him and Tom to fill them. Although *Sea Witch II* could descend as deep as 36, 000 feet — the depth of the Mariana Trench — she wouldn't be required to descend to any such depth today. A mere 30 feet below the surface of the gentle waves, the peak of the sand mound awaited their probe for information.

He glanced at the moon pool in the middle. The water was so clear he could clearly make out the shape of the mound of sand below. The structure was far too vertical to be naturally formed out of sand. Already, large sections had broken off and were crumbling down the sides. Veyron began to connect the winch cables to the top of the small submersible.

Tom stepped down the stairs. His eyes first looked at the crystal-clear waters of the moon pool and then at Sam's hardened face. "It doesn't look that deep. I think I could hold my breath and free dive down to inspect the sand mound."

Sam grinned. "You go right ahead, Tom. That water's only just shy of freezing. I think I'll take the comfort of the *Sea Witch II*."

Tom smiled. "Chicken."

Sam ignored him and climbed in through the top hatch of the submarine. He took a seat in the left pilot's chair and slid it forward. He felt for the main battery switch, positioned in front of the joystick, and flicked it on. The series of red backlit lights illuminated the gauges and controls. He slid his hand backward and gripped the joystick, which sat between the two forward seats. Glancing to see that no one was near the propellers, he squeezed the joystick. The electric motors whirred into life. He adjusted the control to the left and then the right to confirm each propeller was spinning correctly.

Tom shuffled down the hatchway. "On second thoughts, if you're taking the easy way out, I may as well tag along with you."

"I thought you might," Sam said.

"Where are you up to?"

"I think we're just about right to go, if you want to close the hatch."

Tom stood up to close the hatch, but a set of fingers stopped him. The hatch opened fully and Matthew leaned inside with a cell phone. "Sam, the Secretary of Defense wants to speak with you before you dive."

"Really?" Sam cringed. "Was it too hard to tell her I was already under water?"

Matthew shrugged as if to say it wasn't his problem and

handed him the cell phone.

Sam took it. "Good morning, ma'am."

"There's nothing good about this morning, Mr. Reilly. It's been one whole God damn series of screw ups!" Her words were crisp and pugnacious. "Have you found the *Gordoye Dostizheniye?*"

"Not yet." Sam wondered what interest she could possibly have in the lost Russian cargo ship.

She took an exaggerated breath and then sighed. "That's one thing, at least."

Sam waited for her to tell him what was on her mind. When she didn't, he asked. "Ma'am, I really need to put a submarine in the water. May I ask what I can do for you?"

"How long until you locate the *Gordoye Dostizheniye?*"

"I have no idea. At this stage, I'm still not a hundred percent certain we're even searching in the right place."

"The Russian Navy have their own recovery team on its way. Our intelligence suggests they'll be on the site within another twelve hours. I suggest you find the wreckage and salvage it within eleven hours!"

Sam smiled. "That's not a lot of time to locate a ship and retrieve something."

"That's all you have. If we miss this window we'll never get another chance to recover it. The seabed is less than a hundred feet deep throughout the entire area. You've achieved more in less time before."

"I probably knew where the shipwreck was then." Sam knew the gripe wouldn't get him anything. "What do you need me to recover?"

"A shipping container. Its number is 404."

"A shipping container!" Sam was incredulous. "You know there's still a chance this is a rescue mission? As you pointed out, these are relatively shallow waters — there may be air pockets within the ship where life might still be preserved."

"Forget about those lives. This takes priority."

"Really?" Sam asked. "What's inside container 404?"

"That's not your concern. It's more secure than a bank vault — so don't even think about trying to enter it. Your job is to retrieve it before the Russians arrive."

# Chapter Five

S AM FELT THE submarine shift as he strapped himself into the pilot seat. To his right, in the copilot's chair, Tom had commenced cross-checking the startup procedure using the mnemonic HACHIT — checking the Hatch, Air supply, Controls, Harnesses, Instruments and Trim.

Outside, Veyron confirmed the winch hook and cable were correctly connected and the overhead hatch was sealed properly.

Sam waited until Veyron climbed off the back of the submarine and then asked, "Are we ready to get this sub in the water?"

"You're good," Veyron confirmed.

"Thanks." Sam turned to Tom. "You happy?"

Tom flicked the running lights on. "Systems all check out. We're good to go."

Sam depressed the radio transmitter. "*Maria Helena,* this is *Sea Witch II,* we're good for launch."

"Copy that *Sea Witch II,* safe journey and good luck." It was Matthew who replied, his professional monotone voice comforting in its familiarity.

In front of them, Veyron adjusted the controls for the crane.

"All right, gentlemen, here we go."

Sam shifted slightly in his seat as the *Sea Witch II* was winched into the moon pool. The submarine rocked gently as she was lowered into the seawater. He braced himself on two grip bars, but there was minimal movement in the gentle sea.

"*Maria Helena,* we're ready to release the tether and commence our dive," Sam said.

"Copy that. Releasing the tether," Matthew replied.

Above, Veyron climbed on top of the submarine's dome and disconnected the hook and cables. Thirty seconds later, Sam watched him step back onto the edge of the moon pool and give him the thumbs up.

Sam nodded in return and flicked the ballast switch. Water began flooding into the tanks, while air bubbles gurgled to the surface. "Okay, Tom. Let's find the *Gordoye Dostizheniye.*"

The *Sea Witch II* dived to a depth of 60 feet. Sam stopped the water intake and leveled her into neutral buoyancy. In a heads-up display across the front of the dome, a GPS screen overlapped the bathymetric map of the seafloor. He then started the forward propellers, located at each end of the twin hulls. They whirred quietly as they moved the sub towards the strange mound of sand.

Sam brought the submarine down right in front of the large mound of sand. The clear water and ample sun from the surface penetrated to give a clear vision of the strange formation. It looked like the remnants of a forty-foot sandcastle, with its features weathered away into a crude mound by the first wave of the incoming tide.

The sandcastle was already starting to deteriorate under the sea's constant movement. Large chunks, the size of a medium sized car, had broken off and fallen to the ground. On the seabed, bizarre grooves were marked into the ground.

"What do you think those are?" Sam asked.

Tom studied the seabed for a moment. "If I didn't know better, I'd say those grooves almost look like a giant hand raked its way through the sand."

"Yeah. That's pretty much what I thought, too."

"What if it wasn't just a thought?"

Sam's lips curled into an incredulous grin. "You think some giant built this sandcastle?"

Tom shook his head. "No, but what about a giant sinkhole?"

San ran his eyes over the strange grooves in the seabed again. They formed almost perfectly straight lines, etched deep into the sand. It would take a lot of energy to do that.

"It's a possibility." He shook his head in disbelief. "I'm not convinced, but I don't have anything else right now."

"What do you want to do about it?"

Sam positioned the *Sea Witch II* directly over the mound of sand. "Take the controls, and keep us as close as you can to the sand."

"Sure. What are you going to do?"

Sam gripped the twin joysticks in his hands that controlled the manipulator arms, which protruded from each of the submarine's pontoons. Each arm had a reach of twelve feet forward of the bubble. "Let's see how solid this thing is."

"Don't dig too far," Tom cautioned. "No need to bring the whole thing down on us. I'm a cave-diver, not a doodlebug."

Sam did a double-take and stared at Tom. "A what?"

"You know, one of those bugs that digs a hole in the sand… never mind. Just be careful."

Sam sighed heavily. Relaxed his shoulder and gently took control of the twin manipulator arms. He slowly drove the robotic arms into the crest of the mound. He felt no resistance in them whatsoever. The fine white sand known as glacial silt parted like powder.

He watched as the crest was replaced with a thick dust cloud of the fine sand. "What the hell?"

Tom moved the submarine backward — the last thing they wanted was the murky cloud to be sucked into their impellers. "Whatever that is, it wasn't here a few days ago. That's for sure. This is glacial silt. It will disappear in a few days."

"Agreed. Take us around to the base. I want to try the ground penetrating radar."

Tom positioned the submarine about twenty feet back from the base and Sam adjusted the transducer until it lit up a clear image of the mound of sand. There was no doubt about it. The entire thing was soft sand. There was no steel from the bridge tower of a cargo ship or any other sign of a manmade structure.

Sam shook his head. "I'll be damned, but I'd say the ground just opened up and swallowed the *Gordoye Dostizheniye* whole!"

Tom said, "What do you want to do about it?"

"There's nothing we can do. We'll need to wait until we can bring in a large-scale dredging vessel. But where the hell we're going to find one of those this far north, I have no idea."

# Chapter Six

*Cloud Ranch, Southwest of Mesa Verde National Monument, Colorado*

B RODY FROST WOULD have never, if someone had told him years ago, that his work buddy on a Colorado ranch would be a white guy from New York. Whoever heard of a cowboy from New York? Except the kind from that old movie, Rhinestone Cowboy. What a joke. But Malcom Corbin was okay, even if he was a greenhorn. Easy company. Didn't talk much.

Today, he and Malcom were riding one of the mesas on the Cloud Ranch, looking for strays and unbranded calves. The weather was typical for July in southwestern Colorado — sunny, hot, no clouds in the sky. The strong breeze that often blows at the top of the mesa on such a day was not present. It would have been welcome, though. The damp bandana Brody wore around his neck would have cooled him better with a bit of wind.

Malcom, riding several yards away, gave a short whistle, catching Brody's attention. When he looked over, Malcom lifted a lazy arm and pointed toward the mesa's edge. There a young calf was resting in the shade of a bush.

"Where's his mama?" Brody called.

"Yonder," Malcom said.

"Yonder?" Brody had to laugh when Malcom tried to sound

Western. "Seriously?"

He looked where Malcom was pointing. Sure enough, a cow stood listlessly. Not much feed or water up here. If they didn't get her down to better pasturage, she'd die, and her calf with her. He nudged his horse with his knee, and the gelding obediently turned in the direction of the cow, while Malcom dismounted and cautiously approached the calf. Neither wanted to spook the animals that could easily panic and run over the edge, where a 500-foot or more, sheer drop would kill them quicker than any lack of water.

Concentrating on the cow and his slow approach, lasso ready in case she bolted, Brody edged closer. He was focused so much that he didn't notice at first when the wind picked up. He managed to flank her and began to crowd her back toward her calf, when he heard Malcom swear.

Brody asked, "What's wrong?"

"Dust in my eye. Where'd this wind come from?"

For the first time, Brody noticed the stirring in the sagebrush at his horse's feet. As he watched, it became strong enough to swirl and eddy around the gelding's legs. But a few yards away, where Malcom stood calming the calf, it was moving fast enough to give Malcom some trouble.

Malcom looked up. "I'll be damned, where'd that come from?"

"No telling," Brody answered. "Sometimes it just starts blowing. This looks strange, though. Look how it's like a river in this one spot."

The two men stared in wonder as the sand and dust coalesced into what did indeed look like a current of fast-flowing red-brown water, nearly a mile wide, with calmer air on either side of it.

"What the hell? You ever see anything like that before?" Malcom asked. He leaned down to get a closer look at the debris flowing past him. Suddenly, a stray gust took his hat, and despite his swipe at it, the hat joined the wind current and flew toward the edge of the mesa. "Shit! I just bought that Stetson," he swore.

Brody shook his head, and dismounted, careful to stay out of the midst of the red-brown current. Malcom also dismounted again, and both laid their reins over a stunted juniper tree, signaling their mounts to stay put. Brody secured his own hat to his saddle horn.

The two walked toward the edge of the mesa, skirting the side of the strange wind current, which was now as tall as Malcom, at about six feet. In contrast, Brody himself was more than a few inches shorter, at five-foot-six.

Brody got down on his hands and knees and then stretched out full-length on the ground before belly-crawling to the edge. He'd never liked heights, and this one was no different. Below, the glint of water in a year-round spring-fed trickle caught his eye. He didn't see Malcom's hat.

"It's gone, bro."

"Damnit to hell! I paid a fortune for that hat," Malcom swore. "I've got to try to find it."

"I told you the $100 hat was fine, buddy. You had to have the fancy one."

"It doesn't matter. I'd be going after the $100 one, too. I'm not made of money," Malcom answered. "How do we get down from here?"

Brody sighed. The greenhorn was going to get himself killed. "Follow me." He led Malcom well away from the torrent of wind, and started a careful descent.

Any kid growing up in the Four Corners area had scrambled up and down red rock cliffs. Called slickrock locally, it isn't truly slick. Sandstone has enough texture to provide grip for the right kind of shoes. Cowboy boots aren't the right kind. But subtle grooves formed by erosion, along with narrow cracks and ledges, can provide a route for the experienced climber, which Brody was. He thought about having Malcom take off his boots. Even thought about taking off his own. Macho pride stopped him. It was going to be a hairy climb down, though.

Tense moments followed as Brody picked his way to the bottom of the canyon. He was fearful that at any moment, Malcom would lose his grip and come tumbling down on top of him, sweeping both to their deaths on the rocks below. Forty-five minutes later, they reached the bottom.

An entirely different ecosystem existed at the bottom of the canyon. In spring, snowmelt from miles away would feed the stream, which must have also been fed by an up-canyon spring to still have water in it at this time of year. Sand stretched for yards on either side of a lazy dribble. Trees, mostly cottonwood, clung to the sides of the canyon, and scrub juniper took advantage of any sand-filled crack in the rock. The two men walked up the canyon to see if they could spot the place where the strange wind flowed over the top. Malcom kept his eyes on the ground, while Brody searched the trees where Malcom's precious Stetson might have been caught.

Both were surprised to find the debris riding the wind above their heads and being drawn farther up the canyon. Even weirder, there was a similar current of sand and other detritus flowing down from the opposite side of the canyon to join the flow on their side.

"What do you make of that?" Malcom asked, scratching his head.

"It's impossible," Brody answered. "That would mean the wind is blowing from the opposite direction on that side. It doesn't make sense."

As if they'd thought of it simultaneously, both men turned and began moving up the middle of the canyon, stepping into and over the little stream to follow the wind. A mile later, they rounded a bend and found the wind's destination. It made even less sense. Every particle of sand, bit of dried sagebrush or tumbleweed, and fleck of juniper bark was flowing into a good-sized cliff dwelling village carved into the rock a couple hundred feet up the cliff side opposite their mesa.

"Whoa, look at that!" Malcom said. "Did you know that was there?"

"No," Brody replied in wonder. "I bet no one does. That must be almost the size of Mesa Verde or the Chaco Canyon ruins. If anyone knew it was there, there'd be a road blasted into this canyon and hundreds of cars would be honking at us right about now."

"You mean we may be the first to see it?" Malcom asked.

"Since the Ancient Ones who lived here left it," Brody answered. "I wonder if they…"

"They what?"

"No one knows where the Ancient Ones went, or why they left so suddenly. They just up and abandoned Mesa Verde, and there are a lot of theories but no answers. Maybe this pueblo has answers. I have a buddy who works for the Park Service at Mesa Verde. He's an archaeologist. I should call him and ask about this one."

"Wait. This could be something to make us some money. Didn't all those old Indians have gold and silver? What if it's still here? I mean, if no one knows about it. And besides, I bet my hat's in there. I've at least got to go see if I can find it."

"Don't believe all you hear about gold and silver. Silver, maybe. More likely copper and maybe some turquoise. I don't know if the Anasazi traded with outsiders or not. Let's go ahead and look for your hat and then get those strays back to the ranch. When we get back, I'll call my buddy."

"As long as you don't tell him exactly where it is," Malcom answered. Brody could see the gleam of gold fever in his eyes.

"Okay. Come on, let's go find your hat."

The climb to the cliff dwelling was easier than the descent to the bottom of the canyon had been. A hand-and-toe ladder had been carved into the vertical stretches of sandstone, and worn paths angled up in a switch-back fashion where possible. The hard part was staying on the cliff-face while being buffeted by the stinging sand particles borne on the wind. However, they reached the village in short order and began exploring.

In the center of the pueblo, they found the kiva—the underground circular vault used by Puebloans for spiritual ceremonies and political meetings. It was easy enough to spot, as the wind led straight to it and poured in through an area of the roof that had fallen—in a sort of tornado-like spiral dust devil.

Brody felt a supernatural chill and shivered despite the ninety-degree heat being only slightly lower here in the canyon than on the mesa. "Dude, I'm not sure we should go in there. It's sacred."

Malcom turned an astonished gaze on him. "Sacred! I didn't know you were religious."

"I'm not. But there are things about my people and our ancestors that you don't know. It kind of creeps me out to enter a kiva uninvited."

"Who the hell's going to invite you? In case you haven't noticed, this place has been deserted for a very long time," Malcom huffed. "I'm going in."

Brody took a breath in and shook his head, gripping the side of the cliff for balance. "Suit yourself, but I'm not going anywhere near that kiva."

Brody watched as Malcom circled the kiva until he found the ladder leading down into the cylindrical structure. It was made of stones piled together without mortar, but carved into the bedrock so that the above-ground enclosure was only half the total height. It was roofed with saplings laid in a flattish conical manner, with a ladder leading down into it through an opening in the roof. As they had noticed, part of the roof was missing toward the open side of the pueblo, where the wind was pouring in. The normal entrance was on the opposite side.

Brody approached more reluctantly, only rushing to the ladder when he heard a shout from within. He scrambled to the top and looked down into the gloom, but couldn't see Malcom. The wind in the kiva was circling like a tiny tornado.

"Malcom! Are you okay? What's happening?"

There was no answer.

"Malcom! Are you hurt?"

Just then, a flash of white startled Brody into ducking away from the kiva entrance. To his horror, he realized it was Malcom's face, frozen in a rictus of fear.

"Malcom!" Brody shot back up the ladder so quickly he nearly fell into the kiva. As he watched, tracking Malcom's body as it circled lower and lower, he feared Malcom was dead.

*But how?*

And then, his eyes finally adjusted to the darkness, dread stole over him as he saw Malcom's body sucked into the largest sipapu he'd ever seen, in the floor of the kiva. From inside, a wail of dread and terror rang out and echoed up the sipapu then tumbled into the circling wind in the kiva.

*What the hell? Could Malcom still be alive?*

Brody scrambled back down the ladder and ran to the edge of the pueblo. Climbing back up the cliff side as fast as he could, he could think of nothing but riding back to the bunkhouse at full gallop and gathering others to go and rescue Malcom. A superstitious dread overcame him halfway up.

His mind returned to the stories his father used to tell him of the Navajo witches who once protected and now haunted ancient kivas. Known as Skinwalkers, they represented the antithesis of Navajo cultural values. They were the evil reflections of goodly medicine men and women, performing twisted ceremonies and manipulating magic in a perversion of the good works medicine people traditionally performed. In order to practice their good works, traditional healers learn about both good and evil magic. Most could handle the responsibility, but some became corrupt and tormented.

*Could there still be Skinwalkers inside?*

He could think of only one person who might have answers. His best friend from high school, Kevin, had once jokingly told him to call if he ever found a big sipapu. He'd bet his life this one qualified. The sipapu was a hole in the ground, usually no bigger than a finger, located at the center of every kiva. It was a ceremonial reminder of the place where Southwestern Indians emerged back into the world after their long migration underground.

Only then did he notice that the weird wind was dying down. By the time he'd scaled the canyon wall and got back to his horse, it was completely gone. There was no sign a wind had ever scoured the top of the mesa, stolen a Stetson, and most likely led a man to his death.

# Chapter Seven

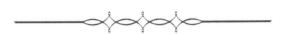

I T WAS 6:25 A.M. when the *Saharan Bucket* arrived on the scene and a little over twenty-six hours since the *Gordoye Dostizheniye sank.* The 55,000-ton deep sea dredging vessel had been seconded from its port of Anchorage in Alaska, where it was in the process of clearing glacial silt from the entrance to the harbor.

Sam Reilly watched as the mammoth vessel came alongside the *Maria Helena.* It was at least four hundred feet long with a bridge tower standing five stories above its deck. Along the deck were a series of giant pipes protruding twenty feet into the air, connected to muscular engines and designed to pump the sand and debris from the seabed.

The inflatable Zodiac was lowered into the water and Tom ran Sam across to the *Saharan Bucket.* The swell of the shallow water of the Bering Strait had picked up, but was still relatively mild, and the little runabout skimmed across the ripples.

Sam thanked Tom for the lift and climbed the steel ladder fixed to the side of the dredging ship's starboard hull. Behind him, he heard the small motor of the runabout increase its pitch as Tom returned to the *Maria Helena* to continue a progressively wider search pattern of the surrounding area for the *Gordoye Dostizheniye.*

He reached the top of the ladder and climbed over the gunwale onto the deck.

"Sam Reilly?" A man in his late forties, with a well-groomed dark beard greeted him.

"That's me." Sam smiled, politely and offered his right hand.

The man took it in callused hands and shook, warmly. "Brendan Miller. Captain of this fine vessel."

"Thanks for getting here so quickly." Sam glanced at the array of powerful machinery that lined the deck. It all appeared so well maintained and clean that it would have brought a smile to the face of the matron of any military hospital. "You made good time from Anchorage."

"Like every sailor, we're still praying for survivors."

"All right. Let's get started." Sam breathed in deeply through his pursed lips. "I should let you know there's minimal chance of finding any survivors, but you never know. If there's any, it would be impossible without your vessel to reach them."

"Why is that?"

"It's a strange theory and might require some sort of leap of faith."

"Go on." The captain turned to walk. "You can tell me on the way to the bridge."

Sam followed. "When we arrived here in the early hours of yesterday morning, the sea was perfectly still. There was no evidence of any wreckage, or maelstrom. No icebergs. And yet, a moderate sized cargo ship apparently disappeared beneath the sea within minutes."

"Okay, I'm listening. What do you think happened?"

"There was a tectonic shift."

"An earthquake?"

"Nothing too dramatic. Just a simple rumble of tectonic plates. The result of the movement caused a sinkhole in the seabed below, which then drew trillions of gallons of seawater inside. During the subsequent vortex, the *Gordoye Dostizheniye* was pulled under. Seismic monitors recorded a minor tremblor."

The captain's thick bushy eyebrows narrowed. "But you haven't located the ship yet."

"No. But we've found a large conical mound of sand." Sam paused at the top of the third flight of stairs. "It's a longshot, but if I'm right about the vortex theory — the only possible explanation for there being no flotsam or other evidence of the wreckage — then the wreckage of the *Gordoye Dostizheniye* is lying directly underneath that sand."

"You think the sand is covering the bridge tower?"

Sam shook his head. "Not immediately beneath it. We've already used ground penetrating radar. The mound is filled with loose sand. But I'm hoping we'll find a cargo ship buried somewhere below that mound."

"Like you said, it requires a leap of faith." Miller shrugged. "Without anything better to go off, I'm willing to take that leap."

"Good," Sam said. "And if the *Gordoye Dostizheniye* is buried… there might still be survivors trapped inside the hull."

# Chapter Eight

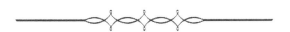

THE BRIDGE OF the *Saharan Bucket* gave the *Maria Helena* a run for its money when it came to high tech gadgetry and information systems. Hydrographic grade multibeam echosounders, sub-bottom profilers and sound velocity profilers provided a visual masterpiece of the ground below in an array of colors.

The bathymetric image showed a series of colors at the warm end of the spectrum — reds, orange and yellows — depicting the shallow area of the Bering Strait. To the south, the image shifted through the greens and blues of deeper water. At the center of the image, a conical tower formed in yellow.

Sam stared at the image. "If that is the *Gordoye Dostizheniye's* bridge tower, it's so shallow I could reach it with a single breath."

Captain Smith shook his head. "It also means that if anyone is trapped down there, they're less than sixty feet from the surface and completely helpless."

"All right. Let's see what your machine can do to help them."

The captain made a few signals and the large auger dredge was lowered from a gigantic crane at the bow into the ocean. The head functioned like a cutter suction dredger, but instead the cutting tool was a rotating Archimedean screw set at right angles to the suction pipe. The dredge was a self-propelled version that allowed the system to propel itself without the use of anchors or cables.

The entire ship vibrated under the strain and a few moments later, Sam watched as thousands of gallons of sand and water was expelled a hundred feet into the air aft of the *Saharan Bucket*.

Captain Miller noticed his curiosity, and said, "The turbidity shroud on auger dredge systems creates a strong suction vacuum, causing much less turbidity than the conical basket-type cutter-head and so they are preferred for environmental applications. The vacuum created by the shroud and the ability to convey material to the pump faster makes auger dredge systems more productive than similar sized conical type cutter-head dredgers."

Sam grinned, like a kid in a candy shop. "Nice piece of gear you've got here."

"You'd better believe it. Some of the best dredgers in the world are up here. It's because of the glacial silt."

"Really? What about it?"

"As the name suggests, the silt is formed by fine particles of rock ground by the movement of glaciers. The particles become fine and powdery, but microscopically more accurately resemble razor sharp gravel."

"So, it's damaging to machinery?" Sam asked, thankful that Tom had made the decision to back the *Sea Witch II* away from the cloud of glacial silt from the crest of the mound and protect the props from real harm.

Miller nodded. "Like you wouldn't believe."

Sam ran his eyes over the rest of the display instruments. To the right were a series of computer screens that monitored the dredging equipment in relation to bathymetric images of the seafloor in a series of depth isobaths. The monitoring software then used Real Time Kinematic satellite navigation to accurately record where the machine had been operating and to what depth.

Sam watched clearly, as the auger head was positioned at the side of the conical tower of sand. The captain adjusted the position with the adept movements of a single hand on a joystick. The device moved forward and began devouring the sand.

Thirty minutes later the auger head was positioned in the middle of the empty pile of sand. Sam stared at the monitoring equipment. It was obvious the sand tower was nothing more than that. He asked, "Would you feel some sort of resistance if the device struck the metal of a ship?"

"Sure we would. There'd be vibrations following up the line that would try and tear my ship apart."

"So, it's just sand?"

Captain Smith crossed his arms. "I don't know what to tell you Mr. Reilly. Really, I don't. The sand's soft. No doubt about it. The ground below has been recently stirred up. That's for sure. But I couldn't even hazard a guess about who or what did it."

"Can you dredge any deeper?"

"To a point. We're already forty feet below the seabed. More sand and debris will keep coming in the farther we go."

"The recently turned over sand continues as deep as forty feet?"

"Yeah. Much deeper." The captain nodded. "It's as though an old gigantic sandworm just bored its way through the surface and swallowed the sea whole."

"Would a submarine earthquake cause anything like that?"

"No. It would stir up the sand. That's for sure. But that's where the similarities end. This is almost a perfectly circular tunnel of weakened sand with the diameter of a quarter of a mile. More like a sinkhole than a shift in the tectonic plates."

"You think it's big enough to have swallowed a moderate sized cargo ship?"

The captain thought about it for a moment. "It would need to drag it down vertically—like stern or bow first, but, yeah... I think it's possible. I've never seen or even heard of such a thing happening before, but it's possible."

Sam nodded. "Any idea what could have possibly caused such an event?"

The captain shook his head. "Beats the hell out of me."

# Chapter Nine

*Big Diomede Island, Bering Strait*

THE SENIOR FOREMAN stared at the large chart pinned up on the wall opposite his desk. He drew a quick breath and shook his head in frustration. It depicted an overly simplistic vision of the various stages of the Transcontinental World Link. An idea which had been bandied about by politicians, engineers, and wealthy merchants since 1890, when the first Governor of the Colorado Territory, William Gilpin, first proposed the idea of a vast cosmopolitan railway linking the US with Europe in a series of railways. More than a century later, Russia, Canada and the US had finally agreed on putting that plan into practice.

It all appeared easy enough on paper. The Bering Strait crossing included a bridge and a tunnel spanning the relatively narrow and shallow waters between the Chukotka Peninsula in Russia and the Seward Peninsula in the U.S. state of Alaska. With the two Diomede Islands between the peninsulas, the Bering Strait could be spanned by a bridge and a tunnel. There would be one long bridge connecting Alaska and the Diomede Islands, and a tunnel connecting the Diomede Islands and Russia. The earth bored from the tunnel could be used as landfill to connect the two islands. So far, the project had faced repeated political, engineering, and financial setbacks. The original feasibility study overlooked the most complex unknown in the construction industry — people.

That's where the problems occurred. It had already been a frustrating day for Michael Gallagher, the foreman of the Canadian-led heavy construction crew. He ran the palm of his hand through what remained of his rapidly thinning, gray hair. He had as much respect as anyone for the First Peoples, but those on this god-forsaken rock of an island were driving him crazy.

Although the Russian-owned Big Diomede Island had been uninhabited by the native Yupik people since they were expelled during World War II, the tribal people who lived on its neighboring island of Little Diomede complained that the tunnel boring would disturb the soil, possibly releasing evil spirits into their world. They pointed to claims by distant relatives of the damage done by the US Northeast Cape Air Force Station on St. Lawrence Island in the Aleutian Islands during the Cold War causing cancer in the native population. The statistics eventually showed that their rates of illness were no higher than other people living in Alaska. Even so, the base was eventually removed and millions of dollars were spent on the cleanup.

The 110 permanent indigenous residents of Little Diomede challenged the Transcontinental World Link project. First, they'd delayed construction of the runway on the old site of the Russian military base. Even though the project had won the court battle, protesters often deliberately got in the way of the dangerous equipment, causing further delays. The foreman had dealt with clearing the runway of trespassing protesters today already, so the plane carrying parts for his Big Bertha class tunnel boring machine could be landed.

Now he was on his way to quell a rumor among his men that the Yupik workers he'd employed to placate the local First Peoples were secretly sabotaging the big machines. There was no need for them to do that, he thought savagely. The borers were temperamental enough on their own. And the near-vertical portion of the tunnel they were working on wasn't easy on them. Nevertheless, they had to get deep enough to establish a secure base for the long horizontal bore toward the Russian mainland.

"Which operator is making the most noise?" he asked his assistant.

"The one in the forward machine," came the answer.

"Figures." He'd have to stop all work in the monster machines following their leader to safely approach the forward borer. Another delay.

Gallagher stepped out of his demountable office, put his hard hat on and climbed into one of the company's mine shuttle cars — a High Mobility Multipurpose Wheeled Vehicle, more commonly referred to as a Humvee. Unlike its lighter civilian equivalent, called a Hummer H1, this was originally military hardware and one of four the company had purchased cheap from one of the bases that had closed down in the early 2000s. With its four-wheel drive, it was an effective shuttle car to move engineers and miners from the surface to the main boring machines far below. This one had a utility tray at the back, sort of like a pick-up truck, that had never been used.

The thing was enormous, but that didn't matter. The tunnels were going to be big enough to accommodate a three-lane highway and the Humvee was only going to be used to ferry people from topside to the lead boring machine. The one nicknamed Big Bertha after Seattle's first female mayor, where the machine was first commissioned.

He turned the ignition and the vehicle's 6.5L V8 turbocharged diesel engine roared into life. He dropped the park brake and put his foot down hard on the accelerator. For nearly six thousand pounds worth of light truck, the Humvee took off at a spritely pace.

Gallagher drove down the recently built construction road from the old base to the entrance to the first shaft of the boring tunnel. Blacktop had already started to break away from the new road base, where the unimaginably heavy boring machines were maneuvered through. Ten minutes later, he reached the entrance of the tunnel.

He gave his ID to the guard who approached his window. The man recognized him immediately and handed the card back to him and waved him through. Gallagher switched on his headlights and drove through.

Five minutes later, he came to a stop where several engineers and machine operators were standing around talking among themselves as though they didn't have a care in the world. Perhaps they didn't? It wasn't their problem that over a hundred million dollars of boring equipment, including Big Bertha was sitting there doing nothing but costing the company a couple hundred thousand dollars a day. And while they were all enjoying a leisurely chat waiting for the machine operator at the head of the convoy to get a move on, he had to explain to the key stakeholders in the project that despite the already almost insurmountable cost overruns, they were still a long way off having to declare the Bering Strait Crossing a total boondoggle.

He switched off the ignition and climbed out of the Humvee. Each of his workers tensed, as though caught by the headmaster for truancy, as Gallagher approached. He shook his head. What did they think was going to happen? The forward machine operator had defiantly pulled the plug. He was bound to come down and get things moving again, today.

Gallagher looked at the group of engineers and machine operators. "All right, where is he?"

"Who?"

"The schmuck who decided today he'd found his balls and decided to cost the company a couple hundred thousand dollars in delays."

"Bill's sitting in his rig," Mark, the tunnel manager for the day shift, said.

"What's his problem, anyway?"

"I don't know. He says the drilling head's struck something."

Gallagher shrugged. "The damned machine designed to slice right through granite for God's sake. So, what's the problem?"

"I don't know. You go talk to him."

Gallagher, realizing he wasn't getting anywhere talking to this bunch, walked toward the lead boring machine, past where the two smaller boring machines had stopped working and his assistant and the crews of both the rear borers followed. Gallagher approached the last of the gigantic tunneling machines.

He watched as the monstrous piece of heavy machinery lurched forward ahead of him. He heard the operator swear. It was immediately followed by a loud explosion, which shook the ground in the tunnel.

Gallagher ducked, instinctively expecting the roof to collapse. When it didn't come down on him, he cautiously rose and looked toward the front of the tunnel, where the machine was toppling, almost in slow motion. The foreman couldn't make sense of what he was seeing at first.

Then, with sudden understanding as the heavy machine disappeared into the newly created fracture in the tunnel wall, he yelled, "Run!"

# Chapter Ten

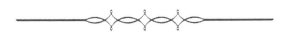

G ALLAGHER TURNED AND ran with the rest of the crew toward the landward end of the tunnel. He expected the freezing sea to come pouring into the tunnel at any moment. Instead of icy saltwater, what followed him was a sustained blast of warm air, carrying dust and other debris. With the rest of his operators, he stumbled, choking, out of the mouth of the tunnel.

Dirt, filth and debris began raining down from above their heads, where the funnel of air spread out in the open and slowed down until it could no longer carry the weight of the dirt and debris it bore. The men stood in clumps, everyone with expressions of confusion.

*What the hell just happened?*

They waited a good thirty minutes for any signs of seawater running up to greet them. When it didn't, Gallagher concluded that the collapse had not been from above, and they could reasonably expect to go and see without drowning.

He led the group back into the tunnel, running again with the hope of rescuing the crew of the forward machine and fighting the gale of hot air and debris every step. When they reached the spot where she'd last been seen, there was no sign of the borer. Only an abyss large enough to swallow her, and ahead, a wall of volcanic gabbro where the foreman would have expected sedimentary bedrock.

The workmen gathered around the perimeter of the hole, trying to peer down into the abyss. However, the still-flowing heated blast drove them back. From what they could tell in brief glimpses with safety goggles protecting their eyes but not the skin of their faces, the machine was not visible.

It appeared the borer had broken into a previously undetected underground cavern. There was no telling how deep it was without specialized equipment, and no chance to form a rescue party from here. The whole crew were presumed dead. The foreman's day was now officially a disaster, but nothing like the poor men who'd gone down with the borer.

"Let's get out of here. There's nothing we can do," he said, with a defeated sigh. The source of the hot air and the detritus it carried was above his pay grade. Let the bigwigs figure it out. He'd have all he could handle keeping his crew from mutinying.

Three hours later, a mine rescue team, two senior engineers, two geologists and one anthropologist arrived. They had been flown in from Anchorage to Wales by a fixed wing aircraft and then from Wales to Big Diomede Island by helicopter. Not a bad effort, Gallagher realized, to pull a group of experts to such a remote part of the world within such short notice.

The mine rescue team donned protective equipment, breathing apparatus, and made their way into the boring tunnel. At the same time the senior engineers, geologists and bigwigs began to try to figure out what happened, what was continuing to happen, and what to do next. Meanwhile, the entire construction camp was being buried under a layer of red sand, grit, and more. The foreman didn't know what to make of the miscellaneous small animals, bush fragments, and oddest of all, bones from both large and small animals being brought up from the cavern by the howling wind. Neither did anyone else.

Gallagher sat in on the frequent meetings, but seldom had anything to contribute. It was his suggestion, though, that brought in a forensic anthropologist to identify the bones. Most were cattle and coyote, which meant they could have originated anywhere on the mainland. That in itself was odd enough. Another oddity — there were no reindeer bones. Reindeer were prevalent in both the Russian and Alaskan peninsulas. Even many of the surrounding islands, such as the Aleutian Islands, had had reindeer introduced and were still herded as a source of subsistence meat.

Oddest of all were the human bones. Not so much those that were of obvious prehistoric origin. The Diomede islands, after all, were thought to be one of the last exposed portions of the land bridge between Asia and North America that existed during the Pleistocene period. The anthropologist was stunned by the size of some of the bone fragments though. They suggested that the origins of those bones were much more modern.

Other than providing a little more information, it made no difference to the foreman's dilemma. He needed to get his crews working again, but before he could do that, he needed more information about that cavern. Would moving the bore hole a few feet or yards to the side save the project? Or would it risk losing another crew and costly machinery? Until someone could tell him that, he was at a standstill.

The engineers couldn't tell him that, though, until the freakish gale stopped. And the geologists couldn't tell him when that would happen. They couldn't even tell him why it was happening. Frustration mounted among the crew, the experts, and the various stakeholders in the project. Nearly eight hours after the original incident, they were still waiting for answers, while the geyser of hot air and copper-colored dust continued unabated.

As the senior engineer from the overall general contractor for the joint Russian/Canadian/American project made his way from his latest inspection of the sinkhole toward the main construction trailer, Gallagher was startled to see a traditional

American ten-gallon Stetson cowboy hat drifting down through the fall of debris. It landed close to his feet. He picked it up, dusted it off, and tried it on for size. It fit.

Gallagher grinned. He shook his head over the ridiculousness of his day. "Can someone please tell me why we haven't heard from the mine rescue team yet?"

# Chapter Eleven

*The Pentagon*

THE SECRETARY OF Defense read her morning briefing. At the end of a long list of notes requiring her attention and action for the day, there was a curious incident of an enormous earth-boring machine disappearing into an abyss off Big Diomede Island that caught her eye. It wasn't likely to be anything for her office to worry about, but interesting all the same.

She called in one of her more trusted science advisors. She showed him the location of the *Gordoye Dostizheniye* on a map and asked if the two incidents could potentially be related.

The science advisor answered without questioning why the Secretary of the world's largest military was concerned about a Russian shipwreck and a mining accident. "Highly doubtful. It's fifteen miles between the two locations by sea, isn't it?"

"I think so. Could both of the incidents have been caused by the same underground event?"

"I don't see how. The report from Big Diomede mentioned that the air coming from the cavern was hot and full of dry red sand and dust. Even if it were water and sea sand coming out of there, the sea temperature in the Bering Strait is barely above freezing now. The disparate temperatures suggest there's no relationship."

The Secretary nodded. "You're right. That will be all."

After he left, she studied the satellite images of the Bering Sea. A puzzled frown formed between her brows. She didn't like coincidences. She especially didn't like this coincidence, touching as it did on a sensitive matter. She called in her Deputy Secretary.

"I need someone to comb recent news articles for strange weather and geographical phenomena in North America and the Pacific."

"I'll get one of the staff on it," he answered. "When do you need the results?"

"Yesterday," she answered.

# Chapter Twelve

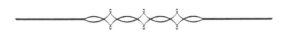

THE DEPUTY SECRETARY dutifully assigned a junior staff member to the task, telling him there was no hurry. Afterward, he left the Pentagon and drove across the Potomac toward downtown D.C. On his way, he dialed a number from memory.

A man answered on the third ring. "Yes?"

"We may have a problem. Meet me at Tosca, in the bar."

Satisfied that he'd be met, he made his way across the 14th Street Bridge and skirted the National Mall on his way to the restaurant. Once there, he seated himself on the next-to-last barstool near a wall and waited for his contact to arrive.

Shortly after, the contact took the last chair. As they perused the menus and savored their first glasses of wine, the contact spoke softly. "What's up?"

"She's interested in the ship," the Deputy Secretary answered.

"How would she even know about it? You're being paranoid." His contact gave a slight shrug. His job was to monitor the Secretary, and notify his boss if she showed any sign that she had recent knowledge of their project. She hadn't been involved with the group for many years, and as far as they knew, she wasn't aware it still existed or had the same agenda it always had. If she was aware, they didn't know if they could trust her now. But this didn't seem like much of a threat, or any reason to believe she knew more than she should.

"No. She's researching geographical phenomena," the Deputy Secretary insisted.

"What difference does it make? The stone's gone. The whole damned ship is gone. We have to start over, so stop worrying."

"It concerns me," the Deputy Secretary answered.

"I'll take care of it," his contact stated firmly. "There's no need for you to concern yourself further. Do I make myself clear?"

"There's something else, you need to know."

"What?"

"The Secretary of Defense received a report today that might change everything."

His contacted nodded. "I'm listening. What was in the report?"

"There was an accident at the Transcontinental World Link. Apparently, the tunnel boring machine punched through something it wasn't supposed to and disappeared into some sort of abyss." The Deputy Secretary swallowed. "It's unlikely, but I wondered if there was a connection."

The contact laughed. "Forget about it. I already have a man working there. He'll take care of it."

"Are you certain?"

"Of course, I'm bloody well certain. You do your job, I'll do mine."

Downing the rest of his wine in one swallow without regard to the fine vintage, the Deputy Secretary slammed down his wineglass. "Don't let your confidence lead you to make a serious mistake," he snarled. "I've lost my appetite. I think we're done here."

His contact returned the snarl with a supercilious smile. "Don't forget. We put you where you are, my friend. Don't let your ambition lead you to believe you can have us remove her without good cause. She was once a friend." With that, he set his own wineglass down gently and left, leaving the Deputy Secretary to pay the tab.

# Chapter Thirteen

*Bering Strait*

S AM WATCHED AS the Russian Admiral-Gorshkov-class frigate continued its grid survey of the area toward the northern end of the Bering Strait. It had arrived overnight and had been uninterested in any communications with him or any one of the other search vessels for that matter. Not that it bothered him. What was he supposed to tell them? It looks like the *Gordoye Dostizheniye* was swallowed by a sinkhole, but there's no evidence of her wreckage anywhere? No. It wouldn't be an easy conversation. Besides, the Secretary of Defense was still waiting for him to update her with his progress. One hard conversation would do him for today.

With a new hot coffee in his hand he briskly climbed the series of steps and entered the bridge of the *Maria Helena.* The ship was currently at anchor. At the navigation table Matthew was calculating whether or not they had enough fuel to continue their original project, or if they needed to divert to Anchorage to refuel — presuming the rescue mission was officially canceled.

Sam said, "I've spoken with the Coast Guard. They've changed the search to a retrieval mission. No longer a rescue mission."

Matthew looked up. "It's been two days since the ship went under. That's fair enough. Are we staying on to help, or returning to our original project?"

"Most likely we'll return to our original plan."

Matthew asked, "Have you spoken to the Secretary of Defense?"

"It's on my list." Sam took a gulp of coffee. "Any news from the Russian frigate?"

"Yes. I spoke with its captain about an hour ago on the radio. I told him what we'd found and what we think has happened."

"And?"

"He told me he thought I was lying and that he would conduct his own investigation."

"What the hell does he think's going on?"

Matthew laughed and shook his head. "I know, right! It was a cargo ship that went under. Yet they're treating it like there's been some sort of clandestine plot to steal state secrets."

Sam didn't laugh. Instead, he felt like he'd been kicked in the guts, as he recalled the Secretary of Defense's insistence that he beat the Russians to the wreckage and retrieve shipping container numbered 404. He forced himself to grin. "Yeah, go figure. Oh well, it won't be our problem much longer."

"Good." Matthew returned to his charts.

Sam picked up the satellite phone next to the helm and brought up the Secretary of Defense's number. He pressed enter and the phone rang.

"Did you retrieve it?" she asked, immediately.

So, small talk was out. Sam stepped out onto the aft balcony and paced. "No. I couldn't find it."

"The shipping container?"

"No. The *Gordoye Dostizheniye.*"

"You're meant to be the best in the business. How did you lose a ship in less than a hundred feet of water?" Her words came out vitriolic. "You were given its precise GPS coordinates where it sank for God's sake!"

Sam grinned. It had been a while since he'd been the recipient of her dissatisfaction. "We think the *Gordoye Dostizheniye* was dragged under by a giant sinkhole. We brought out a dredging vessel to clear the ground below, but if the ship's down there, it's a long way down."

"How long?"

"Well. Nothing came up on our ground penetrating radar, which was able to infiltrate up to a hundred feet below the seabed."

"Do you think there might a series of tunnels below the seabed?"

Sam thought about it for a moment. "It's one possibility."

"And if there was such a tunnel, and part of it collapsed, could that have caused the sort of sinkhole you're talking about — something big enough to devour all traces of the *Gordoye Dostizheniye?*"

"Sure. It's definitely a possibility if the tunnel was large enough. The thing is, there's no evidence of any sort of subterranean tunnels anywhere north of the Aleutian Islands. Heck, there isn't even any evidence of volcanic activities that could have once caused a series of lava tubes. So, I think it's all still in the highly speculative category."

Sam waited for the Secretary of Defense to reply. When she didn't, he asked, "Don't you think?"

Instead, she asked a new question. "Is the Russian frigate still surveying the Bering Strait for the *Gordoye Dostizheniye?*"

"Yes."

"Did they ask where you thought the ship disappeared to?"

"Yeah. Matthew spoke with her captain about an hour ago."

"What did he say?"

"The truth. We have no idea where she went."

"Good. Hopefully he'll keep scouring the seabed long enough for you to reach Big Diomede Island."

"What's on Big Diomede Island?"

"The first stage in the construction of the Bering Strait Crossing."

"That whacky idea for Russia, Canada and the U.S. build a tunnel for a bullet train linking the three countries?"

"That's the one. But not just an idea. Construction began several months ago."

"You don't say?"

"Yes," she responded dryly. "Let me cut to the chase. Their Big Bertha class boring machine punched a hole through the stone, into a large cavern. So far, they haven't been able to retrieve their machine or its crew."

"You think the two incidents are connected?"

"If it isn't, it's an awfully strange coincidence."

"What do you want me to do?"

"The same thing I asked you to do for me yesterday. Locate the *Gordoye Dostizheniye* and retrieve the shipping container 404."

"Do you think the construction team are going to be happy for us to go searching for your secret container while they're resolving a disaster?"

"They will be. They're scouring the Alaskan countryside for a rescue team."

"A mine rescue team?" Sam asked. "Didn't they have their own team available to go in already?"

"They did. But the team never came out again."

"Great. And you'd like us to offer our services?"

"No. I'm ordering you to find that shipping container. I'll contact the construction company and tell them you're on your way."

# Chapter Fourteen

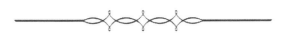

I T WAS ONLY a few minutes later that Elise notified him of a call from British Columbia. The Secretary of Defense must have had that CEO on speed-dial. If he was to help out the crew on the Transcontinental World Link project he would need information. The Secretary of Defense may have a department researcher, but Sam had the best data-miner in the world.

"Elise, get me everything you can on a Canadian drilling company losing their tunneling machine to an underground sink hole. Then cross-reference it to any other unusual geologic events in the past month."

"On it," she replied.

With that, Sam picked up the ship-to-shore satellite phone. "Sam Reilly."

"Mr. Reilly, my name's Russel Wheeler. I have it on good authority that you're the best there is at underground salvage, and more importantly than that, you just happen to be nearby my tunnel boring project on Tomorrow Island. Is that true?"

Sam grinned. "My mother taught me not to brag, sir, but we can certainly try our best to assist you. I hear you've lost a valuable machine down one heck of a sinkhole?"

The CEO's voice was solemn. "Her crew of five is our first

priority. Their families deserve to know their fate for certain, and to have their remains returned to them if what we fear is true."

Sam liked the man. He'd known men, including his own father, for whom the expense would be first on his mind. "Of course, sir. We'll do our best, but as you can imagine, by the sounds of what I've been told we're unlikely to find any survivors."

"I understand." Wheeler paused for a moment and then spoke, "Do you have any idea what possibly caused it?"

"No, sir. We've only just been made aware of it."

"If you can get to it, I'd like to recover my workers, dead or alive, and then get an evaluation of whether it's worth trying to recover the machine."

"Sure. We'll see what we find." Sam took a deep breath, held it and then said. "The rescue mission and any assistance we can provide for the recovery of those trapped inside is on the house. If we locate the boring machine and you want our help to retrieve it, we'll talk about the price. Does that sound fair?"

"More than fair. We'll be happy to pay according to standard Lloyds Open Form terms if we ask you to do the salvage of the machine."

It was the first time he'd heard an owner accept LOF without preamble. "That will work fine. Out of curiosity, what's the machine worth?" Sam asked.

"She was originally built by Hitachi for Seattle's Alaskan Way Viaduct replacement tunnel for $80 million U.S. Of course, she had a $20 million-dollar overhaul before she came to us," the CEO answered.

Sam whistled. It would be a nice little salvage job, if it could be done. He wouldn't know until he'd seen the situation first-hand. "Well, we'll have to see what we're up against," he remarked. "We can be on-site within the hour. Does the island have a helipad?"

"Yeah. Right next to the entrance to the boring tunnel. Despite its name, Big Diomede Island is tiny. You can't miss the helipad. But, Reilly, be aware we have a weird localized turbulent air weather condition here, apparently originating in the bore hole."

"Is it affecting the landing pad area?"

"No, but I thought your pilot might want to know."

"Great, I'll let her know," Sam said. "We'll take the helicopter and see them as soon as we can."

Sam wasted no time, but contacted Matthew with the change of plans immediately. Moments later, he felt the change in the ship's engines. A few minutes after that, Tom predictably arrived at Sam's cabin door.

"What's up? We're moving."

Sam pretended shock. "Really?"

"Cut the crap. Where are we going? Or is it a surprise?" Tom could match Sam sarcasm for sarcasm.

"Come in, take a load off. I'll fill you in."

While Sam told Tom all he knew from the Secretary and the CEO of the drilling company, Tom stayed silent. When Sam stopped talking, he waited for Tom's response. Tom had a slight smile, and appeared to be thinking it all over.

"I can see the wheels turning in your head, buddy," Sam said. "What do you think?"

"I think I'll take a sinkhole without sand in it over one with sand in it any day," Tom quipped. "Yeah, I know that's what you think happened to that ship. And I don't have a better answer. But I'm glad we're not going to try to dig in and dive it, frankly."

"What do you make of the hot wind coming out of the sinkhole where the tunneling machine went down?"

"Hard to say. I guess my first thought would be it bottoms out in an underwater fumarole. If that's the case, we're going to need some serious safety equipment to get to the machine, if it isn't already submerged in magma," Tom's expression changed as he considered the implications. "And the abyss might be filled with lethal gases, too!"

Sam grinned. "Not so anxious to switch from a dive under unstable sand to climbing voluntarily into an active volcano, huh?"

"I've had better offers." Tom grinned.

"So, we'll need to get some climbing gear, breathing apparatus and exposure suits ready. We'd better round up Veyron and plan for the worst. If the situation isn't that dire when we get there, so much the better. Genevieve's going to drop us off as soon as we're good to go."

# Chapter Fifteen

THE SEA KING'S rotor blades began turning slowly, accelerating until they reached lift-off rotation. Genevieve firmly gripped the collective control lever beside her seat and the cyclic-pitch control column in front of her, easing the helicopter off the aft deck of the *Maria Helena*. The helicopter hovered for a moment, before she dipped the nose, applied the throttles, and headed south.

In the back of the helicopter Sam sat reading a series of notes Elise had prepared for him on the Transcontinental World Link. Once he was finished with the basic concept of the project, he moved on to information regarding the gigantic boring machine. Finally, he examined the geologist's survey of the region. The Diomede Islands were primarily composed of Cretaceous-Age granite or quartz monzonite, meaning the islands were formed through glacial movements and not volcanic activity.

He shook his head. None of it made any sense. If the Big Bertha boring machine didn't disappear down some sort of lava tube, where did it go?

Genevieve asked, "Which island are they boring into?"

Sam said, "They're running a land bridge from Alaska to Yesterday Isle, and then a tunnel from Tomorrow Island to the Siberian Peninsular."

"Why do they call the islands Yesterday and Tomorrow?" she asked.

"Because the international date line runs straight through the middle. Big Diomede is twenty-one hours ahead of Little Diomede."

"Go figure."

Sam looked up. They'd been in the air less than ten minutes, but already Big Diomede was visible through the plexiglass, with Little Diomede just beyond it. The entrance to the first stage of the tunnel came into view a few seconds later. A couple hundred feet back from the entrance was a large pile of quartz, stretching more than fifty feet in the air and three hundred feet back. Those rocks, he'd read, would be used to join both islands together. Closer to the tunnel entrance, contrasting the white mountain of quartz, was a pile of red soil twenty feet high.

Tom asked, "What the hell is that?"

Sam watched as a small contingent of men in mining overalls and suits made their way toward the helipad. He said, "I have no idea, but I think we're going to soon find out."

Genevieve spotted the helipad next to the main entrance. She made one reconnaissance circuit and then put the Sea King down. She left the rotors turning while Sam, Tom and Veyron began removing the equipment. When Tom came to grab the last crate, he leaned into the cockpit and kissed Genevieve's lips.

Genevieve pulled back an instant later. "Don't let Sam lead you astray. You know how stupid he can be, right?"

"I know. I'll look after him," Tom said.

"Hey, I'm right here," Sam said. "I can hear you, you know?"

Genevieve looked over her shoulder and smiled at him. "That's what I'm counting on, Sam."

Sam grabbed the last kit and Tom slid the door shut. Twenty seconds later, the Sea King was back in the air, returning to the *Maria Helena*. The pile of equipment they expected to use over the next few days were stacked neatly in a row. The small contingent of miners and experts approached.

"Nice chopper," one of the engineers said.

"Thanks," Sam responded. "I guess your CEO contacted you about me."

"Not my CEO," the spokesman answered. "We're consultants, too. Just like you. He did ask us to cooperate with you."

"Fair enough," Sam said, nodding. "So, who's in charge?"

"That will be me." A man in his early fifties approached and offered his hand. "Michael Gallagher. I'm the head foreman for the project. I was in charge when the boring machine punched a hole into the sinkhole. Those are my men down there."

Sam shook his hand. "Understood. All right. Let's get right down to it. What are we looking at, here? Nice cowboy hat, by the way. You don't see many Stetsons around here."

"Oh, I forgot I was wearing it," Gallagher said. "I thought it was odd, too. It came out of that accursed hole in the ground. Just flew up and came to land a few feet in front of me. I've been wearing it ever since."

"Did it belong to one of the crew of the boring machine?" Sam asked.

"No one claims to have ever seen it before," Gallagher said. "Could we talk about the project?"

"Sure. Have you been able to approach the edge of the sinkhole yet?"

"We've been getting closer every day. I know what you're going to ask. We don't think it's an active volcano. The heat is dissipating. I'll let our geologist tell you his theory."

Sam turned politely to the man Gallagher indicated. "Not a volcano? That's good news."

"It sure is," the geologist responded. "Of course, we haven't been able to get down there to test my theory, but I think a fissure may have opened under the main sinkhole. It's letting out heated gasses under pressure, but as the pressure is relieved by the release of gas, it's beginning to close up again."

Sam looked at Tom, who nodded. "That makes sense. Any idea whether the fumarole will open again? What happens if we get down there and it releases more superheated gas?"

"Then you get fried," the geologist answered cheerfully. "I can't honestly predict what it will do. We're far north of the convergent boundary the runs by the Aleutian Islands. We wouldn't have expected any earth movement here, or very little."

"And yet..." Sam prompted.

"And yet, the borer broke into an enormous sinkhole, and the heated wind gives us our only clue...that the sinkhole is related to the fumarole that's spewing the heat. Sorry, but that's all I can tell you. I haven't had the equipment to explore enough to prove any of it. It's just a theory."

Sam was lost in thought for a moment, and then nodded. "Has anyone been monitoring the heat level?"

"They didn't have the equipment to do it until we got here," the geologist reported. "It did raise the temperature level in the tunnel to about 80 degrees Fahrenheit, which is pretty significant. Outside temperature was averaging in the upper 40s to low 50s Fahrenheit during the day, slightly cooler at night. The tunnel temperature was a few degrees cooler than that, just above freezing."

"And since you arrived?" Sam prompted.

"Outside temps have risen slightly, which is normal for the season. Tunnel temperature has fallen slightly, to around 75. Temperature of the wind stream is hovering just below 80 now. When we got here, the wind was stronger and the heat in the center of the stream was near 150. No one could get near the edge to look down into the tunnel. They didn't have the equipment for it."

Tom leaned forward. "And they call that searing heat?" He forced a laugh. "Sam, we have an improved version of the suits we wore in the Sahara."

"That's good. The old version would have been adequate, though."

"Yes, I think so. Are you thinking what I'm thinking?" Tom grinned. His mood had improved since the *Maria Helena* had left the vicinity of the sand mound in the Bering Strait.

"I'm thinking we need a very long line and a winch," Sam quipped.

"We have both, but it will take a few hours to get the winch in place," Tom said. "Should we get some sleep first?"

"Good idea. We'll start first thing in the morning."

The tunnel crew foreman put in his contribution. "We have winches. What are you thinking? You're going down there?" He shuddered.

"I don't know how else we're going to find your machine," Sam said. His grin matched Tom's. This was going to be a walk in the park compared to the prospect of finding a ship under hundreds of tons of sand.

"Better you than me," Gallagher muttered. "You men get your rest. My crew will place the equipment and have it ready for you in the morning. They've had little enough to do for the past few days."

"Thanks." Sam extended his hand and the foreman shook it enthusiastically.

"No, thank you."

Sam said, "We were told you'd already sent a rescue team in?"

Gallagher nodded, but his face was solemn. "We did."

"And what did they find?"

"We lost contact with them shortly after they entered the tunnel."

# Chapter Sixteen

IT WAS EARLY when Sam and Tom returned from the *Maria Helena* to find the senior engineer, the geologist, the foreman, and several of his men gathered around the hole in the tunnel floor. Veyron was there, too. He'd stayed to ensure the winch was set up correctly.

"There's good news and bad news," Gallagher said.

Sam said, "Tell me the good news first."

"Temperature has fallen to about the same as in the tunnel here," Gallagher said.

"That's a good sign, but we're prepared for worse below." Sam didn't demonstrate by showing the thermal suit he wore under his clothes. It wasn't exactly top secret, but he didn't take industrial espionage lightly, and they'd been entrusted with the secrecy of the high-tech cooling suits.

"And the bad news?"

"One of the men from the mines rescue team came out about an hour ago."

"What did he say?"

"He said they never found the crew and that the other three men from the rescue team all died."

"Died... how?" Sam asked.

"Mostly accidents. One made a simple mistake. His carabiner wasn't attached properly to his harness and he slipped, falling to his death. Another one tripped and got his neck caught around his rope, snapping it instantly."

"And the third one? You said there were four men in the mine rescue team. What happened to him?"

"Apparently, he simply clutched his chest like he was having a heart attack or something, and died."

"Any chance he was exposed to some of toxic gas?" Sam suggested.

"Not a chance. They were all wearing protective heat exposure suits and breathing apparatus."

"All right. I need to talk to this guy... what's his name?"

"Ilya Yezhov. But I'm afraid you can't talk to him."

Sam let the name sink in. "He's Russian?"

"Yeah. This is a combined Canadian, American, and Russian project. Our mine rescue team were struggling to put a team together within the first twenty-four hours. Apparently one of their crew was recently injured. Yezhov was on his way to Alaska to do some joint training, and so was seconded for this mission."

"All right." Sam nodded. Given their location, it made plenty of sense where they'd dragged their resources from. "So why the hell can't I speak to him?"

"He's not on the island anymore. He insisted on being airlifted straight away back to Alaska."

Sam frowned. "Really? Why?"

"Yezhov had a very different theory about what happened to my men in the boring machine and his rescue team."

"Go on. What was his theory?"

"He says they were all killed by Skinwalkers."

# Chapter Seventeen

"**S**KINWALKERS?" SAM ASKED, a wry and incredulous curl forming on his lips. "What the hell are they?"

"It's old Navajo superstitious bullshit. Something about evil witches hiding in tunnels or something."

"Navajo… as in Four Corners region of the U.S.?"

"That's the one."

"So, what's an old superstition from the south doing up here?"

"I don't know. We employ a lot of local people from the Yupik tribe up here. For some reason, they seem to share a lot of similar fears and superstitions as the old Navajo Indians from long ago." Gallagher gave him an all-knowing and superior grin that suggested it was all madness. "Go figure, hey?"

"Right." Sam nodded. He wasn't very superstitious himself, but in his experience, he'd learned that superstitions, like all longstanding myths, were often based on some truth. "All right. I'll keep it in mind."

Ignoring the conversation, Tom was harnessing up. Sam soon joined him, after giving the winch operator a crash course on how slowly to lower them, and cautioning him not to retract the line until they contacted him by radio. He reinforced the lesson by saying, "We don't know if there's an open vein of magma down there. If you hear us say get us out of here, we mean bring us out fast!"

The winch operator turned pale. "Yes, sir. I'll be ready."

Sam clapped him on the shoulder. "Good man. Now, the rest of the signals will be one word, and we need precision. 'Stop' means right now. Just in case we're coming right down into the hot stuff. Got it?"

He gulped. "Yes, sir. Got it. And I guess 'slow' means slow down?"

Sam suppressed a grin. "That would be a good guess. Are you ready?"

The winch operator had caught the grin. He took a deep breath and risked a quip of his own. "The question is, are you ready?"

Sam replied, "I was born ready!"

Sam buckled into his own harness, and then checked Tom's, while Tom simultaneously checked his. As well as the DARPA-inspired thermal suits, they both wore a fully enclosed face-mask with a built-in radio, and carbon fiber air tanks attached to their backs, capable of providing up to two hours of air. At this stage, they still didn't have a clue how hot the air was down there, or whether any poisonous gasses had been released.

Sam stepped into the edge of the opening and flicked on his 3000-lumen dive light. The entire sinkhole lit up like an ancient vault being opened to the sun for the first time. He could see that the dark, glassy walls of the cavern suggested it had been formed by some sort of volcanic event a long time ago. He shined his flashlight downward, and discovered that the sinkhole traversed in a steep, but manageable thirty-degree slope. He could see a rough indent gouged into the rocky slope where the Big Bertha boring machine had obviously slid downward. The sinkhole was so deep his flashlight couldn't reach its bottom. If the slope continued at that angle, there was at least some hope they'd still find survivors.

The air inside was still. No sign of molten lava or superheated gasses appeared to be coming from the suspected fumarole. He glanced at his Parallax MQ-2 monitor. The sensor was used to detect lethal gasses. The unit indicated, at least for the time being, that the air was safe. The sensor was capable of detecting all the gases that would typically be found underground, including LPG, i-butane, propane, alcohol, hydrogen, and smoke. It was a critical piece of equipment that could mean the difference between their life and death.

If this was a fumarole, the could expect all the invisible killers. Gasses such as carbon dioxide, sulfur dioxide, hydrogen chloride, and hydrogen sulfide were commonly released in the form of steam.

For all their banter, the situation was deadly serious. If the heat was caused by a fumarole, toxic gases, superheated steam were all a possibility. Whatever caused this, was already deadly and it was only Sam's confidence and experience that drove him forward.

He checked his KGZ-10 oxygen sensor. While toxic gases were their greatest concern, the monitoring of oxygen was also critical. Low levels of oxygen fail to sustain human breathing, while anything above the standard 21 percent found in the natural atmosphere can be just as dangerous in a highly combustive environment. Right now, the device was reading 19 percent, or just below atmospheric, and well within the ability to sustain adequate oxygenation.

Tom looked at him and then at the safety harness. "We could easily walk down there, you know?"

"Sure. But let's keep it on. We still don't know what really happened to the first rescue team. If we get into trouble, I'd much rather have a safety line to pull us back up."

Veyron checked that the two lines would run smoothly over a makeshift pulley system on the edge of the opening.

Sam said, "Veyron, it looks like we can walk down there. Just make sure you leave enough slack for us to descend, but if you see the cable start moving quickly, stop it. Also, if we get into trouble, you'll need to pull us out quick."

"I'll look after it," Veyron said.

Despite his bravado, Sam did have a little apprehension. They were being lowered into a hole of unknown depth, and unknown composition at the bottom. It was rather like being lowered down the throat of a volcano, except that he felt relatively certain there wasn't an active pool of lava at the bottom. If there had been, the temperature wouldn't have been falling... he hoped.

He and Tom had agreed to keep their chatter to a minimum to avoid confusing the operator. It was one thing to do so with their own crew, who were used to it, but using another auxiliary crew could be more dangerous. They didn't want this guy to miss an emergency command by getting caught up in their usual banter.

They descended the steep slope slowly, carefully placing each foot so they didn't slip. The winch operator was releasing the cable at a rate of fifteen feet per minute, and it felt like they were crawling. Sam peered downward, trying to see something through the oncoming dust. The lights were almost worse than useless, reflecting off the suspended dust like headlights in a snowstorm.

After ten minutes, with no bottom in sight, Sam spoke into his radio. "Increase speed of descent to twenty feet per minute."

"Copy that," the winch operator replied.

They continued walking down the steep slope for nearly twenty minutes before reaching the bottom.

Tom's calm voice sounded in his headset. "Slow."

Sam felt a slight jerk as the operator immediately dialed back their speed to under four feet per minute, but it was only another five minutes before the ground below leveled out. To his relief, the only lights were those coming from his and Tom's headlamps. No hot magma right here, anyway. His suit regulated his body temperature at the optimum 98.6 degrees, so he wouldn't have felt the heat unless the temperature on the bottom was more than the suit could handle, but they would have seen the red glow of fiery molten rock had it been anywhere nearby.

Sam used his more powerful hand held-flashlight and swept the room in a slow arc. The boring machine should have been right there, but neither he or Tom could see it.

"Not again," muttered Tom.

Sam said, "Where did it go?"

# Chapter Eighteen

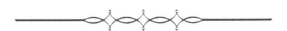

"**W**E'RE BATTING A thousand," Tom continued.

Sam smiled. "Come again?"

"First, we can't find a ship right where it went down, and now we can't find a seven-ton machine that's sixty feet in diameter. Don't you think there's something wrong with this picture?"

"There's definitely something wrong with the first piece. As far as the second is concerned, what puzzles me most is why dust, animal bones, and a cowboy hat flew up from here when the machine landed. If the floor were wet, I'd have thought it punched right through into a vein of magma and melted."

"That would make sense. Except, as you pointed out, the floor in here is dry as some of the bones that came up with that wind."

Sam's eyes followed the grooves in the ground where the boring machine had slid down the steep slope. The tracks disappeared into a new tunnel. He took a compass bearing. The tunnel headed due south. To the right, a second tunnel disappeared toward the north.

He shook his head and laughed. "Is it just me, or does it look like the head of the boring machine kept turning after it slid down the slope?"

"You think it's pulled itself through the tunnel?" Tom asked.

"Must have."

"I think you're right. The question is, however, how far could it have gone?" Sam untethered himself from the lines. Speaking to the winch operator, he said, "We've reached the bottom. Still haven't found the boring machine, her crew or the rescue team. We're going to have a quick look around. We'll let you know when we're back on the line."

Veyron answered. "You didn't find the boring machine?"

"No."

"You're having a rough week, Sam. That's two for two…"

"Thanks, Veyron. I'm still working on fixing both of those stats. We'll be back soon."

Sam checked his Parallax MQ-2 monitor and KGZ-10 oxygen sensor. There were no lethal gasses present, and the oxygen levels were consistent with normal atmospheric levels. Now free from their safety lines, the first order of business was to explore the extent of the chamber. Sam pointed behind him and started to move toward the nearest wall, indicating he'd go clockwise. Tom nodded and walked with him, intending to go counterclockwise when they got to the wall. Sam found the first opening.

He marked the southern tunnel with a fluorescent orange crayon and kept going. Before long, he'd also found an opening that he assumed pointed toward the Seward Peninsula. Again, he marked it with the fluorescent crayon and moved on. Only a few minutes later, he met Tom coming from the opposite direction.

"This isn't a sinkhole," Tom announced.

"What do you mean?"

"It's a volcanic dome. They must have bored too close to the ceiling, and the remaining rock wouldn't hold the weight of the machine. There are lava tubes extending to the north and south back there," Tom answered, indicating the direction from where he'd come.

Sam shined his flashlight at the main tunnel to the south, where the boring machine had left deep grooves cut into the obsidian floor. "Shall we go check out the fate of the machine operators?"

"All right," Tom said.

The ground had a shallow layer of loose sand, the top quarter-inch or so was like the sand that had blown out of the sinkhole when it first caved in. Their feet left prints in the fine red sand, and revealed black sand below it.

At first, they chatted as they walked, putting forth theories on how erosion could have occurred in the tubes, when no wind or water was present to cause it. That led to joking speculation that occasional floods occurred from breeches in the roof of the tubes. Neither believed it, though. It stood to reason that if floods occurred, there would be standing water, or the tubes would be filled by the sea. Instead, it was dry.

The tunnel meandered like an ancient river, constantly trying to find an easier path for its desired course. Sometimes it dipped as much as thirty feet downward, while other times turning sharply to the left or right. The tracks were easy to follow, being carved several inches deep into the obsidian tunnel. At times, the markings struck the walls and even the roof, as Big Bertha appeared to ricochet from each wall of the ancient lava tube, while her powerful motors continued to pull her forward.

Sam said, "Have you ever heard of a lava tube that extends miles into the earth?"

"In general, lava tubes are pretty short. A few hundred feet at most. Not many are as long as a mile."

"So, you think we're just about at the end?"

"Yeah." Tom wore a supercilious grin. "Of course, it might be just like the Kazumura Cave."

"The what?" Sam asked.

"Kazumura Cave, on the Big Island of Hawaii."

Sam nodded. Somewhere in the back of his mind there was some sort of recollection of hearing about the behemoth lava tube. "Go on. What distance did they survey it at?"

"The cave is located on the eastern slope of Kilauea. Kilauea is the most recently active volcano on the Big Island..."

"How long!"

"It was measured just over forty miles in length and a little over three and a half thousand feet deep."

"You've got to be kidding me." Sam stopped. He checked his watch. They'd been walking for nearly thirty minutes. "All right. So, the boring machine... it could be miles farther in, couldn't it?"

"Yeah. What do you want to do?"

"Let's turn around. We'll return this afternoon with more equipment for a prolonged expedition."

Back at the main volcanic dome where they'd first entered the lava tube, Sam stopped again. His eyes focused on the slope toward the surface, where the boring machine had slid down. The gradient somehow appeared softer from the bottom up. Most things did. It was no more than thirty degrees and the stone was solid. It wasn't formed from gravel. It was obsidian.

Tom smiled. "What are you thinking?"

"Do you think we could drive one of those military Humvees down this slope?"

# Chapter Nineteen

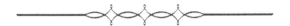

*Cloud Ranch, Southwestern Colorado*

BRODY HAD PUSHED his horse as hard as he dared through the afternoon to reach the homestead on Cloud Ranch. After racing to the bunkhouse on his lathered horse, he found the place empty. He ran to the main ranch house, which was similarly deserted. Frustrated, he turned in a circle, wondering where everyone could have gone. A short distance from the house, he spotted someone coming out of the barn, a woman. He sighed in relief. It was his older sister in the complicated relationships of his tribe. Whites would have called her his cousin, the daughter of his mother's older brother.

"Jenn!" Brody had had a crush on Jenn Williams since he was a toddler and she a pre-teen. Never having found anyone to take her place in his affections, he still dreamed she could be his someday, knowing it was nothing but a dream. She didn't give any sign of returning his worship of her, but she still showed her affection for him as a brother.

Since he couldn't have Jenn, he'd used the few times he'd been in town since going to work on the ranch to find a woman like her. It had proved impossible. Jenn, in addition to being beautiful, was smart and tough. He'd have settled for anyone as beautiful as her, and maybe a little less sassy.

Jenn's lustrous black hair usually hung down her back in a

thick braid. Dark brown eyes set wide, a straight nose with just the slightest upturn at the tip, and the high cheekbones representative of their people formed a pleasing face, culminating in an unusual pointed chin. She wore no makeup on the ranch, but her smooth brown skin needed none. Unlike many tribal women her age, she hadn't begun to thicken through the body from consuming too much of the food introduced by the white man or from having children. Brody didn't know why she was single.

Jenn had used her influence with her boss when Brody had applied for the cowhand position. He had no experience around cattle, but he knew his way around horses. He credited her with his getting the job after his buddy Kevin told him about it many years ago. Since then, he and Kevin had corresponded a few times and they got together when Kevin visited his mother's family on the reservation. Neither had ever married.

"Brody, what's wrong?" Jenn asked, looking at his disheveled appearance. Her brown eyes held an expression of concern.

"It's Malcom! We have to rescue him." He grabbed her hand and started to pull her back toward where his horse was tethered.

She took one look at the horse and stopped, digging in her heels and forcing Brody to stop as well. "Brody Frost! What have you done to this horse? He's not going anywhere, and *we're* not going anywhere until you've taken care of him."

"Jenn, I think Skinwalkers have Malcom. Where is everyone, anyway?"

"Skinwalkers! Brody have you been drinking?" She leaned forward and sniffed his breath, hastily retreating from the stale stench of fear. "Let's sit down. Tell me the whole story."

"There's no time! He's out there..." Brody choked up. The memory of Malcom's last wail of terror formed a lump in his throat that he couldn't clear. He stared helplessly at Jenn, willing her to see his desperation.

She searched his face, and her own changed. "All right. Ben took the others to town. Can we wait for them to get back?"

Brody shook his head in defeat. He wouldn't take Jenn into that awful place, and he couldn't do it alone. Malcom was doomed, if not already dead. Jenn took the gesture to mean they couldn't wait.

"All right. Give your horse some water and get that gear off him. You can groom him later. I'll saddle my horse and find another for you, and we'll go see about Malcom. You can tell me on the way why you think Skinwalkers have him."

Her calm demeanor and sensible plan got through to Brody. At least enough to break through his mental fog. He nodded and walked toward his horse. A few minutes later, Jenn rode out on her mare, leading a stallion for Brody.

Brody recognized the stallion as belonging to Ben Whitecloud, his boss and owner of the ranch. It was a presumption, but he assumed Jenn would know whether it was okay to take the boss's horse. He threw his saddle over the fresh blanket the stallion was wearing and cinched it up, then vaulted into it and nudged the horse into a canter. He'd ridden his at a gallop, but it wouldn't do to injure or wear out the boss's favorite animal. If Malcom wasn't dead already, he probably wouldn't be in another hour, either.

On the way to the edge of the mesa, he filled Jenn in on the events of the day.

"You really found an old cliff dwelling?" she asked in wonder. "How is it possible it's never been discovered before?"

"The area's pretty remote," Brody answered. "And it's hidden halfway down a canyon wall, around a bend from the narrowest part. I don't know what's on the other side, but from this side you wouldn't be able to see it at all."

"And this wind blew from all the way out here into the kiva?" she asked.

"That's what it seemed like at the time," he answered. "But thinking about it on the way back, it was more like the air was being sucked into that sipapu, like Malcom." He shuddered. "One minute he was inside the kiva, and the next he was flying around it and whoosh! In he went. I thought he was dead, but then he screamed. I'll never forget that scream in my life."

"Brody," Jenn began gently. "Maybe that was just a noise the earth made. Maybe it wasn't Malcom."

"It was Malcom. That's why I think Skinwalkers have him. I don't know anything else that could scare him that bad."

Jenn was silent for a while. At last she spoke, again sounding like she was trying to avoid upsetting him. "Brody, if you were being sucked into a hole in the earth, wouldn't you be scared badly?"

"I would if Skinwalkers were causing it," he replied stubbornly. "Listen, Jenn. You shouldn't go with me. I'll go alone, and if I don't come back, you can ride for help. I can't risk them getting you, too."

"Little brother, I'm touched by your concern. But there is something you don't know about me," she confessed. "Our grandmother is a powerful shaman. She taught me to banish Skinwalkers, along with the rest of her craft. I shouldn't tell you this, but I am a medicine woman myself. I am not afraid of them."

Awed, Brody looked at his sister with renewed respect. No wonder she had never married. He felt a little safer in her presence. Maybe he would survive this day.

Brody took a deep breath as for the second time in two days he prepared to face his worst fears—heights and Skinwalkers. He hardly dared even think the name of the latter. It was bad luck to mention them, and he'd already said the name too many times on this day. But being with his older sister made him feel safe, as odd as that was. He was a grown man, after all, not a kid. But even though she was only six years older, she had always protected him and treated him like a favorite.

"We climbed down right about here," he said, watching closely for prints to show him the exact spot where he had led Malcom over the edge. "But the cliff houses are over there." He pointed up-canyon and across.

Jenn followed the line of his gaze. "It looks like the canyon widens before that."

"From the bottom, it makes a turn, and the ruins are around the bend."

"Let's go ahead and climb down the route you took. It might be easier to find the ruins again following your prints."

It didn't matter to Brody. Any route down the cliff face was going to be heart-stopping. But he supposed the one that was already familiar was as good as any. After a few more minutes of searching, he picked up the trail and followed his own prints to the edge.

"It's not too bad," he said, trying to sound confident. He'd probably failed, but he felt a little better about himself. Jenn was right behind him. He felt better about her being the one to follow him down, too. Malcom was okay, but Jenn knew how to negotiate the brittle sandstone and was less likely to fall and plunge both of them to their deaths.

The time of day had changed the light by the time they reached the bottom, and some of the route was deep in shadow. For the first time, Brody realized they'd better move fast or risk having to rough-camp in the canyon. He wouldn't risk the climb in the dark. However, a night in a canyon with Skinwalkers about wouldn't be his favorite option, either. He picked up the pace as he traced their way along the canyon bottom to the turn where the cliff dwelling would reveal itself.

Jenn's gasp of delight told him they'd found it. He was too engrossed in reading the tracks he and Malcom had left earlier to see the village when it first came into view.

"Remember, Jenn. It's dangerous," he cautioned. "We don't know what caused that wind that snatched Malcom, or if or when it might start again."

"I'll be careful," she responded. "But this is extraordinary! Just think, my brother. We may be the first humans to see it in 700 years!"

"That's what worries me," he said darkly.

"Let me deal with any spirits," she answered. "How do we get up there?"

Brody retraced his steps, leading her up until she saw the foot and hand holds, and ran lightly past him to reach the edge of the dwellings.

"Just look at this! I can't imagine living here and not worrying about children falling over the edge." As she spoke, Jenn leaned dangerously toward the open edge of the site.

Brody knew it was neither as steep nor as precarious as it looked. The edge, like any outcrop of sandstone, was rounded and had enough texture to provide good footing even on the downhill surface. Even so, Brody put his hand out in involuntary caution. "That's close enough."

"Don't worry," she said, noticing his discomfort. "I'm good right here, and I won't go any farther."

# Chapter Twenty

JENN TOOK IN the entire view of the canyon. Her eyes swept along the trickle of water at its base, all the way to the end until they reached the turn, moving up to the site of the ancient village. There, her eyes remained locked in admiration for the lost village of her ancestors.

The opening was like a broad, shallow cave—a hollowed-out oval in the sandstone only a few yards deep, but some 40 feet high and perhaps 150 feet wide. In the deepest part of the cave, a complex structure of 3 or 4 stories had been constructed of sandstone rubble stacked with enough skill that little or no mortar was needed. In a few places, a coating of sand-based mud had been dabbed on, either to smooth the surface, or perhaps for decoration. Most of it had fallen away, leaving a patchwork of rough and smooth walls. Openings for looking out or perhaps for defense pierced the walls seemingly at random. Near the top of each structure, ancient beams made of pinyon pine stuck out from the sides.

"Are you all right?" Brody asked.

Jenn smiled and nodded. It was the first time she realized she'd been holding her breath. "I'm just taken in by the vision, that's all."

"I know. It's crazy to think this place has been hidden for so long." He looked at her, his brown eyes studying her for reassurance. "Still don't think the Skinwalkers have taken Malcom?"

"No," she said, with a confidence she no longer quite felt.

She returned her focus on the village. Her first impression was that it was one large structure, but she knew it would have been constructed over a period of years, as the population grew. The irregular height of the stories betrayed the ad-hoc nature of the construction. Some exterior ladders still stood against the walls, and no doubt more would be found inside. Of course, she couldn't trust their integrity after so many centuries. Made of Pinyon branches lashed together with yucca fibers, they could crumble at the slightest touch. Or not, depending on how well this hollow had protected them from the weather. She wasn't going to attempt to find out. But how had Brody and Malcom found the kiva? And why in Heaven's name had Malcom climbed in?

Jenn asked, "How did you even find this place?"

"We were following the wind," Brody answered. "I'm not sure I remember where the kiva was. I was trying to talk Malcom out of climbing in, but he thought he might find gold or silver."

"Are you serious? Didn't you tell him the Ancient Ones were not interested in gold and silver?"

"He wouldn't have listened, and anyway, it happened so fast!"

She stood up and searched for a way down. "Well, the wind isn't blowing now. Let's go find the kiva and investigate what happened to Malcom. I will appease the spirits so we'll be safe. I'll feel better once we're out of the canyon before nightfall."

"Me too."

In truth, Jenn only half-believed the old tales, and didn't put much faith in her own power as a medicine woman. She'd trained with Grandmother to make the old woman happy.

There had been a few incidents that gave Jenn the idea Grandmother had some spiritual and extra-normal gifts, but she'd never felt anything crazy herself. She wasn't going to tell Brody that, though, and shake his faith.

"The kiva is over there," she said, pointing.

"How do you know that's it?" Brody asked. "There are a few circular buildings here."

"Most are for grain storage. See? They are smaller, and there are doors at the bottom to let the grain out. The kiva is big, in a central location, and see, there is the ladder you must have climbed. I can't believe it held your weight."

As she spoke, Jenn had walked toward the kiva, and was eying the ladder dubiously. It was no more recent than the others she'd seen. Likely 700 years old or more, it seemed impossible for the ladder to have survived at all, much less in condition to hold the weight of a grown man. Before she could caution him to be careful, Brody scrambled up it, much the same way as he must have done earlier that day. If nothing else, it proved the ladder was still sound. She didn't hear so much as a creak from the ancient wood.

"Come down, Brody. I will go first."

"No," he said. "You are a woman, and should not look into the kiva, or enter it. Stay here, and I will go in and see if I can find Malcom, or his body."

Jenn nodded submissively. Sometimes she didn't understand the ways of the menfolk in her family. Mostly, they embraced the modern world, though the older men were ill-equipped to prosper in it. And then something like this happened, and even the younger generation retreated into superstition and standing on the old ceremonial ways. With her head down, Brody wouldn't see her indulgent smile. Men were like children sometimes.

Brody climbed over the wall and presumably down a ladder that was inside, as she lost sight of him. "Brody, keep talking, so

I'll know you're all right," she called. "Otherwise, I'm coming in after you."

"I'm okay," he called back, his voice echoing hollowly from the interior of the kiva. "This is weird. I've never seen a sipapu like this."

"What do you mean?"

"Usually, they are very small holes, not even large enough to put my arm into. And they are in the middle of the kiva. This one is at the side, and large enough to stand and walk into."

"Brother, are you certain you don't want me to come in and banish Skinwalkers?" she called out.

"Do not mention them. I think they are gone, but I don't want them to come back. I will call you if I need help. I am going to walk into it to see how far it goes and if I can see Malcom. You may not be able to hear me from there. You may climb the ladder, but do not look inside the kiva."

Jenn chuckled under her breath. She would comply with his wishes, or pretend to. She'd seen inside kivas before, and there was nothing special about them. A round structure built partially underground. Some had benches around the edges, and most had firepits. The sipapu was usually, like Brody said, a small symbol of the world's navel where her people emerged from their life underground, according to the tales. This one would be no different, except for the unusually large sipapu.

Climbing to the top of the ladder, Jenn called out to Brody. "Do you see anything?" He didn't answer. "Brody? Brother!"

Just as she was about to climb in, his voice drifted from inside. "I don't see Malcom. But you won't believe what I do see. I'm coming out."

Jenn retreated to ground level and waited for Brody to come out and tell her what he'd discovered. In a moment, his head appeared over the wall and he was climbing down.

"We're not the first," he stated.

"What do you mean?"

"We're not the first to have seen this place in 700 years. In fact, I'd say someone's been here in the last month." He produced a fearsome-looking modern weapon. She wasn't sure what to call it, but it looked like the automatic weapons she'd seen in movies.

"What the hell?" she exclaimed, startled.

"Drug smugglers, at a guess," Brody answered. "And I think we'd better get out of here before they come back."

"Wait. What else did you see? Was Malcom inside?"

"No sign of Malcom. Bales of marijuana, by the smell. And crates of something else. White powder. Heroin, or cocaine. Meth maybe? I don't know what that looks like. And guns like this. A lot of them."

"You're right! Let's get out of here!"

It was time to go anyway. Her eyes had adjusted slowly, so she only now realized how dark it was getting. The sun must be all the way down. They'd need to hurry to get to the top of the mesa before full dark.

The next question would be to whom to report all this to, and what to do about Malcolm.

# Chapter Twenty-One

V EYRON STUDIED THE Humvee.

His dark brown eyes flashed intelligence, and his grin beamed with boyish interest, as his eyes swept across the military vehicle. It stood six feet high, seven feet wide and fifteen feet long. According to the manual in his hand, the chassis was a steel frame with boxed rails and five cross-members constructed from high-grade alloy steel. The body was made of lightweight aluminum. It was still painted in the same off-green color that was ubiquitous in the U.S. Army.

Sam watched as Veyron and Tom clambered under the chassis to inspect the drivetrain.

Next to him, Michael Gallagher placed a hand on the side of the truck and began to talk like a used car salesman. "The Humvee is fitted with double A-arm independent suspension front and rear, coil springs and hydraulic double-acting shock absorbers for high off-road mobility. This system provides 16 inches ground clearance in normal load conditions. It has a track of 72 inches. The vehicle offers 40% of slide slope, 60% of climb gradient and 60 inches of water fording capacities, making it an outstanding off-road vehicle."

"Are you trying to sell me your truck?" Sam smiled. "Because you know I just need to borrow it, right?"

"No, no. I'm just trying to let you and your engineer friend make an informed decision on whether or not this old girl can make it to the bottom of the sinkhole."

"What do you think?" Sam asked.

It was Gallagher's turn to smile. "If you could walk down the slope, then this here vehicle can drive you down it."

"Do you want to drive it down for me?"

"No sir. No, I do not."

"Okay." Sam watched as Veyron, followed by Tom, slid out from under the vehicle. His eyes turned to Gallagher. "I suppose in that case, I'd better wait and see what my engineer believes."

Veyron turned to Gallagher. "What sort of payload does she carry?"

"She's one of General Motors's expanded capacity vehicles, designed to carry higher payloads with same performance levels as other Humvees. It weighs 2.5 tons and has a payload capacity of roughly 5,100 pounds. It's powered by a turbocharged 6.51 V8 turbo diesel engine."

Veyron nodded. "So, if they can find the crew of the boring machine, it will still be able to climb out of the sinkhole while carrying the additional bodies?"

Gallagher nodded, and Sam noted that Veyron left out whether those bodies would be dead or alive.

"Well what do you guys think?" Sam asked, "Can it be coaxed to drive down the internal obsidian slope of the sinkhole?"

Tom's eyes were wide, like a kid at a monster truck exhibition. "In this? We'd eat that sinkhole up."

He turned to Veyron. "What do you think?"

"I've measured the gradient of the sinkhole. It's thirty-two degrees at its steepest, following the course the boring machine took on its way down. According to the Humvee's specs, it should be able to manage it with ease." Veyron smiled. "Of course, I'd stay wide from the right-hand side of the slope, where the gradient nudges pretty close to fifty degrees. The Humvee might just be able to handle it. More likely than not though, one of the wheels will lock up and you'll end up doing cartwheels down the sinkhole."

"Keep to the left, and we'll be fine?" Sam met Veyron's eye.

Veyron nodded. "Course, I'm glad it's you taking this thing down there and not me."

Tom grinned. "Come on, Sam. She's a beautiful vehicle. Think of it like taking your dad's Rolls Royce Wraith out for a country drive."

Veyron said, "Only in this case, it's a subterranean volcanic tunnel, a hundred feet below the seabed, in an area where the last living person to enter ran away complaining about Skinwalkers haunting its abyss."

To Sam it appeared more like a predator than a mine shuttle, but given the terrain they needed to navigate, it might just be just what they were after.

He shook his head and smiled. "All right. Let's load up the equipment and go find that boring machine."

# Chapter Twenty-Two

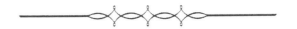

T OM CLIMBED INTO the Humvee.

He searched the dash for a keyed ignition switch. There was none. Military Humvees didn't have any. Instead, a three-position lever controlled off, run, and start. He flicked the lever toward start and the brutal 6.5 L turbo diesel grunted into life. He grinned like a kid suddenly being given the keys to a tank. He pushed the gear-lever into drive.

Next to him, Sam sat quietly, as though he was trying to remember why he suggested such a ridiculous notion as driving the Humvee down into the sinkhole in the first place. Both men wore their DARPA-produced thermal suits, in case the temperatures down below suddenly became less than hospitable. In the large storage hold between the two front seats were a pair of face masks and ultralight carbon fiber air tanks. They weren't taking any chances. If the air quality changed farther down the tunnel, they would be prepared for it.

Tom held his foot on the brake and revved the engine. "Are you ready to descend into the lava tube?"

Sam made a thin-lipped smile. "Not really, but I'm not going to feel any better about it by waiting around."

"That's the spirit!" Tom said.

He released the clutch and the Humvee crept forward. Tom made a quick lap of the crushed stone path that circled the edge of Big Diomede Island until he was confident in the large vehicle's dimensions and awkward controls.

He stopped the Humvee at the entrance to the main descending boring tunnel and switched on the powerful headlights. The dashboard lit up with the soft red glow familiar in military machines that were designed to be used in darkness.

"All right, here we go."

He turned the Humvee into the tunnel and slowly drove down the initial ten-degree gradient of the first bore tunnel. Two miles in, the gradient increased to twenty degrees. The Humvee didn't even complain. It was designed for steep approach and departure gradients of sixty degrees.

Tom spotted the gaping hole in the ground up ahead, where the massive boring machine had punched through the top of the volcanic dome and fallen through. He slowed the Humvee and brought it to a complete stop. He pulled up the park brake and switched the engine off. With the gear in neutral, he shifted the transfer case into low range and started the engine again.

He asked, "How's our air quality?"

Sam glanced at the Parallax MQ-2 monitor and KGZ-10 oxygen sensor. "We're good."

Tom nodded. He released the clutch, and the Humvee crept toward the dark opening where the ground disappeared. The front tires met the small mound of rubble at the entrance. The hood lifted upward as the Humvee mounted the stones undeterred, and a moment later, the hood dipped—as they began their steep descent into the obsidian abyss below.

# Chapter Twenty-Three

S AM GRITTED HIS teeth and held his breath.

It felt like one of those poorly developed theme park rides—a cross between a rollercoaster and a make-believe safari experience—only in this case, there were no rails to keep their vehicle from rolling off the edge. His seatbelt webbing dug into his waist and shoulder, as gravity tried to wrestle him from his seat. The engine grunted with restraint as it refused to release the four wheels from the confined speeds of their low range gearing. Through the windshield the headlights revealed a cliff-like slope with no ending. Thirty feet to their right, the gradient looked more like a sheer cliff.

Sam said, "Keep it light on those brakes. The last thing we need is for one of the tires to lock up, and send us tumbling down this damned lava tube."

Tom smiled. "Relax. This thing was built for this!"

Sam gripped the edge of his seat until the whites of his knuckles showed his all too obvious fear of death. He doubted very much that the original engineers from General Motors had anything like the sloping volcanic tunnel in mind when they built the Humvee, but he decided now was not the time to interrupt Tom's confidence.

Ten minutes later, the Humvee's hood leveled out and they were back on horizontal ground. Tom brought the vehicle to a stop, switched off the engine and went through the process of changing the gear differential back to high.

When the process was complete, he started the engine again, and continued down the horizontal tunnel. The ancient lava tube was nearly eighty feet high and wide enough to fit three Humvees. Even so, Tom kept the speed below ten miles an hour.

They drove on slowly for thirty minutes before the previously straight tunnel took a major left turn. No sign of the drilling rig. Beyond that, it dipped lower, and the character of the tube began to change. A few miles further on, they encountered rubble in their path, and stalactites hung from the ceiling.

"I wonder what could have caused it to alter its path so radically."

"Older rocks, probably," Sam answered without much thought.

"Rocks?" Tom queried.

Now Sam put forth his theory of how the tubes had formed. "You know the Kookoligit Mountains area is a shield volcano. These lava tubes were probably formed at the time of the eruptions that created them, wouldn't you agree?"

"Sure. Whatever you say." Tom grinned.

"Well, the geologist told me this area is thought to be one of the last above-water vestiges of the land bridge that connected Asia and North America. He said it's characterized to the west by Cenozoic deposits, and to the east by older Paleozoic and Protozoic deposits. I figure when the lava intruded between the strata to form these tubes, it ran into a different layer, maybe one that turned it, and ran along the seam between the layers for a while. What do you think?"

"I think it's as good a theory as any. What do I know?"

It was Sam's turn to grin. "You know more about caves than

anyone else I know."

Tom shrugged, as though it was merely academic. The tunnel would be whatever it was, and that was it. The tunnel leveled out again, and Tom increased their speed to thirty miles per hour, although it was open enough that he could have gone much faster.

Twenty minutes later Tom jammed on the brakes.

In front of him, a series of twelve-foot-high stalactites had been broken by the slow-moving boring machine, and now littered the tunnel in an awkward mix of stony fragments, like oversized pick-up sticks.

# Chapter Twenty-Four

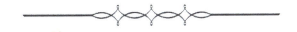

S AM GOT OUT of the Humvee and studied the splintered heap of stalactites. Tom followed him, and squatted down in front of the military four-wheel drive so he could study the approach to the large rocky outcrop.

"Do you think the Humvee could mount this?" Sam asked.

"Not a chance," Tom replied, looking up at their obstruction. "But we could probably pull a few of those stones down with the winch. We wouldn't need to shift them much to make a rocky step that the Humvee could overcome."

"How many hours do you think it will take?"

"A few. That's for sure."

Sam glanced at his wristwatch. It was nearing midnight. "Let's make camp here for the night. Get some rest and we'll work this problem in the morning."

"Sounds like a good plan." Tom grinned. "Want to take a short stroll on the other side of those rocks?"

"Sure. Why?"

Tom made a wry smile. "I have a gut feeling that we're getting close to the end. I hate the thought of camping overnight only to find out in the morning that the boring machine's just on the other side."

"All right. Let's be quick though. I'm kind of beat."

They climbed the barricade of stalactites and continued further south on foot. Both men carried heavy backpacks that were filled with essential supplies, such as basic medical equipment, ropes, and their breathing apparatus and carbon fiber air tanks.

The tunnel continued on a relatively steep descent. Thirty minutes in, Tom stopped. And looked up at a large series of wet stalactites. "Dude, this isn't good. This means there are fissures above us that are letting in seawater. Now I am nervous."

"I've never seen you nervous about stalactites before," Sam observed.

"We've never been twenty miles from the way out of the cave and under hundreds of feet of ocean with no way of knowing what's above us before," Tom retorted. "Even with our dive tanks, if this thing floods, we'd never be able to swim twenty miles on the air supplies we have."

Sam didn't bother to remind Tom of their previous explorations below the sea bed, or that the tube they were following most likely intruded into a stable layer of sedimentary Cenozoic strata over six miles in depth. He didn't even bother to mention that the water above that was hardly hundreds of feet deep. Even the relatively shallow depth of probably 100 feet of sea above them would kill them with its initial downward pressure well before they would drown.

"How far do you want to go?" Sam asked.

"Not far. I'm dog-tired," Tom admitted.

They quickly returned to the rubble pile and the Humvee. Tom found a little sand to cushion his ground mat, and was lying face-up on it, his eyes closed.

"Is it my turn to cook again?" Sam mock-whined.

"Cook or don't cook. I don't care, and I'm too tired to eat." Tom switched off his headlamp and pretended to snore.

Sam found a spot a little farther back and laid out his ground mat, then sat on it and dug in his pack for a meal of jerky and granola. The gourmet freeze-dried meals Genevieve had packed for them would require lighting the compact gas burner and using some of their precious water. He supposed they'd make it back before they'd resort to those.

Sam didn't know whether it had been minutes or hours since he'd fallen asleep when he woke to Tom shaking him urgently.

"Sam, come on, wake up, buddy."

"What's wrong?"

"Smell that?" Tom asked.

"No, what?" Still groggy, Sam struggled to understand where he was, why it was so dark beyond Tom's helmet light, and what could possibly cause Tom to panic.

"Salt water, and something dead." Tom's voice was grim.

The words penetrated Sam's fog, and he shook off Tom's hand. Becoming more alert by the second, he sat up and grabbed his own helmet, turning on its light.

"Where's it coming from?" he asked.

Tom shook his head. "I can't tell, but it wasn't in the air when we went to sleep."

"Okay, well, we know it isn't in the main tube," Sam suggested.

"We don't know that," Tom replied. "I had a bad feeling about that tube after we turned the bend. What if it's caved in, and the water's rising?"

"If that's the case, I'd think we'd be wet," Sam argued. "We're at the same level here as the main tube where it opens to this one."

"We may well be wet before long. We should get out of here, if we can."

"Okay, let me just get my gear packed."

Spooked by Tom's urgency, Sam scrambled up and followed

him. He risked a look back toward the bend in the main lava tube, but saw no water.

"Tom! Wait! Hold up," he called.

Tom took another couple of steps and then came to a halt and looked back.

"Look, Tom. No water," Sam called. "Let's go back and see if it's coming up the rise, or not. We'll have time to outrun it."

"Don't count on that." Tom's slow steps betrayed his reluctance, but he walked toward Sam anyway. "If the rock above collapses, these tunnels will be filled with water faster than you can blink an eye."

"So, we know the lava tube hasn't caved in."

"What makes you so confident?"

"Because we're not wet yet."

"You're right." Tom smiled. "Let's continue down the tunnel. We must have been closer than we thought to the end."

They walked quickly, ready to turn and run if they spotted the smallest trickle of water. But even after reaching the bend and walking to the edge of the section where fallen rock and stalactites cluttered the cave, they saw no water. But now he smelled what Tom did — salt water, and the stench of death.

"What the hell?" he asked, expecting no answer.

In the main tube, they'd been walking side by side and fully upright. Now Tom fell in behind Sam and they continued single-file. They'd gone only about three miles when Sam stopped abruptly, causing Tom to nearly crash into him from behind.

"What?" Tom asked.

"Are you seeing this?" Sam's voice was filled with wonder.

He didn't know when the character of the cave had changed. Hadn't noticed that they'd emerged from the lava tube into the sedimentary rock. But before him lay an underground grotto unlike any he'd ever seen before. The dome of the cave was vast, like a cathedral, but on a scale that he wouldn't have believed if he hadn't been looking at it. At his feet, a still pool of water that looked like malachite in the light of his helmet lamp. Not a ripple marred its mirror-like surface.

Sam shined his flashlight across the water.

Fifty feet into the subterranean lake he spotted the circular features of the giant boring machine. It had pulled itself along the entire length of the lava tube only to be eventually stopped by the soft base of the shallow lake.

Tom removed his backpack, caught his breath and said, "Let's see what's waiting for us inside."

Sam could guess what gruesome find was waiting inside the boring machine. "All right."

He doffed his pack, and waded out after Tom.

The water was warm, approximately eighty-five degrees Fahrenheit. A very comfortable temperature for a swim, even without a wetsuit. The water was no more than knee-deep.

"An underground spring must be warming the water," he called.

"Makes sense," Tom said. "Hurry up, will you. What's taking so long?"

Sam quickly caught up in the shallow water. When he reached Tom's side, his friend immediately waded farther out. Sam was peering into the water, wishing his light wouldn't reflect off the surface, as Tom approached the edge of the boring machine.

In front of him, Tom swore loudly. "You've got to be kidding me!"

Tom's shout brought his head up with a snap. "What is it?"

Beyond the boring machine, almost at the limit of Sam's vision, something huge lay on its side in the water. Tom's incredulous cry echoed off the cathedral ceiling far above them. Listing heavily to its portside were the broken remains of the Gordoye Dostizheniye.

# Chapter Twenty-Five

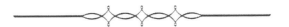

*Ignacio, Southern Ute Reservation*

**B**RODY STOOD MUTE with misery while Jenn laid into the officer manning the front desk at the Ignacio police department.

"What do you mean, it isn't your jurisdiction?" Jenn shouted.

"I'm sorry, but Cloud Ranch is outside the city limits. You'd need to talk to the tribal police, but the crime is outside their jurisdiction. They'll pass it to the FBI."

"I don't care who they send, just tell me where to report what we've found," Jenn said, making an obvious effort to control her temper.

"Well, it's not that easy," the officer said, leaning back in his chair. "I can make the call, but you might as well go home. They won't be in any hurry to take your statement."

Jenn put her fists on her hips, standing with arms akimbo like every woman has done at one time or another when faced with male stupidity. "And why not?"

Brody knew that tone. It spelled danger, but the officer seemed oblivious to his imminent peril. "Do you know how many officers they have, and how much territory they cover? And how many drug reports they get every day? They don't have time to investigate all of them, and they don't have jurisdiction to prosecute, as I said. The FBI is spread too thin, too. Unless we hand them a neat little case, all wrapped up in a bundle, they'll decline to prosecute because nobody out here is getting hurt. They're more concerned about the victims in the city than any of us out here on the rez."

"That's absurd," Jenn sputtered. "What about the white guy who disappeared? Are they interested in him?"

"That's another kettle of fish," the officer explained. "White guy. No Indian has any jurisdiction at all. It's a Federal case, and you don't know he's dead. You don't even know if he's been kidnapped. If and when you find his body, let us know if it looks like foul play. Then maybe the Feds will take an interest. Or maybe not. That's the way it is," the officer said, shutting down further argument. "Go on home. Someone will be out to take the report in a few weeks, maybe."

With two spots of red coloring her cheeks, Jenn whirled and nearly ran down her brother. "Come on, Brody. We'll have to deal with it ourselves."

"Deal with what? Malcom's disappearance? We can't go looking for him in that cave system. I don't know about you, but I'm not anxious to run into Mexican cartel members armed with guns." Brody spat on the ground. "Let Ben decide what to do. I'm done with it."

"I thought Malcom was your friend," Jenn reproached him.

"He was okay. I don't think I'm ready to die for him." Brody had heard enough. Skinwalkers were one thing. Armed cartel members were another.

As if she'd read his thoughts, Jenn asked, "How do you know it's a Mexican cartel? Maybe it's one of us. I mean the tribe. Pretty sure it's no one on the ranch."

"Come on, Jenn. We may live out in the middle of nowhere, but we get TV. Internet even. Sinaloa is active everywhere in the Southwest. Other cartels from Mexico, too. We're between two of the major smuggling routes from Juarez."

Jenn cast her eyes downward. Brody recognized she'd conceded. He was as sure of his assumption as he was his own first name. And equally sure Ben wouldn't be interested in messing around in that sipapu, either. Malcom or no Malcom.

# Chapter Twenty-Six

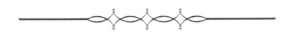

"**T**HAT'S QUITE A story." Ben Whitecloud gave Brody an appraising stare. "You weren't drinking at the time, were you, Brody?"

Insulted, Brody clenched both fists.

Jenn stepped between them. "Ben, you know my brother does not do that. He's telling the truth. We have been to Ignacio to report it, but the authorities want nothing to do with it."

"What makes you think I do?" he retorted.

"The way I see it, it can go one of two ways. You can continue to let criminals use your land for drug running, or you can gather your employees and clean out that sipapu to show them they are not welcome. And by the way, have you forgotten we do not know what has become of Malcom, your employee? Don't you feel any responsibility toward him? What's it going to be?"

Jenn challenged him with flashing eyes. She didn't care if Brody learned she and Ben had once been an item, or that she had broken it off because Ben couldn't stand her independent spirit. He'd have fired her if she hadn't been indispensable to his business. Of that she was certain. Out of respect for a man she'd once loved, she tried not to challenge him often. Out of concern for her brother and the right thing to do, she did now.

Ben blew air forcibly from his cheeks through pursed lips. "All right, Jenn. What do you suggest we do?"

Jenn smiled sweetly. She'd won. "At first light, we take everyone we can arm and go there to see if the drugs are still there. If so, we take them and deliver them to the Ignacio police. They can decide what to do with them. Some will continue to look for Malcom and bring him or his remains out. If the drugs are not there, we'll do the same, but leave some men to guard the entrance in case a new delivery of drugs shows up.

"After that, we should post lookouts to see who brings them, and how often."

Ben sighed. "Is that all?"

Ben couldn't help being sarcastic, Jenn knew well. And she had handed him a tall order. There were no more than a dozen hands on the ranch. All of them were needed for ranch duties.

"Almost. Once we have evidence, *you* need to contact the FBI. Our tribal police are not willing to get involved."

"Me?" he yelped.

She crossed her arms.

"All right. Tell the others to be ready."

Jenn smiled as she left Ben's study. He'd be slamming things down on his desk as soon as he thought she was out of earshot. But he'd do what she asked.

# Chapter Twenty-Seven

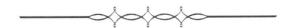

B RODY LED THE way over the edge and down the red sandstone cliffside. If he had to do this very often, he'd be cured of his fear of heights, which would not be a bad thing. Behind him, Jenn and six of Ben's ranch hands made their way carefully, hunting rifles strapped to their backs. All wore stoic expressions.

When they reached the ruins, Jenn took over. "Watch your step, and do as little damage to this sacred place as possible. Who will stay with me and stand guard?"

The men shuffled their feet, until one volunteered. Brody suspected none of them wanted to go with him, but offering to stay with Jenn would make the others think the volunteer feared the spirits of the sipapu. It was a no-win situation. Jenn nodded her acceptance of the volunteer and turned to Brody.

"Be safe, my brother." She waved the man who would stand guard with her to a spot where the two of them could set up crossfire but be safe from each other's shots, then sank to her knees behind an outcrop.

Brody took one look back before leading the others to the kiva. His sister was braver than he was, and it shamed him.

Reaching the kiva, he asked for volunteers to go further into the sipapu with him, two to carry out the drugs, if they were still there, and three to go with him and carry out Malcom's body if they could find it. Once again, feet shuffled, but it didn't take long for four to step forward. "One more," he said. "We must be able to split into twos if the sipapu leads to a cave system." The three remaining men stared each other down until one dropped his eyes and stepped forward. Brody hoped they wouldn't find splitting up necessary. Whoever paired with that one would not have a good partner.

He led the way up the ladder and into the wide hole.

"This isn't a sipapu," one of the men remarked. "It's a cave."

"Do you see another sipapu?" Brody responded with heat. "And a strange wind was being drawn into it. Don't forget that Malcom was sucked in against his will."

"So you say," the same man answered. "How are we to know you didn't kill him for violating the kiva?"

It didn't deserve an answer, but Brody answered anyway. "If I'd done that, why would I have led you all here to bear witness to murder?"

The others nodded and murmured, and the first man backed down. "Lead the way, then."

The entrance required the men to crawl in, but immediately opened up tall enough for every man to stand at full height, and wide enough to go two abreast. They went in single file anyway. Brody conceded that the one who'd challenged him had the right of it. It did look more like a cave than a sipapu. Maybe it really was the Great Sipapu that his childhood friend had believed in. There were more practical matters to consider for now. He switched on his flashlight as he entered. The light at the bottom of the kiva wasn't strong enough to penetrate the sipapu for more than a few feet.

As before, he found the stash of drugs within a few yards of the entrance, but no sign of Malcom. After a short consultation with the others, they decided to move all the drugs out into the kiva proper before going on. Then the two who were supposed to get them out could help find Malcolm before finishing the job.

That task complete, Brody again led the way in. As the group of men went farther, what was clearly a cave system opened into a larger room. Here they found sleeping bags, food supplies, and other evidence that people stayed here on occasion. Brody and his party paused to ready their weapons.

Everyone seemed nervous, and Brody was no exception. He was the only one who had just a handgun, a Heritage Rough Rider .22 caliber revolver that had caught his eye in a pawn shop in Ignacio. It looked like the revolvers all men in old Western movies carried, with a six-inch barrel, a grip finished with wood, and weighing nearly a pound. It was no weapon with which to challenge a drug cartel. The six-shot cylinder would be entirely inadequate in a gunfight, but it was the only one he had.

For the first time, Brody wanted one of the others to lead, but they all hung back until he reluctantly pushed on, circling the cave counterclockwise until he found an opening that led out the back. He motioned the man behind him to come with him, and sent the others to continue around the room.

"If you find another opening, two take it, and the other two keep going. If not, follow us when you come to this one again."

Brody had to duck to walk through the opening, but the passage soon opened wider again, with more head room and the space for Brody and his partner to walk abreast. They'd walked for maybe a couple of miles before he thought to cast his light at their feet. The cave floor was covered in soft sand, and there were thousands of impressions in it, as if it had been used as a passage from here to somewhere for many years.

He shined his flashlight onto it. "Look at that. Where do you think they were all going?" he asked. It was rhetorical, but his partner took it as literal.

"How would I know?"

"Never mind." Brody continued walking, now and then

pointing the flashlight down to see if the footprints continued.

"There's something weird about this cave," his partner remarked.

"What?"

"It's more like a tunnel. I've never been in a cave that was so long and narrow. And if I'm right, It's pretty straight."

Brody had to agree. It was strange. A sudden noise behind him made him crouch and point his revolver down the tunnel. But then he recognized the shout. "Ho! Where are you guys?"

"Here," he called. "How many are you?"

"Two."

Brody stopped and sat down on the soft sand to wait. When the others approached, he asked if the other two were exploring a different cave.

"No. They found the end of their tunnel, and we found the end of ours. They're heading out to finish with the drugs. We just came to tell you."

Brody hung his head. He and his companion must have walked for an hour. It didn't seem likely they'd find Malcolm or his body this far inside the tunnel. Maybe the drug dealers had done something with it, or maybe they'd captured him.

He looked around the group and told them what he was thinking. "Should we go back? If they're in here, they probably have guns."

"This is a weird cave, man," one of the newcomers answered. "I'd like to know where it goes."

"Where it goes is none of our business. Have you forgotten the drugs? Do you want to be in here when whoever put them there comes back?" He pointed his flashlight down. "Look."

As the others examined the impressions, Brody stood impatiently. "I'm leaving," he said finally. "Use your own flashlights if you want to go on."

He began walking back toward the entrance, not looking back. This cave, or tunnel—whatever it was—gave him the creeps. He couldn't wait to get out of it, back into fresh air and safety. He'd gone perhaps half the way back to the large room when a change in the air made him reach for his revolver. He was too late.

A dark shape emerged from an alcove in the cave wall, and before he could bring his revolver up, Brody felt a blow to his shoulder. He cried out, but the next blow was to his head, and he blacked out.

# Chapter Twenty-Eight

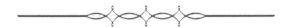

*Cathedral Grotto, Somewhere Beneath the Bering Strait*

S AM STARED AT the wreckage of the *Gordoye Dostizheniye*. More than a dozen shipping containers were strewn throughout the sandy beach at the opposite end of the volcanic grotto, previously concealed by the boring machine. The golden sand was a direct contrast to the jet-black obsidian that surrounded it. No more than thirty feet into the shallow waters were the undamaged remains of the giant boring machine.

It looked perfectly at home in the grotto, like some sort of unworldly machine of the future. It's massive Archimedean screw jutted out from behind, like something one would expect to find on the set of Journey to the Center of the Earth.

Tom swept the entire cavern with his flashlight. "It might take some time to find that container."

Sam said, "Especially since we're not looking for the container to begin with."

"We're not?"

"No. The Secretary of Defense might still think the priority is the retrieval of her shipping container, but I'd still like to place the value of any of those machine operator's life at the top of our priority list."

"All right, let's see what's inside the boring machine."

Sam followed Tom to the back edge of the boring machine. It looked like an enormous sewage pipe sticking out of the subterranean lake.

Sam flashed his light inside. "Anyone in there?"

No response.

Tom said, "The heat alone would have killed them."

"We don't know that for certain. I've seen the specs. That drilling head's more than a foot thick of reinforced steel, and the cylindrical tail of the machine is surrounded by concrete. It might have acted as a significant shield."

Sam gripped the curved side of the tunneling machine and climbed the gap of roughly two feet to get inside. A high-water line extended three feet above the flooring, suggesting that when the Big Bertha machine first entered the grotto, the lake was much higher but had since receded.

He shined his flashlight across the floor. There were deep shoeprints imbedded in the muddy silt where the now receded water once settled. On second examination, they were unlikely to be shoes, but more heavy workmen boots. Whatever they were, there was no doubt in Sam's mind that they revealed the movements of someone who found the boring machine in the lake and climbed inside to see what was inside, before returning again—and not from any survivors.

Tom said, "Any chance they belong to one of the surviving machine operators?"

"No way in the world." Sam followed the imprints with his flashlight. They started at the end of the boring machine, went inside beyond his sight, and then came out again. "All this black volcanic silt occurred after Big Bertha struck the lake, not before."

"So, who the hell's been down here before us?"

"Didn't Gallagher say that another rescue team went into the sinkhole before us?"

"Yeah, and he said all three of them were killed under unusual, albeit natural circumstances." Tom smiled. "Didn't he blame it on some sort of wraith or something?"

"Skinwalkers," Sam corrected him. "Once powerful Navajo medicine men and women who allegedly turned into evil witches, and took the form of any number of wild animals in order to murder people. It's said that in more present-day civilizations, they have been forced to retreat into subterranean cave systems to hide."

"So how did some sort of ancient superstition from the Four Corners part of the U.S. find its way this far north?"

"No idea. I once heard that the Yupik people, the native inhabitants of the regions of modern day Canada, Alaska, the Aleutian Islands and Eastern Siberia, all shared surprising similarities with the Navajo people in terms of spiritual beliefs and ancient myths."

Tom climbed up into the boring machine, next to Sam. "Was there ever any hypothesis for it?"

"No, none."

"All right." Tom shrugged, indifferently. "Let's forget the ancient history lesson and go see what we have."

Sam followed the steps all the way to the inside end of the boring machine and the back of the giant drill head. There was no one there. And no sign of anyone getting injured or killed there. He spotted the operators' chairs. They appeared intact. Sam and Tom both flashed their lights around the tunneling machine, searching for any of the machine operators.

There was nothing.

No bodies.

No blood.

And no sign anyone was ever injured inside the boring machine.

Sam said, "If they didn't die here, where did they go?"

# Chapter Twenty-Nine

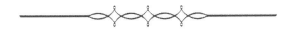

S AM STEPPED OUT of the boring machine and back into the open grotto. He shined his flashlight around the outer edge of the subterranean lake. The water reached the obsidian walls throughout the entire area, with the exception of a golden beach of sand rising from the glossy black obsidian at the eastern end. The grotto was large enough that he still couldn't make out where the lake finished. As he scanned the area as far as he could see, he decided that lake was a poor description of what they'd found. Instead, it was much more like a subterranean sea.

"Is there anybody out there?" he yelled.

The sound echoed for a few seconds before the grotto became once again lost in total silence.

Tom asked, "Do you want to check the other side of the lake, see if we can find the missing crew?"

"Yes, but not now." Sam checked his watch. It was getting late. "It could take an hour or more to reach the other side. We still need to get back to the Humvee. Now that we know it's safe to drive down here, I think we're better off returning to the surface and getting an entire team down here to help search."

"All right, sounds like a plan. What about the ship?"

Sam fixed his eyes on the *Gordoye Dostizheniye.* "Let's go climb on board. We'll get a better idea what we have to work with and what we're going to need to get from the *Maria Helena* to access the main hold."

Tom nodded his agreement and they both waded toward the ship.

She looked like a modern cargo ship, with a flat deck forward, and a tower-bridge aft. The bow rose high out of the water. A significant section of her aft section remained underwater, suggesting the otherwise shallow lake eventually became deep in the middle. The ship was listing at a forty-degree angle to her portside. A large gash had ruptured her hull two thirds of the way along—through which, nearly a hundred or so shipping containers had been expelled and now lay strewn throughout the lake and sandy beach.

Along her hull were the words, *GORDOYE DOSTIZHENIYE.*

"At least we know we found the right one!" Tom said.

Sam laughed. "How many ships were you expecting there to be down here?"

"Not many, but we've been having a bad run lately. I thought we might have come across the wrong one." Tom ran his eyes across the ship. Mostly out of the water, it appeared bigger than he was expecting. "Where do you want to start?"

"The bridge," Sam said, without hesitation. "According to the schematics the Secretary of Defense sent me, the *Gordoye Dostizheniye* is divided into six separate cargo compartments below decks. We need to find the ship's manifest if we're to have any hope of locating container numbered 404."

Tom looked at the gash in the hull. "I guess that's our entrance."

Sam nodded. "Looks like it."

The shallow bottom of the lake dropped sharply as they approached the opening, until they needed to swim the final twenty or so feet.

Tom pointed his flashlight at the razor-sharp protruding edge of the hull, where the thick steel had been torn open. Sam nodded, recognizing what was potentially the most lethal part of boarding the ship. They carefully checked the other side for similar risks and moved toward the middle of the opening.

Confident they could enter the ship, Sam carefully swam along the surface toward the center of the opening. He stopped for a moment and swept his flashlight around the gash, and then inside. He then slowly swam through, and into the hull.

On the other side, he turned around. "It's fine. Keep to the center."

Once inside the hull, the ship looked surprising undamaged. Despite being mostly intact, the ship was still listing at an awkward angle, which meant maneuvering aboard her was like being part of a Picasso painting. They negotiated the stairs and ladders like a jungle-gym, climbing over and around the supports as if they were playground toys, eventually coming out onto the foredeck.

From there the deck canted away from them at a steep downward angle. There was no way to walk upright toward the deckhouse. Instead Sam alternately half slid or climbed his way to the base of the bridge tower.

Tom gripped the steel door handle, but nothing turned. "The door's locked."

Sam tried the door, coming to the same conclusion. "They must have tried to batten down their external doors in an attempt to keep her afloat."

He glanced up at the bridge high above. The walls were vertical with no external ladders or means of reaching it. Tom disappeared as he walked right around the base of the large bridge tower. A minute later he returned to the first locked door.

"Any luck?" Sam asked.

"No. There's a second door on the other side, but it's locked too."

"Any chance we can break it in?"

"This ship was designed to travel across the arctic circle. If they've secured the doors from the inside, there's nothing we're going to do about it without going topside for a blowtorch."

"All right," Sam said. His eyes followed the waterline that extended up within a few feet of the aft deck, and presumably flooding everything below. "You know what that means, don't you?"

Tom sighed. "Yeah, we're going swimming again."

# Chapter Thirty

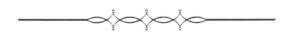

SAM OPENED THE amidships hatch and climbed down the series of grated steps that were now at such an angle that he was required to use the railing as a ladder as opposed to the steps. This section of the hull appeared intact, although the shipping containers had shifted inside. Water extended to within a few feet of the deck.

He shined his flashlight along the gap between the water and the deck. He could only just make out the tips of a number of shipping containers, like giant icebergs breaking the surface. The light struck a steel wall some fifty-feet away.

"That looks like the internal stairwell to the bridge," Tom said. "There must be a door somewhere down there."

"Yeah, about forty feet by my guess. Are you ready for that swim?"

Sam slid into the water and then surface swam to the far end, where the steel internal partition blocked any further movement aft. Tom followed, a few feet behind and shined his flashlight under the water below. The water was surprisingly clear, but they still couldn't identify any door or entrance into the main stairwell.

"I'll go first," Sam said. "If I make it through easily enough,

I'll leave the door open for you. If not, I'll see you back up here in a minute."

"Okay, keep safe."

Sam took a couple deep breaths, and then dipped below. The saltwater stung his eyes and blurred his vision, but he was able to follow the obtuse glare of his flashlight. He kicked his legs until he reached the bottom of the hull, nearly forty feet below. He swallowed gently to equalize the pressure pounding in his ears, and ran his hand along the steel bulkhead for guidance.

He spotted a door toward the middle of the main steel partition that formed the stairwell lining. Sam moved farther along until he could reach the door. The handle turned, but the door could only just open a few inches, and nowhere near enough to slip through.

Sam flashed his light above the door. The edge of a large shipping container that had toppled diagonally on its side was resting against the upper tip of the door.

He placed his hand on the container. There was no thought of it moving anywhere. The thing must have weighed several tons. Sam was about to return to the surface when he noticed his light penetrated part of the bulkhead on the other side.

Pulling himself under and through the gap between the shipping container and the bulkhead, he found a gash in the wall—presumably where the shipping container had smashed against it before settling to its current resting position. He shined his light toward the opening. It was narrow, and sharp, but large enough to fit through.

Sam took a piece of the green chalk and drew an arrow on the steel wall to show Tom where he went. He then swam through the opening, and kicked his legs to the surface of the stairwell on the other side.

He gulped deep breaths of air on the surface.

Two minutes later, Tom's head broke the surface. He took a

normal breath in and appeared settled. More like someone having a casual swim at the beach than challenging the upper ends of the human limits for free diving.

Sam said, "What took you so long?"

Tom grinned. "Just checking the ship out!"

It took only another few minutes for them to climb the steel grates that formed the stairs, open the door and step inside the bridge.

Sam swept his flashlight across the room in one slow, deliberate motion. Once the command center and orderly hub of the *Gordoye Dostizheniye*, it now appeared more like the debauched remnants of a buck's party gone horribly wrong. The intelligent navigation systems and the series of computer monitors for the ship's state of the art control systems had all been shattered.

The pungent smell of death was ripe in the air. There was something else too, something sweet, and almost out of place in the ghastly confines of the bridge. Sam tentatively breathed in through his nose. *Was it tobacco?* Tom covered his nose and mouth with part of his shirt, trying to avoid the smell, and Sam followed suit a moment later.

He then carefully dragged himself toward the communication post at the upper end of the room using a number of fixtures that were permanently attached to the floor as a sort of ladder. Everything else in the control center, including the hapless radio operator's body, had tumbled to what was now the lowest part of the bridge and previously the port side of the ship.

The communications post was a small alcove built into the starboard side of the bridge. Sam gripped hold of the door and pulled himself up. Once inside, he rested his back against the bulkhead next to the door and examined the room.

He imagined the scene in that very room from only a few days ago, and the thought sent a ripple of fear and horror through his spine. As a man who'd spent his life on the sea, he could imagine only too well the words and emotions that consumed the radio operator in his final moments. The confusion, the disbelief, that inability to accept what was inevitable, and finally acceptance and death.

Tom climbed up to the edge of the doorway, holding himself against the frame of the door. "It must have been a horrible way to go."

"Unbelievably so." Sam focused his flashlight on the locked cupboard next to the radio operator's desk, and returned to the task at hand. "Let's find the ship's manifest."

Traditionally, the ship's registry, logbooks, and manifest were stored near the communications room, so that information could be quickly accessed and communicated in an emergency.

Sam turned the key.

*Could it be that easy?*

The cupboard opened. The ship's log was tucked safely in its secured alcove. The registry, outlining the ship's owners was next to it. But the third alcove, labeled, *Inventory Manifest,* was empty.

Sam asked, "Why would the captain remove the manifest?"

Tom shined his flashlight on the sideways leaning desk. A pile of ash formed on the edge of the table and bulkhead. "If I had to guess, I'd say he didn't just remove it, he burnt it, too."

Sam examined the black remains of a thick bundle of paper. A small piece of paper to the right of it had turned a crisp brown, but hadn't quite burnt through. Sam picked it up. The name on the paper was the *Gordoye Dostizheniye,* and on the top of it, he could just make out the words, *Ship's Manifest.*

He carefully ran his fingers through the pile of ash. Nothing remained that could be recognized as its original paper, let alone read. Someone had gone to the specific trouble of ensuring the entire document was burnt through. Everything had been destroyed.

"The damned thing's been burnt through!" Sam shook his and asked, "Why would the captain do that? What was he hiding?"

Tom said, "Not the captain."

"No?"

"Look. These ashes are dry, despite the entire bridge being soaked through. And there's a strong smell of tobacco in the air and there's the stump of a burnt cigarette into the side of the bulkhead."

Sam glanced at the burn mark on the bulkhead. "So? Maybe the old captain was a heavy smoker. Not unusual for the older generation of Russians given their cold climate." His eyes then turned to meet Tom's. "What are you suggesting happened?"

Tom expelled a deep breath of air. "I think someone's been in here since the ship sunk, and that person intentionally burnt the ship's manifest."

# Chapter Thirty-One

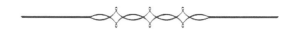

**S**AM LET THOSE words sink in for a moment.

He then grinned. "Well that's going to make it a hell of a lot harder to find the Secretary of Defense's shipping container. She's going to be pissed, but we'll have to do it the old-fashioned way and search every damned part of the ship."

"It could take days."

"Or weeks," Sam pointed out. "Come on, let's go back topside and start again tomorrow. We can bring Veyron and Genevieve with us, while I'm sure Gallagher will be keen to inspect the boring machine."

Tom said, "That still doesn't answer the other question."

Sam expelled a breath of air. "Who the hell's been on board the ship since she sank, and why did they go to the trouble of finding the manifest and burning it?"

"Exactly."

"I have no idea, but when we get top-side I'm going to contact the Secretary of Defense and get some answers. By the looks of things, she's not the only person who wants to find whatever's inside shipping container 404."

At the back of the bridge was a small open deck. Sam stepped toward it, expecting to have to unlock the door, to get out.

Instead, as his hand gripped the handle, it turned easily.

Sam grinned. "The door's unlocked, and the hatches haven't been battened."

Tom nodded, realization dawning on him. "The crew never had time to lock all the hatches. They hadn't even considered that as an option. That means the door downstairs was locked by our unexpected guest, as a means of slowing down our search for the ship's manifest."

Sam stepped out onto the deck. Using his flashlight, he searched the subterranean lake for any sign of the intruder. The water was still. If he or she was down there, they weren't in the water. Not that that mattered. The ship was massive. Plenty of places to hide if anyone wanted to remain hidden.

He turned to Tom. "Come on, let's go get some help."

Twenty minutes later Sam and Tom had worked their way out of the *Gordoye Dostizheniye*. Sam started to swim toward the shore. His feet soon found perch on the solid obsidian ground knee-deep below the water.

He flashed his light across the lake, trying to orient himself with the original tunnel through which they'd entered the cathedral grotto. His bearings were slightly off and it appeared as though he was approaching the wrong side

"Hey Sam!" Tom swept his flashlight in a wide arc and then stopped, with it fixed on a shipping container toward the beach. "You're going to want to see this!"

Sam turned around. His eyes fixed where Tom's light had shined. On the edge of the shipping container were the numbers 404.

# Chapter Thirty-Two

**S**AM'S EYES ROLLED across the numbers, in disbelief.

"That's the one. That's our container." He spoke the words softly, frightened whoever was looking for the same container was still out there, listening.

Tom asked, "Any idea how we're going to remove it?"

"No. It would be impossible to shift something that size to the surface without anyone detecting it. Better we open the container up, and remove whatever's inside."

"Didn't the Secretary of Defense say something about the shipping container having some sort of state of the art security system?"

Sam said, "There's always a way in."

"She's going to be pissed."

Sam nodded. They would deal with that when they got to it. He walked around to the end of the container. It was a solid steel wall. He then kept walking and reached the opposite end. Again, there was a solid wall of steel, with no apparent gaps.

Tom smiled. "You were saying, about there always being a way in?"

"Okay, so someone made the effort to secure this one," Sam

acknowledged.

He ran his hand along the edge of the container and stopped. His eyes turned to a small, covered metallic casing that protected what appeared to be a security keypad.

Sam tentatively opened the metallic outer cover. It swung upward and revealed a standard seventeen key digital keypad. Ten digits with seven modifier keys. He didn't need to try and work out the math. There were potentially millions of alternative combinations. Any way he looked at it, he and Tom were never going to guess the code.

Tom smiled, sympathetically. "There's always a way in to these things, are there?"

"All right, I might have been wrong about that. Come on, let's return to the surface. I'm sure our friend Gallagher the foreman will have some sort of tool he might loan us to cut a hole in the shipping container."

"Okay, mind if I have a go?"

"At what?"

"I'm a pretty lucky kind of guy. I thought..."

Sam grinned. "What? You thought you might just guess the code?"

Tom shrugged. "Sure, why not? We're going to have to cut our way in anyway, so why not try?"

"Suit yourself." Sam stepped away. "But you're more likely to win the lotto than break this code."

"You're probably right." Tom studied the keypad and typed a total of six numbers, followed by six alternative numbers, such as plus and minus and asterisks at random.

Nothing happened.

Sam said. "It looks like you guessed wrong."

"Or maybe I just need to press enter?"

"Come on. Let's get back to the surface, I'm wrecked. I could use some sleep."

Tom pressed enter.

A moment later the sound of heavy hydraulic locks started to move from inside the shipping container. He smiled broadly. "Well, what do you know… it says I'm a winner!"

Sam turned to face the shipping container. His eyes widened and he opened his mouth to speak. The last of the hydraulic locks completed their movements and the massive vaulted door slowly automatically opened in front of him. "You've got to be kidding me."

Tom smiled, gloating like a bad winner at cards. "Beginner's luck?"

"How did you know?" Sam persisted.

"I told you I was born lucky."

"How, Tom!"

"It says so." Tom pointed to the now fully opened door. "Right over there in black permanent marker."

Sam's eyes darted to the outward facing section of the shipping container's door. The writing was dark and barely visible inside the darkness of the cathedral grotto without the direct aim of his flashlight. He smiled. "I don't know what the Secretary of Defense wanted, but it appears someone on board the *Gordoye Dostizheniye* intended for the salvage crew to find whatever's inside."

# Chapter Thirty-Three

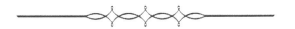

**S**AM STEPPED UP and inside the shipping container.

His first impression was that he was walking into an ultra-secure bank vault, or perhaps a futuristic room for tourists on the International Space Station. He frowned at the description. It would be a poor waste of money to fly all that way only to have a room without a view. Midway across the length of the container, a single mahogany desk was fixed to the wall. The contents of the desk appeared all jumbled up on the floor on the opposite side, where the shipping container was tilted at a near forty-five-degree angle. Sam's eyes followed the debris of stationery to where it lay piled in a neat mess of crumpled pieces. Leaning up against the same edge of the wall was a man.

In life, Sam suspected the man had been considered fair skinned or pale, but now his blood-drained face had a uniquely waxy appearance. The full skin that may have once made his face animated was now gaunt and drawn tight across his jaw bone. His lips were curled upward giving him the surreal appearance of peace—as though his life had been one of torment, and Death had finally released him. The muscles around his eye sockets had contracted one last time leaving his dark brown, nearly black eyes wide open. They stared vacantly at the far end of the shipping container—where a large stone artifact stood fixed in a purpose-built cradle.

Sam tensed and held his breath. "Holy shit! Is that the Death Stone that was stolen from Göbekli Tepe?"

Tom removed part of its protective cloth.

It revealed the image of a comet approaching earth. Four weeks ago, inside the Temple of Illumination and built into a lava tube in the bowels of Mount Ararat, they had first learned about the existence of the stone. It was the last megalithic stone to be discovered in the ancient temple of Göbekli Tepe. The stone was said to depict the return of the same comet that caused the mini ice-age known as the Younger Dryas around 13,000 years ago. Only this time, the cataclysmic even would be much larger, leading to the extinction of the human race. According to the brother of an archeologist who discovered the stone, it was taken to the U.S. for further analysis, but the ship sunk on the way, and the stone was never recovered.

"Now we know why the Secretary of Defense didn't want us to open the shipping container. She knew about it all this time, but never said anything."

Sam returned his gaze on the dead passenger. He imagined the type of death the poor man had suffered and wondered what his part was in this entire thing. How much had the stranger known? Maybe that was why Death seemed so welcomed by him?

Rigor mortis had firmly set in and both his hands were clenched shut across his chest. In his right hand was a single piece of paper.

Tom swore. "Good God, it's a note!"

Sam picked it up and read it out loud.

——◇◇◇◇——

*If you want the human race to survive, you need to convince the Secretary of Defense that this container was empty. The Death Stone needs to be removed in secret and examined by an Astronomer who has no connection with the U.S. Government. He or she will be able to work out what the stone means and what needs to be done.*

*THEY are watching the Secretary of Defense.*

*What she did twenty years ago must be kept secret if you want her to live.*

*If you want anyone to live, you need to look to the stone for guidance. It has all the answers. Particularly the greatest one of all, for which THEY have killed to hide — how to save the human race from extinction.*

*Ryan Balmain.*

# Chapter Thirty-Four

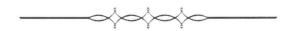

J ENN WATCHED AS the two hands who'd come out of the kiva
headed down the canyon. They'd told her that the cave had
split into three, and Brody had sent them and two others down
the smaller passages just to be sure there was nothing there.
They'd found the end of theirs, and so had the other two, who
volunteered to go after Brody and his companion.

She'd told them there was no sense in waiting and sent them
back to the ranch along with the man who'd been with her. She
assumed Brody and the others would be out soon, and then they
could all go home.

Jenn was as anxious to establish her brother's innocence as to
understand what had happened to Malcom. Brody's story was
so far-fetched that even she had trouble believing it. She
couldn't imagine what the authorities would make of it.

While she waited for Brody and the other three to come out
of the sipapu, she ruminated on what she'd learned from her
grandmother, and softly hummed an atonal chant to settle
Malcom's spirit, if indeed it roamed as she assumed it did. She
hadn't known Malcom well, but from what she'd seen of him
and the fact that her brother considered him a friend of sorts,
she thought he was a good enough guy. He hadn't deserved to
die this far from his family.

At the same time, she was annoyed with him for disrupting the sanctity of the kiva and drawing her brother into a potential legal situation. Brody had always been special to her. The only child younger than she in an extended family consisting of her father's four natural children and his sister's three, not to mention *their* extended families, she was closer to him than to her older sisters and brothers. As his babysitter until he went to school, she'd protected him from bullies both inside and outside the family. She was determined to protect him from the consequences of Malcom's disastrous disappearance in any way she could.

She sat alone with her thoughts for another couple of hours as night fell and the air turned cooler, and she'd begun to be concerned about the four men who were still inside the sipapu. Should she wait for them? Or had they made shelter somewhere inside? Already it would be unsafe to attempt to scale the canyon wall, but she wasn't prepared for a night under the stars.

She was still debating and leaning toward seeking a less exposed position somewhere inside the ruins when a noise alerted her to people emerging from the sipapu.

"Brody?" she called.

"No, he's not with us," came the answer. It was too dark to see who'd answered her.

In a moment, the head of one of the hands appeared at the top of the ladder. "Brody isn't here?" he asked.

"I thought you went to find him?" Jenn answered.

"We did find him. We went on to explore a bit more, but he headed back. He should be here."

Jenn jumped to her feet, alarmed. "How long ago?"

By now, the hand who was conversing with her had climbed out, one of his companions was on the way down the ladder, and the third man was at the top of the inside ladder, waiting for his turn to climb down the outside. The second man reached the bottom and shrugged. "Two and a half, three hours?"

The others agreed. "More like three," the third man said.

"Could he be lost?" Jenn was trying not to panic, but with dark falling she couldn't help but worry about the drug dealers who might be back tonight. She firmly pushed away old superstitions about spirits, though. That was the last thing she needed, and she didn't know who among the three men with her might hold to the old ways despite their modern education.

The others exchanged looks. "Don't think so," the first man finally said. "It's pretty much a straight shot. There are two other tunnels, but one didn't go far, and the other one got really narrow. Even if he'd gone down one or both, he'd have turned around. And we'd have seen him if he came back our way."

"Then what could have happened?" she asked. "And what do you mean by tunnels?" The others hadn't said tunnels.

"There are three narrow passages off the main room after you get into the sipapu. They're long, more like tunnels than caves. I guess he could have gone into one of those other tunnels, and then maybe his batteries died and he's waiting for someone to find him and lead him out," one said.

"Can you go back in and check?" she asked, knowing it was asking a lot. She was still worried about the drug dealers, too. They had to be on the minds of the three ranch hands as well.

"Sorry, Jenn. Our flashlights are just about dead, too. We don't even have enough light to get up the cliffside," the first man answered. "I think we're going to have to bunk here until morning. Brody should be all right. There's nothing in there that could hurt him."

Jenn was worried, but the others were calm enough to help allay her fears. She still didn't want to encounter drug dealers, and she didn't want Brody to, either. But if he wasn't in the main tunnel, he'd probably be okay until they could reasonably get to him. She just hoped he hadn't somehow injured himself.

"Okay, I guess there's nothing else we can do. We should probably find a place to bunk besides right here, though."

Agreeing to stick together, they explored the nearby structures with the last of the remaining light from the flashlights, and found a room with a soft layer of sand deposited inside. It was a tight fit, but they all managed to settle in. Jenn lay awake until the others' steady breathing told her they were asleep. When she finally drifted off, her last conscious thought was to hope Brody didn't get too thirsty or hungry before they found him.

# Chapter Thirty-Five

**B**RODY WOKE TO utter darkness with a pounding headache. He'd never known so profound a lack of light, and at first thought he was dreaming. Then a voice interrupted his thoughts and confirmed he was indeed awake.

"What are you doing here?" The voice was rough, the tone accusatory.

"I'd like to know the same thing," he answered.

It was a mistake. A slapping blow to his face whipped his head around halfway, and made his head throb.

"I'll ask one more time. Don't be a smartass. What are you doing here?"

Brody answered cautiously this time. "I don't really know where 'here' is. I was inside the sipapu to find the body of my friend, Malcom. He got sucked in by some kind of weird wind. That's all I know, honest."

A grunt was all he got in return. In the silence, he was left to wonder how the other person, a man he assumed, had known he was awake. He started to lift his hand to feel and make sure his eyes were actually open, but found he couldn't. Another attempt let him understand that his wrists were restrained somehow. He couldn't reach as far as his face.

As the fog lifted from his brain, he remembered the drugs they'd found. They must have belonged to this guy, or a group he was part of. He considered saying something about it, and thought better of the idea. Better not to let his captor know he had any knowledge of the drugs. Maybe he'd get out of this alive, since he hadn't seen the guy's face.

A hiss, a click, and light suddenly blinded him. So much for not seeing his captor's face. It leered at him from across a small cave-like room, fully visible in the light of the lantern the man had lit. Brody averted his face and shut his eyes, but it was too late.

"You were walking toward the entrance. I didn't see a body," his captor accused.

"We didn't either," Brody explained, continuing to hold his eyes shut. "I thought it was useless to keep searching. I was just leaving."

"We? How many?"

Was this the time to lie? Had the guy already captured the others? Were they all out of the cave by now? Brody had no sense of the length of time he'd been unconscious, but a hollow stomach told him it had been hours, at least. He decided his own health demanded the truth. "I left three others deeper in the main tunnel. Two had already gone out." He didn't mention Jenn.

"Did you see anything unusual?"

Brody thought the guy must be talking about the drugs. He *would* lie about that. He'd already decided. "No. What do you mean?"

"Never mind. We'll see about your story, and you'd better be telling the truth. Why did the two leave?"

"They'd already found the end of their tunnel, and so did the other two men. Two came to find us in the third, and I left them with the guy I was with because they wanted to know where that one led."

"Third…." The stranger stopped himself. "Okay. Wait here." He chuckled and doused the lantern, leaving Brody in pitch black darkness again.

Brody waited, hardly daring to breathe. After what seemed like a long time, he strained all his senses, hoping to detect anyone else's presence with him. Finally, he concluded he was alone. He tried to stand, only then understanding the guy's chuckle. His legs were also restrained, and he couldn't get them under him, no matter what he tried. Eventually he stopped trying and accepted that he might die in this dark place. Unless his captor came back with even worse plans for him.

# Chapter Thirty-Six

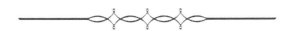

TOM REMOVED HIS backpack and threw it into the back seat of the Humvee, before climbing into the driver's seat. He flicked the ignition switch to the start position and the powerful 6.5L turbo diesel turned over and rumbled into life. He switched the headlights on and made a sharp three-point turn before heading back the way they'd come.

Sam was silent in the passenger seat. Tom guessed he was most likely thinking over the complications of the note they'd discovered inside the shipping container and the logistics of removing the ancient megalithic stone.

Content in the silence of his own thoughts, he concentrated on maneuvering the cumbersome vehicle through the constantly undulating and twisting ancient lava tube. He was able to drive faster on the returning trip, no longer having to take into account any unexpected obstacles.

Twenty minutes into the trip he spotted the short and steep forty-foot hump in the tunnel they'd climbed and dipped down into earlier on the drive in. It reminded him of a short roller coaster with its sharp upward section, short narrow crest and steep descent. He planted his foot down hard on the accelerator and the heavy Humvee picked up speed for the approach.

He hit the steep section at speed and the Humvee rapidly

cruised to the top, slowing down as it reached the crest. Tom grinned. It was hard not to enjoy the ride. And then everything changed — because a pool of dark liquid had formed on the road.

"Stop, stop!" yelled Sam.

Tom jammed his foot on the brake, and the Humvee slid to a stop. "What did you see?"

"Back up, back…"

"What is it?"

"You didn't see it?" Sam asked. "Back up to the peak, just before the crest."

Tom shoved the Humvee into reverse and planted the accelerator again. The engine whined under the restraint of the lower gearing ratio.

"Okay. Stop!" Sam said.

Tom stopped the Humvee and pulled up the handbrake. "What do you see?"

It was unlike Sam to get so rattled all of a sudden. His eyes studied the ground in front of the hood. It was covered in more of that strange reddish-brown dirt they'd found at the base of the volcanic dome. In the middle of the tunnel, a small patch of dark liquid had been soaked up by the soil. At a guess it could have been anything from water to oil.

"Well… how do you suppose that occurred?" Sam asked, unclipping his seatbelt.

Tom shrugged. "The liquid could be anything."

"Liquid? What liquid?"

"On the crest of the hill, there's a darkened area of soil. I thought that's what you were getting so excited about. What were you looking at?"

Sam opened the door and pointed to the ceiling above. "That!"

Tom followed him. His eyes darted to the volcanic ceiling

above, where two sections of the lava tube had come together to form a rocky gap. Wedged into that crevasse were the remains of some unfortunate individual.

His eyes narrowed and his mouth opened as he turned to face Sam. "How in heck does anyone get stuck up there?"

# Chapter Thirty-Seven

IT TOOK AN hour for Sam and Tom to remove the body from the crevasse, using the cabin roof of the Humvee as a climbing platform. Sam studied the body with a cursory glance from the head down. It was covered in so many grotesque bruises that it almost appeared inhuman. What was recognizable was the man's torn jeans and cowboy boots. They seemed somewhat out of place given their location.

"What the hell happened to him?" Tom asked.

Sam said, "I don't know. It looks like he's been thrown around this tunnel system like a moth caught in a vacuum cleaner, bouncing into every edge until his body finally became stuck."

"The strange wind that Gallagher told us about that brought with it all that red dirt?"

"Exactly. But where the strange air vent had come from and how one of Gallagher's men got caught up in the wind this far down the tunnel, I have no idea. He looks more like a cowboy than a machine operator." Sam looked at the body and then back to Tom. "Come on. Give me a hand to move him into the tray and let's go give the bad news to Gallagher so he can identify him."

It took another hour to reach the surface. Tom stopped the Humvee just outside the entrance to the main boring tunnel. Sam stepped out and met Gallagher as he approached.

Gallagher asked, "Any luck?"

Sam nodded. "We found your machine. It's a long way down, but it looks intact."

"Really. That's great news!" Gallagher then tensed and held his breath. "Any news for my men? Or the mine rescue team?"

"I'm sorry. Your men must have been separated from Big Bertha during the accident. It was completely empty when we found it. We found the remains of one person in the tunnel, but I'm not sure whether it belongs to one of your machine operators or a member of the rescue team."

"Can I have a look?"

"Yes. Of course." Sam led him to the back of the Humvee and pulled back blanket they'd used to cover him.

Gallagher took off his hat out of respect and shook his head. "I'm sorry."

"Did you know him well?" Sam asked.

"No. I'm sorry I have no idea who this man is. He definitely wasn't one of my men — and he definitely wasn't one of the men from the rescue team."

# Chapter Thirty-Eight

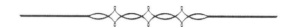

*Cloud Ranch*

O N THE MORNING after their chilly night in the ruins, Jenn and two of the three hands set out to return to the ranch house for supplies. They left the third to guard the entrance, in case Brody finally stumbled out. When they got to the ranch, Ben Whitecloud was not in his office.

"Where's Ben?" Jenn demanded after looking everywhere in the immediate vicinity. No one answered the question, because no one was around to hear it.

She was anxious to accompany whoever was going back to look for Brody. She went into the ranch kitchen pantry to retrieve as many flashlight batteries as she could find, and then went back out to recruit some help. She found one of the two hands she'd sent home the night before in the barn, saddling a fresh horse.

"Ben went into town. Why?"

"Oh. Come with me. I need someone to help me find Brody."

The hand tilted his head. "Find Brody? What do you mean?"

Jenn realized he may not have heard. "Brody never came out of the sipapu last night, and everyone was out of batteries for their flashlights."

"Oh, man," the hand answered. "Okay, wait here. I'll round

up a few of the others and go with you."

Jenn went back to Ben's office, and for the first time, thought about what they might be up against. She called Ben on his cell phone.

"Ben, are you still in town?"

"Yeah, why?"

"Something bad is going on, and I think it has to do with the drugs Brody found inside that ruin. We're in over our heads. Can you get a helicopter?"

"Why do we need…"

"Listen. Brody's missing now. When we find him, he may be hurt and unable to climb out of that canyon. I don't want to risk another delay." She didn't mention they hadn't found Malcolm, assuming the hands had already told him.

"I'll do my best. Wait for me there."

It was less than an hour later when Jenn heard the distinctive sound of the police helicopter overhead. She ran outside. If she could hitch a ride in the helicopter, she could get to Brody even faster. She'd go into the sipapu herself if she had to. The others could bitch about sacred kivas all they wanted. It was her brother in distress, and she was going after him.

She ran back into the kitchen on that thought and collected some food and water to carry with her. Brody would be hungry. Thirsty, too. By the time she got back outside, the helicopter had landed in the broad swath of mown desert scrub that served as the front lawn for both the ranch house and the bunkhouse.

Ben was ducking under the still-rotating blades. She waited for him to run to her.

"Jenn, what the hell is going on?" he asked, his eyes taking in her disheveled appearance. "What happened? Why didn't you come back last night?"

She quickly filled him in on Brody's disappearance and night falling before the other three came out of the sipapu.

"That doesn't sound like any sipapu I ever heard of," he said. A frown began to form between his thick black eyebrows. "What do you want to do now?"

"Fly out there with you, of course," she said.

"Room for only three," he responded. "I'm going, because it's my land and my employee. The pilot. Malcom's body coming back. We can take you out, but not back, so you can't go."

"But we never found Malcolm. I'm going," she said, challenging him with her chin jutting out. "We can send another couple of hands out on horseback, and they can lead a couple of horses for Brody and me to come back on."

Ben swore. "Why didn't you say so? Get them together, and we'll wait for you."

Sending him an exasperated frown, Jenn went to convey the change in plans to the hand she'd spoken to earlier. Why didn't men ever communicate fully? She supposed the hands had just come back to the ranch and turned in without reporting to Ben. But Ben hadn't asked about Malcolm when they were on the phone. She thought he knew. A few minutes later, she boarded the helicopter and put on the headphones the pilot handed her.

"Where do we go?" he asked. "I understand you know the way."

Minutes later, the pilot flew above the canyon, searching for a safe place to land. He found it about a mile up-canyon from where Jenn pointed out the bend that concealed the ruins. As the chopper settled into the soft sand of the wash, he let them know that he was watching a developing weather situation. He'd be waiting for their signal at a spot on the mesa above.

The canyon could be subject to a dangerous flash flood if the cell over Ignacio developed into a thunderstorm, he informed them. According to his topographical maps, the head of the canyon lay within the drainage area. Well-versed in the ways of desert flash flooding, Jenn and Ben acknowledged the warning. They'd get above the canyon floor as quickly as possible, and try to find a route that approached the ruins from there. Even though there wasn't a cloud in the blue, blue sky, a rainstorm from tens or hundreds of miles away could create a raging flood in the bottom of the canyon where only a trickle ran now.

Ben told Jenn he judged they could travel the easy route on the canyon floor to get to the ruins, and then they'd have to determine the next move. He had a radio to communicate with the chopper pilot, and would check the weather report as well as scout a route up the canyon wall opposite the direction of his ranch.

Until then, Jenn hadn't considered the logistics of getting Brody to the chopper if he couldn't make it on his own. In truth, it was just as problematic as what they'd already rejected. Carrying a dead weight of almost two hundred pounds up a sheer cliff wall wasn't practical for two men, much less one man and a woman. "We can't possibly carry him up there!" she exclaimed. "How were you planning to do it?"

"Rescue basket," Ben answered. "The cliff is lower on this side, and I think the pilot can come down into the canyon a bit, even though it was too narrow to land just below the ruins. But we'll have to climb out."

"You forget, I'm not going out with you. I have to go with Brody."

Ben looked back at her, an inscrutable expression in his eyes. "I haven't forgotten. I want to check this side for how these drug runners are getting here. You said there was no sign of them on our side."

"I'm sure they come up the canyon from the south," she said. But as she said it, she hesitated. There were no major roads near the mouth of the canyon. By helicopter, or from the other side, there were at least two different routes they could take.

Ben didn't answer, but set a faster pace. "We need to get out of the bottom as soon as possible. Let's pick it up."

With his longer stride, he soon outpaced her, and

disappeared around a bend. Jenn's heart sped up when she looked up and didn't see him ahead of her. "Ben!"

Relieved when she heard him answer, she smiled. They had their differences, but she could count on him. "Nothing. Just can't see you."

"I'll wait, but hurry!" he called back. "I think I'm just below the ruins."

From her journey the day before, Jenn remembered being able to see them easily. She thought he may not have gone far enough to do so, but when she caught up with him and looked where he pointed, she realized he'd found either another pueblo ruin or a part she hadn't seen of the one she knew of. The way up was easier, almost a ramp instead of the hand-and-toe indentations they'd climbed to get to the kiva.

"I don't know," she said. "I'm not sure this is the same ruin. But we might as well go up and check it out."

Without answering, Ben proceeded in front of her and both were soon standing in a much bigger village. A narrow trail led around an outcrop, where Jenn assumed they'd find the part she'd seen before. She said as much.

"Stay behind me. We'd better make sure no one is here."

Jenn bristled, but settled when Ben took the handgun out of a concealed shoulder holster. She hadn't known he was wearing it. Seeing it now, she concluded it was a good idea he was.

They hadn't kept their voices low. Anyone hiding inside one of the well-preserved apartments in the pueblo structure would know they were there already. But would they continue to hide, or come out to confront them? She moved closer to Ben, the instinct to seek protection overriding her usual bravado.

Ben scanned the slits in the adobe walls that passed for windows. Evidently, he was able to satisfy himself that no one was there, so he headed for the trail around the outcrop with Jenn in close pursuit. Neither spoke as they cautiously eased around the blind corner.

As Jenn had suspected, the part of the ruins she was more familiar with lay just on the other side. As the trail widened and then disappeared into the broad area between the structures and the edge, she overtook Ben and led the way to the kiva.

Ben radioed the pilot that they'd arrived and asked how long he could wait.

"Weather report's deteriorating," he answered. "I'll go to the top and wait there as long as I can."

"Okay. Some of my hands should be there soon," Ben answered.

Jenn waited until he'd signed off, and then said, "Ben, will you help me look for Brody before you go looking for the drug runners' route? I'm afraid to go in there on my own."

It cost her a great deal of emotional currency to say it. The fact that it was true wasn't as important as the fact that it was the only argument that might sway him, in her opinion. Her observations had concluded he was far more concerned about criminal activity on his land than the death or disappearance of a couple of hands. She was disappointed in him.

Ben gazed out into the canyon, making her wonder if he was looking for the hands that were supposedly on their way to help her. To her relief, he agreed.

"Okay. Let's go get him out."

# Chapter Thirty-Nine

*Inside the Sipapu*

**B**RODY WOKE AGAIN, this time certain he was conscious though the conditions hadn't changed. He was certain he was awake, or as certain as he could be. He'd never been hungry in a dream before, so the fact that his stomach thought his throat had been cut was probably an accurate clue he was awake. He moaned.

The sound echoed, making him believe he was still alone. After so long in the darkness, his hearing had become more acute. He heard no breathing, no rustle of bat wings or the almost-audible squeaks they sometimes made. He'd assumed from his captor's conversation the night before that he was still in the cave system he'd entered through the sipapu.

Now he concluded that it was a more extensive system than he knew. Jenn would be moving heaven and earth to find him, but would she have the resources? There was no way to know where he was in the caves, or whether his location was so hidden that no one who didn't already know it was there could find it. How long could he survive? Would they give up looking for him before he died?

Most puzzling of all, why was he still alive? His captor could have killed him, and Brody had no idea why he hadn't. Somehow, the thought gave him hope. Maybe there was a chance for him, which made it all the more puzzling why they hadn't found Malcolm.

With hope came powerful thirst. He began to feel around his body as far as he could reach, trussed and tethered as he was. If his captor had left him some water, he could live for days. His emotions became a roller coaster as he discovered that if there was water in the cave, it was out of his reach. Thirst turned to obsession. As the hours passed, Brody could not stop himself from repeating an endless loop of hope, followed by despair, until he thought he might go insane before rescue or death occurred.

At last, he howled in utter frustration. Tears came then, despite his attempt to stop them. He thought it might seal his death warrant if he wasted a drop of moisture that remained in his body. With a Herculean effort, he forced himself to become dispassionate and stop crying.

It was then that he picked up a distant sound. Someone was coming.

"I see you haven't died yet," the gravelly voice observed.

"Why haven't I?" Brody answered. As before, the blow came without warning, but this time Brody felt the movement before the back of his assailant's hand connected with his cheek. He avoided the worst of the blow by turning his head. "How can you see anything?" he asked out of genuine curiosity.

Light bloomed in the darkness, causing Brody to wince and shut his eyes. "My secret," the guy drawled.

He held out a canteen, and Brody nodded. "Please."

Cool water slipped down his throat and dribbled from his chin. He couldn't swallow fast enough, and mourned the loss of the drops that didn't make it into his mouth. Too soon, the guy withdrew the canteen and capped it.

"How much would your people pay to have you back?" the guy asked.

"My people are poor. They would give everything they have," Brody said. "But they don't have much." He believed it was the truth.

"What about your employer, Ben Whitecloud? What would he give?"

Brody thought about it. "I don't know," he said. He truly didn't. Ben wasn't a bad man, but his relative wealth had come hard for him. And he owed Brody nothing more than his wages.

"What if we wanted him to turn a blind eye to our presence here in return for you? Would he do that?"

Brody hoped so, but he found he couldn't know. He didn't know Ben that well. "I hope he would. Honestly, I don't know."

"You'd better pray he will. Now that he knows we're here, that's a problem for us."

Brody didn't think that called for an answer, and he stayed silent.

"Who's the pretty woman with him?" The question came after a few minutes of silence, during which his captive had taken something out of a backpack and was chewing on it. Brody was focused on the food and almost missed the question.

"What?"

With exaggerated patience, the guy held out a piece of jerky, which Brody snatched at with his teeth. Too quickly, the guy pulled it back.

"You want this? Who's the woman with Whitecloud?"

Brody was genuinely confused. "With him where? At the ranch? Probably my sister, Jenn Williams." Immediately he regretted his answer, in case it put Jenn in danger. Just as quickly, he changed his mind when the guy held out the jerky again, and this time let Brody catch it between his teeth.

"Not at the ranch. They're in the ruins. It looks like they're going to come in and look for you. Whether they find you, and whether they get out of here, depends on how Whitecloud answers. Hope you enjoy the jerky. It could be your last meal."

With that, the light went out again and Brody heard his captor's steps fade into the distance. Brody's loop of hope and despair gained a new emotion — fear for Jenn. He began to pray to the Catholic God in whose school he'd been educated, and to all the spirits of his people, that she forget about him and go home to safety, or that Ben had the right answer.

# Chapter Forty

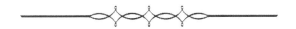

*Anasazi Ruin*

"**Y**OU KNOW, YOU shouldn't come in here," Ben said. He was at the top of the kiva wall, preparing to descend the ladder inside.

"It's a little late for that," Jenn snapped. "Are you seriously going to tell me you believe all that nonsense?"

"Don't you?"

Ben's question brought her up short. If she were honest, she'd have to say she half-did. Her grandmother had believed it and had trained her in the ancient medicine. But her modern education made her reject it as nothing more than superstition. When she'd told Brody she could banish Skinwalkers, it was only to reassure him.

But there was something weird and mysterious about Malcom's disappearance. Nothing in her experience explained it. It seemed more closely related to the old tales than to anything Jenn knew of modern life. She was spooked, and that's why she'd asked Ben to help her in the first place. It didn't mean she was going to let it stop her.

"No. Not a word. Get over and out of my way. I'm coming up." With that, she began to climb the ladder to the top of the wall, noting with satisfaction that Ben's head was sinking below the top on the inside of the kiva.

A few minutes later, she stood beside him at the bottom of the kiva, taking in the details.

"It's not all that impressive," she observed.

"Probably all the furnishings were taken when they left here," Ben answered. He put his hand on the smoke-blackened ceiling. "Do you want to lead the way?" His smile was mocking.

"Go ahead, my handsome prince," Jenn mocked in kind. Her sweet smile was meant to take the sting out of it. Why she was flirting with her ex while her younger brother was possibly in mortal danger didn't have an answer, and so she didn't try. Ben winked at her before ducking into the opening they'd called the sipapu.

Ben's voice floated out to her. "Man, it's dark in here."

Jenn followed him in, switching on her flashlight. "The hands told me there were three openings leading out of this room. Two don't go far. The third leads far into the cliffside. It's where Brody was when he reportedly came back out on his own after they told him Malcom's body wasn't in the other passages. The others said there were no significant side-caves in there. Brody never came out, and the others didn't see him when they did."

"He has to be in one of the shallow ones," Ben reasoned. "He must have lost his way, maybe when his flashlight gave out. He's probably waiting for someone to get there with a light."

"Maybe so," Jenn remarked. "It's as good a place to start as any. From what they told me, it's the first opening on the left."

Ben put his left hand on the cave wall and kept it there as he walked. Jenn followed, watching their shadows dance on the walls and ceiling of the cave as they avoided stumbling over rubble in the cave. Before long, they found the opening and went inside, immediately having to duck as the ceiling was much lower.

"I don't think this one is very promising," Jenn said, dodging a stalactite. The passage was narrow and obstructed by both stalactites and stalagmites.

"You never know when these things will open up into bigger rooms," Ben said. "I remember visiting Carlsbad Caverns when I was a kid. I'd think we were at a dead end, and then we'd go around a corner, and there was another big room."

A few yards farther along, they'd come to what appeared to be the end of the cave, but Ben spotted an opening no more than knee high. Ben dropped to his hands and knees. "Wait until I can see if this is passable."

"Why would he crawl in there? Surely he'd know it was the wrong way to get out?"

"No telling what he was thinking if he was stumbling around in the dark. Maybe thought it would be a good place to hide if the drug runners came in?"

That made sense, Jenn thought. "Shouldn't I go in first?" she argued. "I'm smaller."

"You're not afraid of what might be in there?"

"What?" she asked.

"Snakes, spiders, scorpions, Skinwalkers." Ben's tone still mocked her.

Jenn suppressed a grin. "I know better than that. Snakes would have been at the entrance. I'll watch where I put my hands. *You*," she added, "better be careful of Skinwalkers. *I* have my medicine pouch. Move over."

Jenn dropped to her hands and knees, hesitated as she swept the couple of feet before her for unfriendly insects, and then crawled into the small passageway. By the time she had to drop to her belly, she was convinced Brody couldn't have come this way. Surprisingly, it opened far enough for her to crawl on hands and knees again, and within a few yards had broken into a larger room. Just like Ben had said it might.

She crawled out, then turned to call back through the passage.

"It may be tight, but I think you can get through. There's another room here."

Ben's faint answer was, "Coming."

Jenn didn't wait for him. The room was smaller than the one at the kiva entrance, but another tunnel-like passage led out of it. She started down it, and came face-to-face with a lurid red Z painted on the wall. She gasped and flinched back.

"What is it?" Ben's voice startled her again and she jumped.

"Baby, what..."

Ben's widening eyes indicated he'd seen the graffiti. "Oh, shit. Jenn, we've got to get out of here."

"What does it mean?" she asked.

"Los Zetas," he answered. "That's their sign. It must have been their drugs you guys found. The FBI will listen now, if we live to tell it. We've got to go."

"Not without Brody," Jenn said, though her entire body was trembling.

"Baby..."

"Don't 'baby' me," she snarled. "I thought we had that straight. I'm not your baby, and I'm going to find my brother."

"I just meant, I mean — I'm sorry, Jenn. He's probably dead."

She felt tears spill over and roll down her cheeks. "Then I'll find his body." She turned back and felt blindly for where the passage led. Then she felt Ben's hands on her shoulders.

"This way," he said gently. He guided her to the right, where the passage turned, keeping his hands on her shoulders as her tears cleared and she led the way.

It was clear that the passage had been carved from the living rock. The sides were straight, the passage just wide enough for one person, and barely high enough for Ben to walk upright. They hadn't gone far when a voice called out from beyond.

"Who's there?"

"Brody?" Jenn whispered. Then more urgently. "Brody! Is that you? Please, God, let it be you."

"Jenn, thank God. Get me out of here, before he comes back."

Jenn stumbled forward, with Ben on her heels. "Who did this to you, Brody?" She found him lying on his side, his wrists tied together, and his ankles both tied and tethered to a ring set into the wall.

"I don't know. Do you have any water?"

She fumbled for the tube from her camelback and fed it into his lips. "Here. Don't drink too much at first. Take it slow."

Brody sipped, then tongued the valve out of his mouth. "Get me loose."

Ben was ready with a pocket knife. He stepped forward, knelt, and began sawing at the bindings between Brody's ankles. While he worked, Brody told them what had happened, though he couldn't remember much.

"Someone knocked me out. I woke up here. He's been back twice, and gave me water and a little jerky."

"This is a Zeta's hideout," Ben explained. "I wonder why they didn't just kill you."

"He told me they were going to ransom me. In return for you leaving them alone, Ben."

"Over my dead body," Ben snarled. "Their poison is killing our youth. As soon as we get out of here, I'm going to the FBI."

"I'm sorry to hear that," a new voice answered. "You see, that's a problem for us."

# Chapter Forty-One

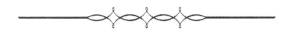

S AM EXPLAINED TO Gallagher what they'd found inside the cathedral grotto, including the discovery of the *Gordoye Dostizheniye,* their need to retrieve the strange stone artifact, and that it would need to remain a secret. The foreman had agreed to provide the heavy lifting equipment and whatever support was required to remove the stone while his own crew were down there making plans to retrieve the Big Bertha drilling machine. However, he noted the machine would most likely need to be dismantled before it could be brought back to the surface.

It wasn't until shortly after lunch time that Sam and Tom, along with a small convoy of three Humvees, made their way back down into the strange volcanic tunnel. Gallagher had decided to come, too, so that he could see first-hand what they were dealing with. At the front of the procession was a twenty-ton all terrain Lift King—something Sam decided was a cross between a forklift and a Sherman tank.

The Lift King made for a slow journey, but there was nothing they could do about that. It was a real stroke of luck they could even get such a machine in to retrieve the Death Stone. At the back of the convoy, a team of engineers ran a long line of phone and power cables along the side of the wall. Sam noted that

Gallagher was already thinking ahead and recognized that any attempt to dismantle and retrieve Big Bertha was going to be a drawn-out process of many weeks. Therefore, he wanted direct communication lines set between the worksite and the surface.

It was three in the afternoon by the time they reached the small barricade of fallen stalactites that had blocked their Humvee from originally reaching the grotto. The Lift King operator made short work of the barricade and the team continued to the cathedral grotto.

Tom parked the Humvee to the side of the subterranean lake and switched its engine off, but left the spotlights shining to cover the volcanic vault in light. Sam climbed out into the water. He along with the rest of the crew all wore waist high wading pants to stop him from getting wet in the shallow water while they worked. He looked at Gallagher, who was getting out of the back of the same Humvee with a big grin on his face.

The rest of the convoy parked in a neat line to the side of him.

Sam said, "Well… what do you think?"

Gallagher looked up at the giant grotto. "I've never seen anything like this and I've been working underground since I was sixteen!"

"Do you want to go see your beloved boring machine?" Sam asked.

"Yes please."

Sam switched on his flashlight. "Follow me."

Gallagher turned to his second in charge, who was getting out of the second Humvee in the convoy. "Let's get the men to set up some external lighting. I want this place to look like it's permanently daytime."

"Understood, sir."

Tom said, "I'll go give them a hand."

"Thank you." Gallagher looked back toward his 2IC and said, "And tell Ross and Tim I want one of them standing guard on

Big Bertha the entire time and the other at this entrance in case anyone tries to come or go without my permission."

"Yes, sir."

Sam looked at Gallagher. "You brought security?"

Gallagher nodded. "They're armed, too. Both licensed and carry pistols, too. I'm not taking any chance of someone causing any mischief to my damned machine now that we found her — especially since you told me you've seen evidence of someone boarding that Russian ship since the accident."

Sam watched Gallagher's eyes light up like a father reunited with his only child, climbing up into the boring machine. The foreman ran his hands lovingly over the various instruments, checking what worked and what didn't.

When Gallagher was finished Sam asked, "How is she?"

Gallagher smiled. "She's in a better condition than I would have ever expected. Heck, there's barely a scratch on her. Do you have any idea what this means?"

"That you saved your shareholders a fortune?"

"More than that. It means the construction of the Transcontinental World Link can continue. We're barely meeting budget as it is. If we'd lost Big Bertha, the project would have almost certainly been scrapped."

Sam grinned. "I'm glad we could help."

"You have no idea how much you've done for us."

Outside the boring machine the workers had gotten the external spotlights working. As they warmed up, the entire north side of the cathedral grotto lit up.

Gallagher stepped out of the boring machine and into the water again. The *Gordoye Dostizheniye* shined under the lights and the scattered shipping containers reflected the lighting. It must have triggered his memory, because a moment latter, Gallagher turned to Sam and said, "Okay, let's go see that ancient stone you're trying to steal."

Sam's lips thinned at the suggestion. "I assure you what I'm doing is perfectly legal…"

Gallagher's eyes narrowed. "You think salvaging an artifact off a recently sunken ship before anyone realizes it's down here is legal?"

"All right. So, it's not legal." Sam made a show of a deep sigh. "But I can give you my word that it's more important than anything else on earth that I remove the stone before anyone else finds it."

Gallagher shrugged. "You found my machine and saved the company nearly a hundred million dollars. I don't care one iota if it's legal or not—I'll help you get your stone."

"Thank you."

"Which one of these containers has it?"

Sam pointed at one about a hundred feet away.

"Do you know how deep it is out there?"

"Not very. Maybe one to two feet at most. No more than knee-deep."

"Where does it get deep?" Gallagher asked.

"About twenty feet off the Russian cargo ship. Everywhere else appears to be the same shallow depth."

Gallagher nodded and then made a sharp whistle that echoed throughout the grotto. He called to the all-terrain Lift King driver. "Follow me."

Sam, Tom and Gallagher waded through the water toward the specialized shipping container, followed by the Lift King.

He checked the photo on his cell phone which showed the security code and then keyed it into the keypad and pressed enter. The hydraulic locks shifted and the door opened.

Tom stepped inside first. "Sam, you're not going to believe this!"

Sam tensed. "What now?"

"The Death Stone's been removed."

# Chapter Forty-Two

SAM'S REACTION WAS visceral. "No! It can't be."

"I know. That's three things we've lost this week. If you didn't own the company I expect you and I would get fired over this..." Tom stopped, having noticed Sam's face.

"I don't understand. We covered the original outside note that had the code written on it so no one else could get in."

Tom expelled his breath slowly. "That means whoever stole the stone was watching us when we went inside."

"How can someone have gotten to it without us noticing?" Sam asked. "More importantly, how could anyone have moved it out of here?"

"All right. Let's think this through. We know the damned thing didn't leave the way we came in. There's nowhere to hide a machine big enough to move the stone within the lava tube."

"So, where is it?" Gallagher asked, his bushy eyebrows narrowing.

Sam said, "There's only one place we're forgetting..."

Tom asked, "Where?"

"The opposite end of the cathedral grotto."

Sam climbed into the driver's seat of the Humvee. Flicked the engine to start and dropped the handbrake.

"What are you doing?" Tom asked.

"I'm driving to the other end of the lake. They can't have much of a head start on us."

"You don't even know if its shallow enough to drive across."

He looked out past the *Gordoye Dostizheniye* out toward the lake. The cathedral grotto was so massive that it looked like a subterranean sea more than a lake. On the horizon, the still water blurred with the stone ceiling into one, giving the impression of a sea that went forever.

Sam grinned. "Sure we do. Unless someone put the stone on a ship, we know someone picked up the stone in a large vehicle and drove across that lake. I'll keep to the sides."

Tom shrugged. "You're crazy."

"Are you coming with me?"

"Sure." Tom climbed into the passenger seat. "It wouldn't be the first time I followed you on some foolhardy expedition."

"Take this. If you get into trouble, we're all on channel twenty. Also, I've got communications topside if you need me to get a message through to your crew." Gallagher handed him a radio. "Do you two have a weapon?"

"No."

Gallagher shook his head and climbed into the Humvee's back seat. "Ah... all right. I better come with you. I brought a handgun down in case we had trouble."

Sam planted his foot hard and nearly eight thousand pounds of Humvee accelerated through the water. He kept to the left-hand side of the lake and still the bumper created a large bow-wave as it forced its way through the shallow water.

It was another twenty minutes before they reached the lake's far end. The cathedral ceiling had disappeared here. In its place was a giant circumferential opening.

Sam stopped the car and opened his door to look up. "I guess that's the sinkhole that swallowed the *Gordoye Dostizheniye*."

Tom stared at it. One of the largest sinkholes in the world. Now blocked by an avalanche with millions of tons of glacial silt from the seabed above. "The ship must have only just fit through the hole by going bow or stern first."

"The question is, where did the water go?"

"You don't think this lake is the remnants of that water?"

"I do." Sam swept the horizon of the lake with his flashlight. "But the water's no longer high enough to float the *Gordoye Dostizheniye*, let alone travel the few miles back to where it now lies. Also, I've been looking at the edge of the water. The waterline appears to be getting lower."

"It must be draining somewhere."

Sam sat back in the Humvee and closed the door. "And that must be where our Death Stone has been taken."

He put the Humvee into gear and continued driving. Up ahead, there was movement in the water. Not much, but if you watched it for a few seconds, it became obvious that the water was slowly flowing further south.

Tom said, "Just slow down a little. Something's changing up ahead."

Sam dropped down into low. "I see the ripples. What? Are you worried we're about to drive over an underground waterfall?"

Tom smiled. "It had crossed my mind."

"Me too. But I think the gradient change up ahead can't be that steep, otherwise we'd see more of a response from this water."

"Hope you're right."

A few minutes later, Sam took his foot off the pedal and the Humvee slowed. The headlights were being swallowed by a dark opening in the volcanic grotto up ahead. The water near it had noticeably picked up its pace, now racing toward the mouth of the new lava tube.

Sam squinted to make recognition out of what he was seeing. "What is that?"

Tom swallowed. "I've believe that's the subterranean waterfall that doesn't exist."

# Chapter Forty-Three

SAM SHOVED HIS foot hard on the brake pedal.

The Humvee's thirty-seven-inch Goodyear military tires ground to a halt on the bed of obsidian below. The now fast-moving water, being drawn toward the descending lava tube, had little effect on the vehicle's nearly eight thousand pounds of steel.

The entrance showed that the new tunnel was smaller than the lava tube between the surface and the cathedral grotto, but still plenty big enough for the Humvee to enter. Sam lifted his foot off the brake and edged closer.

Tom asked, "What are you doing?"

"Getting my stone back!"

"Whoa… wait a minute. What makes you certain that thing doesn't drop away to our oblivion?"

Sam gently stopped a few feet from the entrance.

His eyes swept from the top of the opening to the bottom. The original waterline mark was above the top of the tube, meaning that an enormous amount of water had already made its way through the tunnel. At the lip of the entrance, the water was less than a foot deep, but was flowing extremely fast, drawn by the steep gradient.

The headlights lit up the new lava tube and Sam followed it with his eyes until they quickly became lost in its depth possibly hundreds of feet below. Along its base, water, no deeper than five or six inches, flowed freely down the twenty-something degree slope, like a giant waterslide.

Tom said, "You can't possibly be thinking about doing what I think you're going to do?"

"Why not?"

"For starters, you have no idea how far down that thing goes or if the Humvee can even fit. And second, you have no idea whether or not the entire section below us is completely full of water."

Sam took his foot off the brake and the Humvee crawled closer. "Sure I do."

"How?"

"Look at the lip of the lava tube."

A small set of tank-tracks — the sort found on a bulldozer — lined the otherwise smooth, black, gloss of the volcanic stone base. There were multiple sets of tracks, as though someone had driven up as well as down the tunnel a few times before, carving deep indents into the otherwise hard stone.

"That's our thief!" Tom said.

And Sam eased the Humvee down into the tunnel.

# Chapter Forty-Four

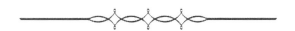

THE HUMVEE CREPT slowly down the ancient lava tunnel, while the shallow water raced by. Sam kept a firm, but gentle grip on the steering wheel. Allowing the heavy four-wheel drive to pick its course. The drop continued for at least a hundred feet and then leveled out into a new volcanic dome. This one much smaller than where they'd just come from, but still magnificent.

The new cavern appeared a little smaller than the field of a football stadium. The headlights were able to reach the opposite end, faintly reflecting back at them from the glossy volcanic stone wall. To their right the water followed a small river. In front, Sam could see the watermark had once flooded most of the volcanic plateau.

He imagined the enormous sinkhole opening up in the cathedral grotto and the unimaginable number of gallons of water flowing down through this tunnel, where it spilled out into the new opening, before flowing to their right, in search of gravitational equilibrium.

"Which way?" Sam asked.

"Keep to the left," Tom said without hesitation. "Our thief will be trying to stay away from wherever that water's heading."

Sam continued to drive.

Up ahead, something else began to reflect his headlights. Something long and straight, spanning the width of the volcanic dome.

"What is that?" he asked.

Tom said, "Keep going. It looks almost like railway tracks."

Sam drove the Humvee straight ahead to the very end, where a pair of railway tracks ran right across the field of obsidian.

He stopped at the railway tracks.

Sam put the Humvee in neutral and pulled the handbrake. He switched on his flashlight, opened the door and stepped out.

To the left the tracks disappeared into a straight tunnel that appeared to go on forever, with the steel railway eventually blending in with the horizon. He turned and faced the opposite direction. The tracks continued into a different tunnel that looked almost identical. About forty feet into the tunnel the tracks disappeared.

Sam shined his flashlight across the railway tracks, trying to see where they went, or if they simply reached their end. The light reflected back at him in a series of ripples.

He smiled, with understanding. "The tracks are covered with water!"

Tom said, "So it appears this tunnel has a small downward slope to it."

Sam took a bearing with his compass. The dry tunnel ran southeast, while the flooded tunnel ran northwest. He tried to mentally picture where the railway tracks could possibly come out and how long it would take to drive.

Tom took a few steps and measured the width of the railway tracks. He grinned. "Well, what do you know?"

"Little, it seems." A wry smile formed on Sam's lips as he saw recognition in his friend's eyes. "What do you see that I don't?"

"Look at the width of the track," Tom said. "It's five feet."

"So?"

"That means it's Russian."

"Why, what size tracks do we use in the States?"

"Four feet eight inches — what is considered standard around the world."

"Russia doesn't?" Sam asked.

"No. They use five feet exactly."

"Why?"

"Defense."

"Really?"

Tom said, "Concerned that their railway lines could be used by an invader, Russia purposely chose a railway gauge that was uncommon and different from their neighboring countries."

"All right," Sam said. "So, unless these tunnels perform a massive U-turn it looks like the lines to the U.S. are open, while we're going to have to wait to take any trips to Russia's for a while."

He got back into the Humvee, worried they'd lost the stone for good this time. He followed the tracks to the east in his process of making a big U-turn and heading back to the cathedral grotto. Maybe there was still time for Elise to work out where the railway line came out.

As he turned left and away from the railway tracks, he stopped. There in front of them rows of large wooden crates were stacked three high. At the end of the crates, standing upright was the megalithic Death Stone.

Sam parked next to it and got out of the Humvee.

He and Tom both swept their flashlight in large circular swaths, searching for anyone waiting for them. Somehow the entire place appeared empty. Sam said, "Someone must have brought it down here to load on a train or something."

Tom nodded. "Sure, but I can't see the forklift they used to load it."

"We need to get it out of here before whoever they are come back."

Gallagher nodded. "Sure, but without anything to lift it with, you're just going to have to wait until we can get down here with the Lift King."

Confident they were alone for the time being, Sam approached the first crate. The lid had a series of metal latches that needed to be slid open to release it. He worked his way through each of them and then opened the lid.

Inside, packaged in rows of ten were Russian PKM heavy machine guns.

Sam said, "Holy shit!"

Tom opened the next crate, which was filled with dozens of AA-12 fully automatic shotguns and 28 round quick release magazines.

Gallagher said, "Good Lord! What is that?"

"If I had to guess, Mr. Gallagher, I'd say you're a little late with your Siberian/Alaskan railroad. It appears mother nature beat you to it." Sam glanced at the mass of weapons boxed along the side of the railway line. "And it appears arms dealers found it first. They've been using it to ship weapons across the Bering Strait."

Tom said, "That might explain the series of accidents your first rescue crew suffered."

Gallagher asked, "You think whoever put these here is still around?"

Sam said, "They're not here now, but they'll be back soon. That's for certain."

"And instead of killing my rescue team the old-fashioned way, they made it appear like they had fallen victim to a series of bad luck... as a ruse to try and sway the rest of my miners to leave the tunnel, fearing the ancient stories of Skinwalkers?"

"Yeah, I think you might just be right about that."

Gallagher swallowed hard. "Then where are they now?"

Sam swallowed the fear rising like bile in his throat. "I have no idea, but I have no intention of waiting here any longer to find out."

Tom approached from the other end of the pile of crates. "I'm sorry to tell you, but I think I found your missing Big Bertha crew, and what remains of your rescue team."

"They're dead?" Gallagher asked.

Tom nodded. "Yeah. Bullet holes in each of them. Clean head shots, too. Double taps. Very professional."

Gallagher tensed. "What about Ilya Yezhov?"

"Who?" Sam asked.

"He was the leader of the mine rescue team we sent in to search for Big Bertha's crew. Why didn't they kill him?"

Sam swore. "He's the one who must have done this. He knew about the arms smuggling operation and came down here to kill your men, and protect his shipment of weapons."

Tom said, "Not just the weapons. He knew about the Death Stone."

That thought sent fear up Sam's spine. It meant this wasn't all about the arms shipment. Someone in government was responsible for the Death Stone.

Could it have been possible that someone intentionally blew a hole in the ceiling of the cathedral grotto to sink the *Gordoye Dostizheniye* and bury the Death Stone?

*Who could organize such a thing?*

He turned to Gallagher. "Can you get a message to the surface?"

"It will have to be relayed through the communications cable by my men at the cathedral grotto, but we should be able to.

What do you want me to tell them?"

"Tell them not to let anyone land on Big Diomede Island. Whoever's behind this, you can count on them being back with reinforcements."

"Okay, okay..." Gallagher said, adjusting his radio. "I'll let them know."

Sam watched Gallagher step away to make the communications. He came back less than a minute later. His face pale and tense.

Sam asked, "What is it? Did you get the message to the surface crew?"

Gallagher's jaw was set hard. "Yeah, but they said that Ilya Yezhov was on his way back with a second rescue team to help."

"You have to tell them to stop him from landing on the island," Sam said, starting the Humvee.

"I did, but how?"

"Anything they can think of. Tell them to place a couple of cars on the runway. We all know its short enough as it is. I can't imagine any aircraft could land there with a Humvee or two parked midway along."

Gallagher said, "I'll tell them."

Behind them, Tom removed two AA-12s and several 28-round quick-release magazines and dumped them in the back seat of the Humvee. He then returned to the first opened crate and removed two PKM heavy machine guns and two boxes of rimmed 7.62×54mmR cartridges.

Sam asked, "What are you doing?"

Tom placed his cache into the back of the Humvee and then fed the 28 round quick release magazines into the AA-12 shotgun, and set it to fully automatic. "I'm trying not to go against my father's most treasured rule."

"What's that?"

"Never enter a gunfight without a gun."

# Chapter Forty-Five

*On-board the Maria Helena*

THE *MARIA HELENA* rested in the shallow waters of the Bering Strait, anchored only a few hundred feet off the coast of Big Diomede Island. Genevieve checked her watch. Sam and Tom had been underground for nearly fourteen hours now — an hour longer than she'd expected. It was probably time she warmed up the Sea King and went over to the makeshift rescue camp next to the main boring tunnel to retrieve them.

She stepped onto the aft deck. It was a clear day, with cerulean blue skies and no cloud in any direction. Her eyes stopped on a white speck to the west, and a moment later she realized it was moving. Genevieve heard the persistent drum of the twin-propellered medium sized cargo aircraft follow. She grabbed a pair of binoculars and examined the cargo aircraft. It banked to the north, and she caught a better glimpse of her fuselage. It looked familiar to her, with its high-set cantilevered wings, twin turbo-props and stalky main undercarriage. Genevieve smiled with genuine surprise at the once familiar aircraft of her childhood.

It was an Antonov An-26.

Built in Russia during the Soviet era, the aircraft had been used since the sixties with production being ceased by the early eighties. Its development was initially funded by the military and based on the An-24T tactical transport aircraft, with a focus on heavy cargo transport. The main difference being that the Antonov An-26 used a retractable cargo ramp with the ability to carry much larger payloads over short distances.

This one was a civilian model. Its presence in the area, given their close proximity to Russian mainland, wasn't so much of a surprise. Nor was the fact that the aircraft was approaching from the Alaskan peninsula and not the Siberian, because workers in the remote areas often came from both sides of the Bering Strait. What surprised her was the fact the pilot appeared to be on approach to land, although she couldn't picture where. She mentally imagined their surrounding islands and coast. It was impossible to think that a pilot of such a large aircraft would try to land on the makeshift runway of Big Diomede Island, which was only designed to take single propellered light aircraft.

Genevieve switched on the radio inside the Sea King to listen to the pilot. The local airwaves were silent. She stepped onto the deck and tracked the Russian aircraft through binoculars. At a glance she saw that the pilot was banking to the left, with its landing gear down and its flaps set down. It was turning onto its final approach with the small, recently established runway.

*What the hell's it doing here?*

She wondered if it was in serious trouble. The runway on Big Diomede Island was built to take light aircraft, single and twin-engine fixed wings, to charter the machine crew who worked on a fly-in fly-out basis. She'd flown over the runway herself in the Sea King. There was no way in the world a large cargo plane — especially an antiquated Soviet era military cargo plane — would be able to land on it.

*They must have some serious trouble to even contemplate such a landing.*

Her ears listened to repeated transmissions from someone on the ground on Big Diomede Island. They were repeatedly trying to contact the incoming aircraft, warning that a Humvee was currently broken down midway along the landing strip, and that it would be impossible to land until they moved it. The pilot remained silent, either because he couldn't hear them or was intentionally ignoring them.

She focused her binoculars on the runway along the mesa in the middle of the island. A big camouflaged Humvee sat empty, parked in the middle of the runway.

*What the hell's going on over there?*

"Matthew, Veyron, Elise, can you get up here?" she shouted.

She returned her focus on the Antonov An-26. Its pilot maintained position on a final approach. Surely, they realize there's no possible way to land an aircraft that size on the runway? Especially now there's a car parked in the middle to block it off.

The aircraft was now flying about fifteen feet directly over the crumpled heap of rocks that lined the island and just before the runway. The Humvee was no more than a couple hundred feet away. She held her breath as she watched the debacle unfold. The pilot would be hard pressed to take off again before colliding with the Humvee.

*Move the damned Humvee…*

Her eyes darted toward the pilot of the aircraft.

*Pull up! For fuck sake!*

She then spotted two flashes. It happened so quick, and was so unexpected coming out of a civilian aircraft, that her mind struggled to accept what she'd seen.

And then it was over.

The Humvee exploded in a mass of fiery destruction, being thrown far to the side of the runway and the aircraft's wheels kept rolling along the runway.

What just happened? Did the pilot really use air to surface missiles?

She kept the binoculars fixed on the aircraft. The retractable cargo ramp lowered to a horizontal position, and several motorcycles rolled out the back.

A moment later, the Antonov An-26's nose lifted and the aircraft was back in the air, having completed its touch and go landing.

The rat-a-tat-tat sound of hundreds of firecrackers exploding now resonated from the island.

The radio in the Sea King was suddenly live with frantic messages. She stepped closer and heard someone shouting, "People are shooting at us! We're taking fire!"

She grabbed the microphone. "This is the *Maria Helena*. Please confirm. Who are you being attacked by?"

There was no response.

Elise ran up the stairs from onto the deck. "What's going on?"

"There's trouble on the island. I'm not sure what, exactly." Genevieve shook her head in disbelief. "But I think someone just said they're under attack!"

# Chapter Forty-Six

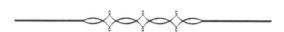

G ENEVIEVE SAT IN the cockpit of the Sea King helicopter, with its blades turning at speed. She would be in the air as soon as the other three were on-board. The radio was switched on, but there had been no more communications from the island. Even the sound of gunfire had finally died down to an occasional burst.

The copilot's side door opened and Elise climbed in, looking like a petite version of Tomb Raider. At each thigh she wore an Israeli-built Uzi, and in her hands, she was carrying a large automatic rifle. She rested the weapon across her lap, closed the door, and removed the side window so that she could shoot if she needed to.

Genevieve grinned. "You brought an M24 bolt action sniper rifle?"

"What?" Elise shrugged, undeterred.

"To what might end up being just a demonstration by locals unhappy about the building of a tunnel through their sacred land?"

Elise smiled. "You said get the firepower."

Veyron carried the Gatling style Browning .50 caliber heavy machine gun and attached it to its mount on the left side of the rear helicopter door. Behind him, Matthew carried a rocket launcher. Neither man spoke.

Genevieve glanced at Matthew. "You brought an RPG 7 rocket launcher. What the hell do you think you're going to do with that?"

Matthew, by far the most conservative and mild-mannered member of the crew, shrugged. "Elise didn't tell me what was going on. Just that the Big Diomede Island camp was under attack, Sam and Tom are still there, and you wanted us to bring enough firepower to end it. Did I miss anything?"

Genevieve grinned. "No. I'd say, that just about sums it up."

Elise handed her a Glock 31. "Just in case we have trouble and you need to put us on the ground."

Genevieve took it and nodded, not even wanting to think about what that would mean. She checked the magazine was full and holstered the handgun over the right side of her hip. Her eyes then swept the Sea King's instruments. Happy with what she saw, she lifted the collective, and took off. The Sea King hovered twenty feet off the ground, before she lowered the nose and made a beeline toward the Island camp — leaving the *Maria Helena* alone to swing on her anchor in the idyllic waters.

Veyron asked, "Do you think it's one of the local Yupik tribes?"

"Not likely. I heard machine gun fire in the background."

It was a short trip. Less than a minute before they were overhead of the main camp, and roughly a mile from the entrance to the main boring tunnel. In an instant, she knew they were in trouble. Genevieve hovered for a moment, as her eyes swept the landscape. The entire place looked more like a warzone than a public construction site. Bullet holes riddled the buildings, dead bodies of the construction workers lay motionless where they were lively minutes earlier, and expensive machines now burned.

There was nothing left. Someone had killed every last one of them.

Genevieve rotated the Sea King in a wide circle. Nothing moved down below. "Can you see anything?" she asked.

"Nothing," came the unanimous response.

Then, Elise said, "There. Nine o'clock. I have a visual on two motorbikes!"

Genevieve glanced at her nine o'clock position. There were two men riding KLR 650 endurance bikes, wearing completely black helmets and body armor.

It was as much as she was going to see. An instant later, she heard the sound of gunfire and shoved the cyclic control to her right, banking away from the shots.

Behind her, she heard Veyron release the Browning heavy machine gun. Bullets sprayed the ground where the riders had been moments beforehand.

"Anyone got eyes of those bikes?" Veyron shouted.

"I got nothing," Genevieve replied.

Each of them searched their respective angles out of the helicopter. Genevieve swept the area with her eyes trained for any sign of movement. The bikes must have hidden somewhere, but where? There was no vegetation high enough to provide any concealment.

Her eyes stopped on one of the small lodges used to house the fly-in fly-out workers. "They're in the buildings!"

A second later she heard the M24 bolt action sniper rifle fire. Her eyes shifted from Elise to the building below. A motorcycle crept out of the front door.

Elise squeezed the trigger again, and its rider fell to the ground.

An instant later, the second motorcycle shot through the back door and out onto the roadway that led to the main boring tunnel. Genevieve didn't wait an instant. Instead, she dipped the nose and followed the motorcyclist.

Up ahead, she spotted another three bikes enter the tunnel. Her eyes fixed on one of them, who had now turned around, firing at them.

She banked to the right and then flew a wide arc behind the tunnel's entrance. Veyron fired another burst of .50 caliber rounds, hitting one of the riders — and then all of the remaining motorcycles disappeared into the tunnel.

The Sea King carefully rounded the tunnel and came down to hover fifty feet away and perpendicular to the entrance, so that Veyron could line his heavy machine gun up neatly — but there was no sign of the riders.

Genevieve sighed. "All right, it looks like I'm going to have to put us down if we want to follow them."

Five feet off the ground, she heard the momentous grumble of the earth being torn apart. She swore as she pulled the collective lever up hard, and the Sea King rose swiftly into the air. A thousand tons of quartz, gravel and sand ripped through the tunnel in a single blast, landing hundreds of feet away from the entrance.

Genevieve fought with her controls to keep the Sea King in the air as the blast-wave struck. She swung the helicopter in a three-hundred-foot arc away from the entrance, and slowly watched with horror as realization dawned.

Elise glanced at the distorted rubble below. "Did the tunnel just cave in?"

Genevieve shook her head. "No way. That amount of blast had to be from dynamite or C4!"

"That's going to take months to reach anyone who was still down there." Veyron looked at the rubble. "Tell me our boys weren't still down there!"

Genevieve swallowed hard. "They were meant to be back an hour ago..."

# Chapter Forty-Seven

SAM LED THE convoy of three Humvees through the meandering lava tube toward the surface. With his foot pressed down hard on the accelerator, the heavy vehicle ran the constantly twisting, winding, and undulating tunnel at speeds more appropriate to a bobsled or a theme park ride than an armored vehicle.

In the front passenger seat, Tom silently checked each of the weapons he'd taken from the arms cache. While in the back Gallagher continued to try and reach anyone on the surface via radio, but they had gone silent since his first transmission.

Sam reached the crest of the dip where they'd found the cowboy's body, and then quickly descended into the straight section that approached the bottom of the first volcanic vault, where Big Bertha had first punched her way through the volcanic rock and into the ancient world.

Sam spotted the uphill track rising to the main tunnel up ahead. Mentally he picked the route and prepared himself for the steep climb, but he never reached the incline. Instead, he heard the most frightening sound anyone below ground can possibly hear — the rumble of a cave in — and he jammed on the brakes.

Boulders the size of cars came rolling down the steep incline up ahead, destroying everything in their path. He shoved the gear into reverse, but the other Humvees were in his way and hadn't yet seen what was coming. Instead, he moved the gear into drive and accelerated quickly, keeping his eyes fixed on the smaller opening to a separate tunnel toward the north of the volcanic dome.

He swerved to the left and braked as a small boulder came rolling down in front of him. The instant it passed, he was back on the accelerator. He needed to reach that second tunnel, if they were going to survive the landslide of falling rubble.

Behind them, the men in the second Humvee weren't quite so lucky. A fragment of obsidian the size of a small bus struck them, crushing the entire vehicle and its occupants as a though it were nothing more than a fly being swatted.

Sam entered the second tunnel and drove about fifty feet inside before coming to a rounded turn, stopping so that he could watch the disaster unfold outside the tunnel, while still leaving enough room to continue driving farther into the tunnel if he had to do so. The last Humvee in their small convoy pulled up to a stop behind them.

He stared out the window, watching until the last of the debris finally stopped falling. In its wake the entire area became choked with dust and fine particles of crushed stone, making it impossible to see the remains of the crushed Humvee. Not that it mattered to Sam. He didn't need to see it to know that all the men inside were crushed.

As the dust settled, Sam moved the Humvee closer to the entrance of the tunnel to see what was left, pulling up so that he faced the tunnel, in case he needed to get out of there in a hurry.

Tom said, "The track's been destroyed!"

"Not just the track!" Sam's eyes swept the area above. "The tunnel's caved in."

"Or been intentionally destroyed," Gallagher said.

At the back of the dark tunnel where they'd taken sanctuary, a series of glowing lights lit up the tunnel, like the malevolent and piercing eyes of ancient predators.

"What the hell?" Tom said.

Sam said, "We've got company."

# Chapter Forty-Eight

FIVE MOTORCYCLE ENGINES started up simultaneously, their engines purring loudly in the confines of the tunnel. The series of single headlights shined right at the Humvee. The riders wore black armor with matching helmets, giving them an unnaturally menacing appearance. The engines revved in unison, like a bunch of wild dogs restlessly awaiting their release into the wild to hunt.

Tom gripped the handle of his AA-12 shotgun as he studied the riders and grinned. "Let them come. We're ready."

Sam held his position, as though he was still trying to decide whether to try and outrun them or fight. "We don't know what they have?"

"We might not know what they have, but we know we're in a military grade armored vehicle and we have plenty of firepower." Gallagher reached for the PKM heavy machine gun and fed the first chain of its ammunition belt into the receiver. "I just wished we'd thought to arm the other crews better."

Before Sam could make his decision, bullets started to spray their windshield, causing a small series of fine splintered stars to form.

Tom said, "Swing around to the side, and I'll let's see if our new-found friends are still interested in playing once they know that we're armed."

"All right."

Sam moved the Humvee another ten feet forward into a curve. Tom opened his door and fired half a dozen shots downwind.

Three of the riders were knocked off their bikes, while the other two split up to opposite sides of the tunnel in an attempt to race past. Tom was quick and fired back at the first one, while the second one raced by and out into the main volcanic dome.

Tom swore and climbed back into the Humvee, not wanting to risk being shot at from both directions.

A moment later he heard Gallagher fire a long burst from the PKM heavy machine gun, and the rider who'd slipped past him was killed in seconds.

Tom turned to face Gallagher. "Thanks."

Through the windshield, he noticed two of the riders get up and start firing at them again. They were wearing some sort of Kevlar protective armor. Tom noticed their own windshield wasn't holding up to the task as well. Cracks were beginning to form where repeated shots had caused damage to the internal layers of the bullet-proof glass. Even military grade glass was never really bullet-proof.

Sam raced toward their attackers, sending nearly eight thousand pounds of steel racing toward their unprotected and fragile frames.

The two remaining riders immediately jumped onto their bike and took off. Sam tried to follow them, but the tunnel quickly narrowed and even if it hadn't, the cumbersome Humvee was no match for the speed and agility of the endurance bikes. The two bikes soon disappeared deep into the darkness.

Tom asked, "You got any plans to get us out of here?"

"Not really." Sam confirmed.

Gallagher said, "What about the long railway tunnel?"

Sam's eyes narrowed. "It could be a thousand miles to the mainland — assuming the track even goes to the mainland — we'd run out of fuel long before that."

Tom smiled. "You got a better idea?"

"No."

"I'd rather make an attempt crossing the railway tunnel. Even if we have a long walk ahead of us, it's better than trying to dig our way out." Tom searched for any sign of the motorcycles in the darkness ahead. "Besides, at least that way we'll know we've lost our unwanted guests. I used to ride a KLR 650. Their fuel tanks are tiny. They'll run out of fuel long before us."

Sam looked back at Gallagher. "What do you reckon?"

"It could take months for a rescue party to come dig us out. If we have to walk, I'd rather make a start now."

"All right. That's decided."

Sam circled around, stopping next to the second Humvee. Tom wound his window down and told the driver their plan. With everyone in agreement, they set out for the long journey into unknown.

Behind them, Tom spotted a sudden flash of the motorcyclist's RPG.

It happened so quickly, his mind couldn't register what he was seeing. The armor piercing rocket struck the Humvee next to them. Its detonation had a one second delay. There was recognition in the driver's face, and an instant later, the entire Humvee erupted in a fiery explosion.

# Chapter Forty-Nine

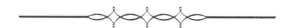

S AM FLOORED THE Humvee and raced out of the tunnel before the riders could reload and get a second shot off. He swerved to the left, rounding the massive boulder and wreckage of the crushed Humvee.

Tom unclipped his seatbelt and climbed into the back seat, preparing to fire some protective rounds at the motorcycles once they caught up. Next to him Gallagher fed another chain of ammunition into the PKM's receiver.

The Humvee sped through the tunnel, up over the crest and into the steep dip below. Sam maintained a moderate speed. He needed to move fast enough that the riders wouldn't have enough time to stop their bikes and fire an RPG, but there was no reason to race—after all, any contest of pure speed and agility, would be won by the motorcyclists with ease.

Behind him, Sam heard Tom fire a couple shots from his shotgun. He then swerved to the left, giving Gallagher room to target their attackers with his machine gun. The motorcyclists didn't fire any shots back. They couldn't fire an RPG while moving, and their hand machine guns—most likely Russian made PP-19 Bizon submachine guns—were unlikely to penetrate the bulletproof glass of the Humvee's rear window.

Soon the motorcycles dropped back, biding their time for a

better opportunity to attack. Sam sighed heavily. He, too, was searching for the right time to make a better attack. Soon, they would approach the cathedral grotto—and then who knows what the motorcyclist would try and do.

"What do you want to do when we reach the grotto?" Sam asked, without taking his eyes of the tunnel ahead.

"Why don't you pull up to the side of the entrance?" Tom answered. "That way, we can shoot them as they come out."

Sam considered the implications for a moment. "Seems fair. What if they reduce the distance between us, cutting our preparation time short?"

"Then we move to plan B," Gallagher suggested.

Sam rounded the barricade of stalactites. "Great. What's our plan B?"

"Keep going until you reach Big Bertha." Gallagher paused, as though he was still thinking it out in his mind. "When you round her, you hit the brakes long enough for me to get out and I'll set up inside. Then, you double back around, and I'll take them out from behind."

"That could work."

The tunnel straightened up and the opening to the cathedral grotto came into sight. Sam gunned the accelerator, and the Humvee started to pick up its pace.

Sam glanced in his rearview mirror. The two motorcyclists had opened their throttles up and were now rapidly closing the gap.

Gallagher said, "It looks like it's going to have to be plan B."

Sam fixed his eyes on the opening ahead. "Or plan C. You two had better hold on!"

"What's plan C?" Tom and Gallagher said in unison.

"This."

Sam jammed on the brakes.

One of the motorcyclists plowed straight into the Humvee's rear axle with a sickening thud. The second rider swerved to the right and shot around them, racing into the shallow waters.

Sam accelerated quickly, but lost sight of the rider and his motorcycle. "Where the hell did he go?"

Tom swept the area with his eyes. "He's got to be hiding behind one of those shipping containers."

"Sure." Sam slowly drove to the left, toward Big Bertha. "But which one?"

There were three shipping containers close enough for the rider to have reached in the time that he'd had.

Sam slowly skirted the left of each of them in the Humvee. When he reached the last one, there was no sign of the last motorcycle or rider.

He frowned. "Where did he go?"

Tom said, "Kill your headlights for a minute. Let's see if we can spot his light."

Sam switched the headlights off and waited.

Their eyes adjusted to the now pitch-dark environment and then they spotted the motorcycle's headlight. It wasn't a direct beam, but a sort of radiant glow from behind a shipping container to their right.

Sam gently released the brake and the Humvee lurched forward at a crawling pace in the dark. Tom and Gallagher gripped their weapons, and lowered their respective windows. They might only get one chance at this.

Approaching the edge of the shipping container, Sam whispered. "Ready?"

"Yes."

Sam shoved his foot down hard on the accelerator and the Humvee leapt forward at speed. He switched the headlights on. The KLR 650 lit up instantly. The motorcycle was resting on its stand, with its single headlight turned on, but no rider to be seen.

"Oh shit!" Sam swore.

He swerved to the right and switched off his headlights again. His front right wheel drove over the motorcycle, and Sam felt it crush under the Humvee's weight.

A split second later, he saw the flash of the rocket launching from the opposite direction, near the subterranean lake's shore. *He must have left the motorcycle running as a ruse, and then swum under the water directly in front of them!* Sam cursed his mistake.

The rocket went wide and struck the shipping container instead, sending a gush of water into the air. The blast-wave struck the back of the Humvee, shoving it forward. Sam gripped the steering wheel hard, trying to fight to keep the military vehicle from rolling.

In the back seats, both Gallagher and Tom emptied round after round of shots toward the rider in the dark. It was impossible to see him in the dark, and even more difficult to know if any of the shots hit their target.

In the midst of the shootout, Sam heard the rider return fire with his submachine gun. It would take a moment for the rider to arm another RPG — even if he was carrying a second rocket — and that was all the time Sam needed to escape. He kept the 6.5L turbo diesel at roar, and concentrated completely on getting away.

With the motorcycle now crushed, Sam realized all he had to do to defeat the rider was get away. They could now drive down the railway tunnel without any chance of the rider catching up.

The sound of gunfire finally ceased and Sam continued driving in silence. After two to three minutes had passed, and he was certain they were now well out of any possible firing range from the rider — even if he'd survived — Sam finally slowed and glanced over his shoulder.

"Well done, gentlemen. It's over."

Tom grinned. "Nice driving. That rocket was close."

Gallagher just stared forward with lifeless eyes.

Tom swore and moved closer to help. "He's been hit."

There was nothing any of them could do to save Gallagher. He'd taken a bullet through the back of his neck and into the base of his spine. He must have died instantly.

Sam continued driving. Tom climbed forward into the passenger seat and neither spoke for a few minutes. Sam concentrated on driving, while Tom simply took it all in.

A lot of people had died in a very short amount of time — all because of the information stored on the Death Stone.

"We need to get the Death Stone out of here and to an astronomer to crack its code. Then, maybe all these deaths will have been worth it, despite their enormous cost. We might still have time to save the human race."

"I know." Tom said, ruefully.

Sam approached the opening to the downward lava tube he watched as the shallow water raced down the slope. The Humvee mounted the lip and began its steady crawl down the steep tunnel.

Despite their tremendous losses, he was feeling positive. They still had half a tank of fuel and two nearly full jerry cans of diesel strapped to the back. All in total, that would allow them to drive nearly a thousand miles along the railway line. After that, he was confident they could walk out of the tunnel. Within a few days, he could regroup with the rest of the crew from the *Maria Helena* and retrieve the Death Stone.

The Humvee leveled out and all of his hopes changed as they entered the volcanic dome where the railway tunnel ran — because in front of them, black smoke billowed from the boiler of a gray steam train.

# Chapter Fifty

SAM ROLLED HIS eyes across the strange relic of the past. An anachronism, surrounded by modern weapons, and military hardware. The steam boiler and engine-house was followed by a coal tender — basically a carriage dedicated to hauling coal — followed by four carriages of varying sizes.

The first one was constructed of wood and looked like it belonged in an old western cowboy movie. Decorative candle lights lit up the inside, revealing it to be empty. The second was made out of steel and clearly for the purpose of carrying heavy cargo. It had already been loaded with all the boxes of weapons he and Tom had discovered earlier and possibly the Death Stone. The third carriage was mostly a flat platform and currently housed a forklift at the front and twenty odd feet of spare space most likely expected to be used for the motorcycles. The last carriage housed a heavy machine gun platform.

Despite the train's size there appeared to be very few occupants on board. Two men climbed down casually from the cargo carriage to greet them. Neither appeared concerned, as they approached with their hands in their pockets. It looked like they were expecting their friends who'd ridden down from the surface.

Sam pulled up right next to them.

Tom rolled his window down. "Good afternoon."

The two men appeared casual as they greeted them, but reacted impressively fast. Each drawing their weapons without asking who he was or what he wanted. Tom didn't wait to see the outcome of their speed, and he pulled the AA-12 shotgun's trigger three times and the two men were dead.

One shot probably would have sufficed.

Sam waited for the sound of more attackers, but none came.

Tom scanned the rest of the train. It looked empty. "That can't possibly be it?"

"I don't know. Let's go find out."

Sam drove up onto the third carriage, parking the Humvee neatly on the flat-bed railway car directly behind the forklift.

He waited for another response, but none appeared. He placed the gear in park and switched off the engine and pulled the handbrake. A moment later he turned the headlights off. Their now very dark world remained silent. Up ahead, he could easily make out the faint glow of the passenger carriage. In front of that, he spotted the flicker of firelight coming from the fire chamber.

Tom handed Sam the second shotgun. "Shall we?"

Sam took it. The weapon was loaded with a fresh 28 rounds magazine. "Let's."

They slowly made their way to the front of the train. Using only the light of the first carriage and keeping their own flashlights switched off, they cleared each carriage.

Inside the first carriage, it felt like they were stepping into a time-machine and being transported to a late nineteenth century carriage for Russian royalty.

The carriage was split into two rooms. Inside the first one, seating was sparse, with three leather embroidered couches and a single matching footstool. Exquisite interior woodwork of rich teak was interwoven with ivory carvings to match the elegant high windows and ornamental candles throughout. At the end of the first room a heavy oak desk stood fixed to the side of the railway carriage, with an old leather chair pulled in close. On the desk was a series of pens and paper, a single Fabergé egg encrusted with rubies. Next to it, an opening of intricate gold had been formed in the desk, and an internet and laptop power cable protruded, in direct contrast to their nineteenth century surroundings.

Sam's eyes widened as he examined the desk. But he left everything where it was, and completed his search of the room, and then continued farther down the carriage. The next one was an open dining room, for no more than five persons.

At the end of the carriage, Sam and Tom split up. One went around the left side of the coal tender to approach the engine cab, while the other went around the right side.

Sam stepped into the cab first, with his shotgun aiming level. Light and heat radiated from the boiler's fire box, through an open stoking door. It struck him as strange that someone would leave it as such. He stepped another foot forward, and felt someone press the barrel of a gun into the back of his chest.

"Put the gun down," the stranger said.

The man had been waiting outside the train, while the light of the open flame had lured him inside. Sam swallowed hard and cursed himself for not checking the dark space outside the train first. He then slowly lowered his shotgun.

"Good, now step into the light where I can see you better."

Sam followed his directions, stepping into the middle of the engine cab. "Now what?"

"Now you can tell me how many of you there are," the train driver snarled.

"Just two." It was Tom's voice that answered. "But I've got the barrel of a shotgun fixed on your head."

"All right." The stranger said, lowering the handgun. "Now

what?"

Sam turned to face him.

"Now you show us how to operate this train."

# Chapter Fifty-One

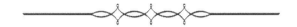

*Inside the Sipapu*

THE STRANGER'S ACCENT pegged his origins as south of the border, but his English was impeccable. Not what Jenn would have expected from a cartel member. She, Brody, and Ben had all reacted differently when he spoke. Brody gave a strangled yelp, Ben had whirled to face the man, his hand snaking toward his shoulder holster, and she herself had frozen, the idea that their deaths were imminent flashing into her mind before the stranger's second sentence was finished.

"Don't make me shoot you," the stranger added. He held his hand out, and Ben reluctantly handed over the pistol he'd only half drawn.

"Easy, man. We can work this out," Ben ventured.

"Of course, we can, *esse.*"

Jenn was jarred again by the slang term for friend. She glanced at Ben, shaking her head slightly. She didn't know what he had in mind, but she was certain that challenging this man in any way would be even more dangerous, if that were possible.

"What do you want?" Ben asked.

"You have something that belongs to us, *esse*. We want it back is all. Of course, we'd prefer you not speak to the FBI about our transaction."

The stranger grinned, his teeth flashing white in the light of their flashlights. "We will need assurances, you understand."

Ben nodded. He looked at Jenn. "It will be all right."

She wanted to tell him not to trust the man, not to give him the drugs. But she couldn't stop shaking, and she didn't want her voice to betray her fear. She stayed silent as Ben and the stranger negotiated their fate.

"I think we will keep the girl here. If you give us back our goods, you may take her with you when you go."

"And what about my man? This is one of my best cowboys. I need him, too."

"In due time, *esse*. You can have him back after we relocate. If your government does not bother us in the meantime. A month, maybe."

"No!" Jenn cried, involuntarily.

The stranger smiled broadly again. "What's this, *esse?* Your woman has another man? Maybe we will kill him for you, if our partnership is pleasant."

"He's my brother," Jenn choked out.

"In that case, we will let your boyfriend decide. Hey, *esse*, why are you still here?"

"I'm not your buddy," Ben snarled.

"Ben, please!" Jenn pleaded.

"You want it back here?" Ben asked, ignoring her.

"Better not. You have hay for your animals?"

"Of course," Ben spat.

"Conceal it within a load of hay and take it to Durango. Write your cell phone number here. We'll tell you where to deliver it." The man handed Ben a slip of paper and a stub of pencil from his pocket. Ben wrote something on the paper and handed it back.

"It'll take a few hours to get back to the ranch from here, and another to get the load in the truck."

Ben still hadn't looked at Jenn again, and she willed him to with every bit of mental focus she could bring to bear.

"Better hurry. I may get bored." The man's leer sent a chill to Jenn's bones.

She didn't want to be left alone with him, but she didn't want to leave Brody with him either. Her mind scrambled furiously for something to say, anything to allow them all to leave together. But she knew nothing would work. The man exuded pure evil, despite his mild tone and cultured speech patterns.

He stepped aside to allow Ben to pass, and then moved back to block the passage.

"Don't bother. I'm not leaving my brother," she said. Ice had replaced the blood in her veins. Only her wits stood between her and whatever disgusting plans the man had for her. She could only hope they'd save her brother, too. A part of her mind began the ancient chants her grandmother had taught her, and her hand went to the medicine pouch hanging around her neck.

The man's hand came up, his evil-looking pistol pointing at her. "What's that?"

"Nothing," she replied, letting her hand fall away. "A token of protection my people wear."

He snorted. Looked down at Brody, still tethered on the ground despite Ben's earlier efforts. "Do you believe in that superstitious crap, too?"

Brody shook his head.

"Just as well. Your spirits won't save you. You'd better hope your boss likes you as much as he does your sister."

Jenn made an involuntary sound. Brody and the other man both stared at her. She wanted to explain to Brody that she and Ben no longer had a relationship, that it had been short-lived, and that he needn't be hurt that she hadn't confided in him. But she couldn't dash his hopes that Ben would do as the man asked, nor was it safe to let the man know she had her own doubts. What would Ben do? She wished she knew.

# Chapter Fifty-Two

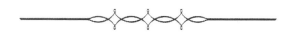

**B**EN LOST NO time in retrieving his radio from his shirt pocket once out of the cave. But inside the kiva, he had no reception, and it took another half hour to climb out of the kiva and then get to the center of the canyon below the pueblo to try again. Still nothing. Maybe the pilot had left.

He steadfastly kept his mind off what might be happening to Jenn or Brody. There was nothing he could do for her except get to the ranch as quickly as possible. Without the chopper, he'd have to take the route the others had taken in and out of the canyon. Fortunately, there had been no rain recently, and their tracks were easy to follow.

He set out at an easy jog, meant to move him quickly without expending the energy he'd need for a long run. If he missed the men who were on their way with horses for Jenn and Brody by even half a mile, it would be a long run back to the ranch. He could only hope they were following the tracks from the other end.

Far to the northeast, the crack of thunder preceded an afternoon storm. Monsoon was early this year, and the parched land would have been grateful had it been sentient. Certainly, the Utes who subsisted on high-desert farming to feed their cattle and horses were grateful. And they all knew to stay out of canyons at this time of year. The sudden downpour would have sent everyone near Ignacio scrambling for shelter, but Ben knew nothing of it.

Overhead in the canyon where Ben ran, the sky was blue, the sun shining hotly on his bare head. He thought about the hat that had started this entire disaster and wished he'd thought to bring one when he'd entered the helicopter hours before. He kept his eyes on the ground and followed the tracks. A little heat wouldn't kill him, at least not inside the canyon. On the mesa was a different story, but he had to believe he'd meet up with the others. They'd have water.

On the heels of that thought came a step that brought him under the willows lining the canyon. The damp sand he'd been travelling over coalesced into a shallow pool of water, left from the trickle that sometimes found the surface in the bottom of the canyon. He bent and dropped to a knee to take a sip.

As he did, he noticed something he hadn't felt before. The ground was vibrating. He stood up, puzzled, and then heard the far-off rumble that told him what was happening. Behind him, and probably traveling far faster than he could, he knew a wall of water choked with fallen tree trunks, mud, and probably animals caught in the flash flood would be coming. He had to get out of the narrow canyon and climb to safety immediately!

Ben ran for his life. As soon as he broke through the copse of willows, he glanced from his feet, where he still followed the tracks left by his employees, to the side of the canyon wall. It didn't matter now whether he found where the others had climbed down and back up. As soon as he spotted anywhere he could get up the wall, he'd go for it. The flood could reach 20 or 30 feet up the walls, he thought. He had to find a spot that wouldn't trap him below that level.

The distant rumble was now a roar, as loud as a freight train. *Don't look back.* Looking back could prove fatal, if he stumbled. And it would slow him down. He was desperate to know how close the water was, while at the same time understanding that if it was close enough to see, he was already dead.

Just as he thought there was no escape, a rockfall appeared as he passed a stand of brush. He veered toward it and scrambled for the top, heedless of the potential for a twisted ankle in the rubble. It led to a crack in the sandstone that climbers would call a chimney, and he climbed that as fast as he could by wedging the toe of his boot on one side and pushing with his hands on the other, his back to the rock.

Below him, a rush of water appeared. The noise was indescribable. He gained the next ledge as the wall he'd anticipated rounded the last bend before his position. Without hearing it, Ben knew he was yelling. He'd never known fear like this, not even when the cartel guy had startled them in the cave that morning. It was going to be a close call, and if he didn't get above the flood, Jenn and Brody were likely to die as well. Desperately, he reached for a gnarled juniper and clung on for his life as he swung his legs up.

His left foot caught a low branch and allowed him to swing himself to a sitting position. Inches below him, a gnarled old cottonwood tumbled in the flood and passed by. His heart was pounding harder than it ever had, and his throat was sore from bellowing out his fear and horror. Behind the filthy wall of mud and debris, the waters were calmer, though still swift and deep. How would Jenn get home, even if the drug runner kept his word and released her?

But he couldn't think of that now. He had a mission, and unless he completed it, she wouldn't be coming home anyway. He looked from side to side. The juniper that was his throne for the moment grew out of a narrow ledge that wouldn't even allow him to stand upright, and there was no way up. Maddeningly, the top of the wall was another hundred feet or more above him. He was trapped until the waters receded.

# Chapter Fifty-Three

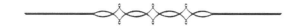

*On-board the Maria Helena*

ELISE PICKED UP her cell phone on the first ring. "Madam Secretary."

She'd left a message with the Secretary of Defense's personal assistant for her to return the call to the ship as soon as she became reachable. That was over two hours ago, and time was short.

"Elise. I've seen the surveillance footage." The Secretary of Defense said, her voice calm and professional. "Was anyone still in the tunnel when it imploded?"

"Sam and Tom, along with about a dozen of the construction crew."

"What were they still doing down there?"

"They were in the process of developing a plan to retrieve Big Bertha from where she'd become lost a few miles down a lava tube." Elise intentionally left out any news of finding the Death Stone.

"Does anyone have a timeframe for removing the rubble and gaining access to the lava tube?" It was reassuring to hear the Secretary's methodical approach to the problem, without a hint of concern over the most likely deaths of Sam and Tom, as well as at least a dozen construction workers.

"Veyron's surveyed the site using ground-penetrating radar. He says he's no expert on what can be achieved, but given the location, and the fact all mining equipment would still need to be brought in and assembled on site, he can't see us opening the tunnel inside of three months."

"So, even if Sam and Tom survived the cave in, they'll starve or more likely die of thirst well before we can get them out. Is that where we're at?"

"Yes."

The Secretary of Defense spoke with the certainty of a person in charge of the world's most powerful militaries. "These people were experts. They rode into the tunnel and disappeared inside before the explosion. They didn't destroy the entrance to that tunnel just so they could die. So let's find out where the other end of that tunnel leads."

Elise took a breath. "You know it's the middle of the Bering Strait, right? The entire tunnel's underwater."

"So? Go find out where it comes out!"

# Chapter Fifty-Four

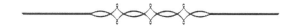

*Washington D.C.*

THE SECRETARY OF Defense's displeasure had been felt—and heard—throughout the offices. Her deputy caught wind of the nature of the disaster via the office grapevine, and made haste to leave before she could descend on him with directives.

From his car, he called the contact he'd met before. This time, he chose an out-of-the-way location closer to his own office. This debacle was squarely on the other agency's shoulders, and he wanted his counterpart to know he wouldn't cover for them this time.

He sat on a park bench, near the street taco vendor whose wares were warming his hands. A few moments after he'd taken his seat, the bench flexed, letting him know his contact had joined him.

"Slumming?" the other man asked.

"I am now," the Deputy Secretary answered. "What the hell went wrong over there?"

"Over there?" The innocuous question, asked with an air of innocent ignorance, infuriated the Deputy Secretary.

"Don't act the fool," he snarled. "You know very well what I'm talking about, or you wouldn't be here. *What the hell went wrong?*"

"A slight hiccup, that's all," the man answered. His intense blue eyes fixed on him, behind thick glasses. "I assure you, the stone is safe."

"Don't ever say that word to me again. Here." The Deputy Secretary thrust the warm, wrapped tacos into the hands of his contact and dug in his suit coat pocket for his flask. He tipped it up quickly and took a healthy swallow. He risked a glance at his companion.

The man was regarding the tacos with a bemused expression.

The Deputy Secretary lowered his voice to a sinister hiss. "He was supposed to make it look like an accident, a natural cave-in. Now I have an entire island filled with dead bodies riddled with bullet holes and a tunnel that looks like someone's tested one of our newest bunker busters on it. Not a cave-in. Not an accident."

"It couldn't be helped. There was a Humvee..."

"I don't care what there was. Four well-respected friends of the Secretary are swearing a team of elite mercenaries on motorcycles came through and killed everyone on the ground, before blowing up the tunnel! Just what did your idiot expect, that no one would question the deaths by machine gun fire?" He snatched the tacos back and ripped back the wrappings on one, furiously tearing into it with his teeth.

"Look, it's the middle of the Bering Strait. Even the news media haven't caught on yet. No one will, if you keep your principal calm. No one knows what happened out there. Make sure it doesn't become a news item." The man pulled a handkerchief from his pocket and wiped at his greasy fingers, his nose wrinkled in disgust.

"And how am I supposed to do that? Everyone in our office heard the Secretary's reaction. She's not happy, I tell you."

The other man shrugged. "I don't know how you're supposed to contain it, and I don't care. That's your problem."

The Deputy Secretary had a moment of blind rage,

visualizing himself choking the man to death with his bare hands. No one, to his knowledge, had ever crossed the Secretary before and lived — figuratively or literally — to tell the story. If she found out he was involved, it could very well be worth his life.

"We'll see whose problem it is if her pet salvage operator or that blasted stone isn't found safe. I wouldn't want to be in your shoes or your boss's." It would be better for him to own up and then shift the blame to Homeland Security, than to have her think it was him.

His counterpart chuckled with no humor. "I told you Ilya Yezhov would come through with it in the end, didn't I? It's safe, but unavailable." He didn't mention Reilly, but the sinister curl on his upper lip implied the worst for Reilly and his sidekick.

"What do you mean? He's sent everyone on our tails!"

"Sure, but by the time anyone can dig that tunnel out and find the stone, it'll no longer matter, will it?"

"So that's how you're justifying this?"

"I do what needs to be done."

"The colony thinks Yezhov's the golden-haired boy, but has anyone stopped to question what a man with his temperament would do in the new world?"

The contact's lips formed an oily smile. "In the new world, a man like Yezhov could do just about anything he pleases. Yes. As frightening as it is, we need just that sort of man if our meagre colony is to survive."

"You're making a terrible deal."

His contact shrugged. "Sometimes you have to dance with the Devil."

# Chapter Fifty-Five

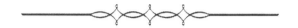

*Inside the Railway Tunnel*

S AM AND TOM had taken it in turns to rest on the large bed they'd found in the first carriage, once occupied by Russian royalty at the end of the nineteenth century. It was potentially a two to three-day trip through the tunnel depending on where it came out on the U.S. mainland. Right now, Tom was sleeping, while Sam was working to keep the train moving.

He shoveled another load of coal into the fire chamber. Sam had quickly discovered that stoking the fire mass was a fine art, rather than a case of simply lumping more coal on a dwindling flame. Matvei, their Russian steam train driver and prisoner, had been defiant in his refusal to help. But once he and Tom started to load more coal and experiment with random levers in order to coax the old train to move, the old man, terrified that his precious machine would be destroyed, had caved and offered his assistance.

Keeping the fire mass at the right heat and intensity required precision. Even to the point where Matvei would instruct Sam as to which size coal lumps were to be fed and where exactly on the fire to put it. It took a while to achieve the desired result at first, and for some time Sam and Tom had found they were constantly trying to correct the speed of the train, by either releasing more steam, or opening the blower to increase steam generation.

"There is a balance," Matvei began. "An ideal value where the fire is most effective. Above this the steam engine becomes inefficient, damaging, and ultimately dangerous to run. Below this, there is not enough steam generated to reach the maximum desired speed of locomotion."

Sam smiled. It was like listening to his dad talk about sailing when he was a kid. The man had obviously spent his life working on steam trains. Instead of being lost to a world of electric and diesel trains, he'd been taken in by a secret organization who were using an old steam train, owned by a Russian monarch over a century ago, to move their illicit products across the Bering Strait.

"Is that enough?" Sam asked.

"Maybe just one more. But not a full shovel, please."

Sam dug the shovel into the coal tender and tipped part of it out again. He glanced at Matvei, waited until the man gave him a reassuring nod, and then fed the coal into the fire chamber. The pressure gauges to the right of the engine cab all started to rise, but the speed dial showed they were still slowing.

Matvei noted it too, although he hadn't looked at the speed indicator. "We're coming to the first of three major hills."

Sam dug the shovel back into the coal tender.

"No, you've already got plenty of heat."

"Then what do we do?" Sam smiled. "Get out and push?"

Matvei ignored his comment. "Below the fire chamber you'll see a grate, and directly under that there is a door called a damper. Opening the damper allows air to flow up from underneath the fire and through it—this in turn feeds the fire and will help generate what is called a steam boost."

"Okay." Sam opened the damper. "Now what?"

"Now you turn the blower on."

Sam pulled the lever to his right and the blower opened up. It was designed to force air up the chimney, which had the effect of drawing air up from the fire and feeding it. Instantly, Sam felt the steam turbines increase their speed and power. His eyes followed the headlights toward the long, empty tunnel and then back. Steam exhaled out of the chimney at the front of the boiler, billowing all the way to the end of the train's carriages.

"There you go. That will do it." Matvei was smiling now.

Sam felt his heart race and breathed deeply. There was a simple joy to helping the old technology run. He turned to face Matvei and said, "You really love your train, don't you?"

"Yes. I never married, but I have been looking after this old girl now for... let me think... close on twenty years now."

"Why?"

Matvei's graying eyebrows bushed together. "Why what?"

"Why this train and why doing this?"

"It's good money."

"Okay that explains your purpose, but why not electric or diesel? Why this old train?"

Matvei made a big show of sighing heavily, as though the question was absurd. "Because neither of those modern beasts could be half as useful to my masters as a steam train."

"Who are your masters?" Sam asked.

Matvei fidgeted with the rope that firmly bound his wrists together. He smiled ruefully. "Don't misunderstand my decision to help you move my train so that you don't destroy her as a willingness to tell you everything. Some secrets, I'm afraid, are worth dying for."

Sam nodded in understanding. He wasn't going to get anywhere by trying to get any more out of him. "Okay. Back to your train then. Why is she better than any modern electric or diesel beast?"

"Electric is obviously impossible here. These are very old tracks, and if you look overhead, there's no infrastructure for electric."

"And diesel?"

"A diesel requires more maintenance. Despite its age, steam engines are surprisingly easy to maintain." Matvei laughed. "And because my master already owned a steam train, so its appearance wouldn't rouse any suspicions."

Sam studied the man's face. He was serious. Had Matvei intentionally given something away about his master? Find the original owner of the steam train and he would find the leader of the secret organization.

"Any other reason you'd choose coal over diesel?" Sam asked.

Matvei swallowed hard. "Sure. More importantly, they'll run in the extreme cold of the new world."

# Chapter Fifty-Six

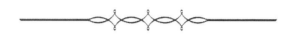

**B**EN WHITECLOUD WOKE with a start as he felt himself falling. As many people had done before him, he often had dreams of falling. A medicine woman had once told him it meant he would die in a fall, but he'd given the information no credence. It was an easy enough way to explain the dreams. And about as believable as the white man's explanation that it meant anxiety.

Today, he thanked his superb reflexes for grasping the juniper in which he was perched and preventing a real fall into the roiling waters below. It was impossible to believe he'd fallen asleep, but the evidence suggested his exhaustion and worry had caught up with him.

Until today, Ben had no reason to be anxious. He was wealthy by the accounting of his people, with a vast ranch and many cattle. It was true he sometimes worried he'd never stop loving Jenn after she broke off their relationship, but she was still in his life. He had time to convince her to come back to him. He needed nothing else.

But now, her safety was in doubt, and he had no way to ensure it. Stuck in this tree, while floodwaters continued to flow past, he could neither go up nor go down. How long would it be before the water receded? And when it did, would the route he'd taken to his refuge in the juniper still be there? Flash floods were known for sweeping away everything in their path. They pounded both landscape and structures, first with a barrage of dead trees, animals, and whatever else they picked up on their way downstream, pushed by deadly, swiftly-moving water.

The noise had receded, though. He wondered how long he'd slept before beginning to slip. Below, froth and occasional floating objects allowed him to judge how fast the water was running, and he knew he had no chance of swimming in it unscathed. But he thought it was several feet lower than the crest had been.

He began to hope it would be over soon, or at least low enough that he could climb down to look for a route all the way up the cliffside. Now that the tracks he'd been following had been washed away, it no longer made sense to find the same route up and down that Brody had taken. He needed to get to the top and strike out for the ranch house as quickly as possible, before the cartel got impatient and did something unthinkable to Jenn.

He was looking to his right, searching the cliff face above him for a viable climb, when he heard the shout. Twisting around, he caught a glimpse of one of the hands directly above him, peering over the side.

"Yo, boss!" the man yelled. "Are you stuck?"

The question didn't deserve an answer. On the other hand, the men didn't know what had transpired today. Their levity wasn't appropriate, but they didn't know it.

"Toss me a rope!" he called.

"Hang on, boss. We're rigging something. Sit tight." Echoes of the man's laughter rang off the cliffside on the opposite bank.

Ten minutes later, a knotted harness snaked to within arm's reach. As he grasped it and wriggled into it, Ben spared a thought for the distance. If the rope had been spliced or knotted together, it stood a chance of giving way, dropping him to his death. Furthermore, he was a solid 190 pounds, and it would take quite an effort to haul him up. He could only hope there were enough men up there to manage the job. But staying in the tree was not an option.

He gave the rope a firm tug, and felt a tug in return. Then, inch by agonizing inch, he began to rise, watching the waters below him as he did.

When he reached the top of the mesa, two pairs of hands grabbed him by the arms and dragged him over the side. He resisted the urge to grab one of the men and hug him for all he was worth, but he did stretch out his hand for a heartfelt handshake.

"Thanks, boys," he said. He glanced beyond them to where the rope stretched toward the horses. Even though he was certain the horses had done the heavy work, it had taken real skill to make sure the ropes would hold where they'd been knotted together, and to keep it from fraying where it pulled over the edge.

Quickly, he explained what had happened, and they agreed there was no point in waiting there for the water to go back to normal. It could take days. They rode back to the ranch at as fast a pace as they could while making sure the horses would make it, leading Jenn's mare while Ben rode Brody's larger gelding.

Ben marveled at the bone-dry ground he was covering. The storm that created the flash flood had missed his land by miles. It was the way of the desert, though, and he'd known of many floods occurring in spots that never saw as much as half an inch of rainfall in a month. This was the first time he'd had to race one for his life, and for the life of someone he couldn't lose. The thought made him spur his mount to greater speed.

When they arrived at the ranch, Ben organized all the hands that could be spared from essential ranch chores to load a hay truck with a hollow core to conceal the drugs. With those loaded, he had them cover it with a top layer and close the back end. It was a big risk. If he were caught with the drugs, he'd spend the rest of his life in jail. Even worse, the cartel would probably kill Jenn and Brody.

He wouldn't ask one of his hands to take the risk of driving the truck to Durango for the meeting. As soon as it was loaded and secured to his satisfaction, he swung into the driver's seat. He set his cell phone where he could both see it and hear it, and attached it to a charging cord to make sure the battery wouldn't die while the phone searched for a cell signal in the background. His ranch foreman slapped the door and wished him good luck.

"Take some of the men and get to that ruin as soon as the water will let you," Ben told his foreman. "Go armed, and be careful."

"No worries, boss," the man answered. "I'll take care of things here. Come back safe."

Ben lifted his hand in the time-honored cowboy gesture that meant everything from 'hi' to 'I've got this,' and then shifted into gear and pulled away with his men watching. In the rearview mirror, he saw his foreman pointing here and there, setting the men to work. They were good hands, and he valued every one of them. He fervently hoped he wouldn't lose another over this debacle.

Ben had been on the road for about half an hour when his cell phone twanged a guitar riff, his ring for an unknown caller. He reached for it and thumbed it on. "Ben Whitecloud."

"Are you on the road, Mr. Whitecloud?" The caller's voice was unfamiliar, but the menace in it matched that of the cartel member who'd captured them that morning.

"I am. ETA 20 minutes."

His caller gave him directions to an equipment rental lot off College Drive. "Drive around back. I'm in a U-Haul truck, and you'll follow me from there."

Ben was growing more nervous as he approached the rental company lot. The business was still open, meaning there were too many witnesses. He wished he'd thought to paint over his ranch logo on the truck doors, but it was too late for that now. He turned in and drove to the back of the lot as instructed, spotting the U-Haul truck as soon as he rounded the building. He flashed his headlights, and the driver of the truck immediately answered with a flash of his own. The U-Haul pulled away, going around the opposite side of the building with Ben following.

From there, they followed a circuitous route in the direction of the airport. Ben muttered to himself that if they'd wanted the goods at the airport, it would have saved him some mileage for them to say so in the first place, as it was much closer to his ranch than the city was. But before they reached it, the U-Haul turned down a private dirt road and eventually pulled into a large barn.

Ben followed. He was met by armed men, who gestured with their semi-automatic weapons for him to step out of the truck. Ben was a peaceful man, but a proud one. His Ute heritage had given him the near-black hair, dark skin and high cheekbones that typified most Native Americans. It had taught him lessons of racial prejudice when he attended agricultural college, but also taught him patience. However, his patience was beginning to wear thin.

"What is this? Just take what belongs to you and let me go. I've fulfilled my end of the bargain."

One of the men surrounding him put a single shot through the lower door of the truck and gestured again. With dread borne of anticipated failure, Ben opened the door and slid to the ground. He stood passively as the same man handed his weapon to another and then patted Ben down, relieving him of the second pistol he'd placed in his shoulder holster.

"Wait here," the man grunted. He took his weapon back from the other man and signaled two to cover Ben. The rest went about transferring the drugs from Ben's truck to the U-Haul, taking some of the hay as well.

When they'd finished, the only man who had spoken directed Ben to face his truck, his hands on the door, eyes straight ahead, and not to move. Ben turned, expecting a barrage of bullets to the back, or a single one to the back of his head, at any moment. Instead, he heard the other truck start up. When it had clearly left the building, he steeled himself for the execution he was certain would come. None of the men who'd threatened him had concealed their faces.

Minutes later, he dared to look around. He was alone in the building. Ben wasted no time in idle speculation about why he was still alive. It was enough that he was. He got into the truck and drove out of the building, still expecting to be shot. But shots never came. He drove at speed to the ranch. No word had come from the cartel member who had Jenn and Brody.

Had he bought his own survival at the cost of theirs?

# Chapter Fifty-Seven

*On Board the Maria Helena*

E LISE STUDIED THE array of computer monitors surrounding her. One, a display of seismic activity from the Marianas to the coast of California, showed no unusual activity. Another, from west of the same coast to the eastern foothills of the Rocky Mountains, showed some minor temblors, but nothing out of the ordinary for the seismically active region.

Still another was scrolling a feed that pulled from various social media sites and more arcane sources. The query was long and convoluted, aiming to tease out any news of something unusual, whether it had to do with geology or not. Elise had constructed it to exclude the usual noise about car accidents, bank robberies, people unhappy with the way they'd been treated at restaurants, stores, or on airlines, and funny cat videos disguised by sponsored spam pages as amazing, shocking, or she'd never guess whatever they wanted her to believe.

Sometimes she rued the day the internet had been opened to the public. On the other hand, for the patient person who knew how to make Boolean logic sit up and beg, it was a rich source of information hiding in plain sight.

She marked a police blotter entry from Colorado for follow-up. A supernatural wind had sucked a man out of a previously-undiscovered Anasazi ruin and into a cave of some sort. Now that was something that didn't happen every day.

Her mind raced to the cowboy Sam and Tom had found wedged into a crevasse in the ceiling of the lava tube yesterday. The foreman, Gallagher, had told them that the cowboy wasn't part of his construction team, or his mines rescue team.

She scanned the report for a photo of the cowboy sucked into the old Anasazi ruin. It was a picture of a very white male, sitting awkwardly atop a horse, with a big hat. He looked more like he was dressed up for the picture than to go ranching. None the less, he had a nice smile, and looked proud of himself.

Elise then brought up the pictures Sam had taken of the cowboy they'd found in the lava tube. She stared at the picture.

*No. Surely it can't be possible?*

A few minutes later, her satellite phone rang.

"What have you got for me?" The Secretary of Defense asked.

"It's a long shot and I'm not a hundred percent certain I believe it myself."

The Secretary of Defense liked immediate answers. "What did you find?"

Elise sighed. "There's one hell of a strange story in Colorado…"

# Chapter Fifty-Eight

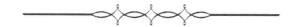

*Inside the Sipapu*

AFTER BEN HAD left, the cartel thug had left Jenn and Brody in the dark cave. He hadn't tied Jenn up, or taken her food and water. Apparently, he'd trusted that her concern for her brother would keep her where he wanted her. With no light, they wouldn't have dared to try to find their way to the surface anyway, she supposed.

As the dark closed in around her, she fought the nausea and panic that came with her fear of enclosed spaces. Brody had been here for more than a day. She could tough it out.

However, the thug had left her with a penknife, which she prudently carried in her medicine pouch. When she told Brody, he laughed. "That's not traditional," he said through hysterical gasps.

"Fortunately for you, I'm not very traditional myself," Jenn answered. She hoped he could hear the smile in her voice, but it didn't matter enough to force it. She reached for him, feeling for the bindings around his hands. Ben had cut through those at Brody's ankles, but Brody hadn't attempted to stand while their captor had been in the room with them, and the man must not have checked.

Once she'd found them by feel, Jenn began patiently sawing through the cords, and before long she'd cut through them. A trickle of sticky moisture indicated she'd nicked Brody's skin at some point, but he hadn't made a sound. When she took her hands away, she felt the shift in the air as he stood and stretched.

"Let's get out of here," he said.

"But we can't see," she objected. Her claustrophobia paralyzed her and she was reluctant to move, in case they took the wrong direction and got stuck.

"It's all right. I know how to get out. Hold onto my shirt, and follow me."

Jenn knelt to feel for her backpack. "Wait, let me get my things." Finding it, she took a swallow of water and held the valve end of the water tube out, bumping it into Brody's body. He took it and she heard the gurgle of the water as he swallowed some. "Okay, I'm ready. Let's go." She slung her backpack over one shoulder and took hold of his shirt with the other hand.

"You don't by any chance have a flashlight in your pack, do you?" Brody asked.

"I do, but the battery is dead. Sorry."

Brody led the way slowly, and Jenn had the impression he kept one hand on the wall of the cave always. She lost track of the turns they made, but made no protest. There was little to choose from, between getting lost and waiting for the cartel guy to come and kill them. She had no illusion that he'd turn them loose, even if Ben got their drugs back to them and returned for her and Brody.

The thought led her to another. "Brody, are you still worried about Skinwalkers?"

"I guess not. I'm more worried about the live evil ones."

"I agree. To be honest, I think Skinwalkers were our version of zombies. And I don't believe in zombies."

Brody gave a bark of a laugh. "You're probably right. But I do believe this. Sound carries in these caves. We should be quiet, in case that guy is still in here."

Jenn fell silent. It was eerie, following Brody in complete silence through deepest darkness. But before long, she saw a faint light ahead. She tugged on Brody's shirt, and he stopped. "What's that light?" she whispered.

"I hope it's the entrance," he said. "We should be nearly there."

Relief flooded Jenn, and she gave Brody a push to get him started walking again. As the light grew brighter, she knew he'd been right. They were in the large cave room just next to the kiva. They'd escaped!

Emerging into the kiva, they heard a sound she couldn't identify. She was right behind Brody on the ladder, even though he cautioned her it might not hold them both. So, she heard when he breathed a soft curse.

"What is it?"

He didn't answer, but climbed the rest of the way out and held out his hand to help her do the same. When her head cleared the top of the kiva wall, she echoed his curse. A few feet below them, water flowed where the lower levels of the pueblo had stood before.

"We've got to climb!" she cried. She looked around for a way up the cliffside from the indentation where the pueblo had been built, and found nothing.

"I think it's as high as it's going to get," Brody said hopefully. "Look, it's mostly smooth water. The head of the flood must have passed already."

"Are you prepared to stake your life on that?" Jenn asked.

"There's not a whole lot of choice. It's either stay here and prepare to hide or defend ourselves if that guy comes back, or go back into the caves. What do you want to do?"

Jenn had to agree. She didn't see a third choice. "Let's get as high as we can and hide. But we need to watch that water. If it starts rising, we'll have to get to the cave and as far from the entrance as we can."

"Sounds like a plan."

They settled for a perch in a nearby part of the apartment-like pueblo, where they could watch the water and still see the kiva wall. It wasn't a good hiding place, but they didn't find anywhere else that met all three requirements. And they agreed that the flood represented the greatest certain danger.

"I wonder when this happened," Brody said. "Do you think Ben got out?"

His innocent question flooded Jenn with dread. "Oh, my God! Do you think he might not have?"

"I guess it depends."

"The helicopter pilot who brought us here said he was watching weather from the up-canyon direction. How long has it been since we found you?"

"Three hours? Maybe four… I don't know, to be honest."

"That's plenty of time for the flood to have made it here, even if the rain hadn't started when the pilot set us down," Jenn mused. "I hope he made it out."

When Brody didn't answer, she kept the rest of her thoughts to herself. She'd never stopped caring for Ben. If he'd died in the flood, she would grieve, assuming she had the chance. But it also meant he wouldn't have made it to the ranch and returned the drugs. And that meant they'd better watch the kiva for the cartel guy to come out, too, and be prepared to meet him with deadly force.

"Brody," she said, after thinking it through. "If that guy comes out of the kiva, we have to kill him."

"What? What are you talking about?"

"If Ben didn't make it, they're going to kill us over the loss of the drugs. Even if he did, that guy didn't cover his face. We can identify him. It's him or us."

"You sure the law will see it that way?"

"I'd rather take my chances with the law than with that man," she insisted.

Moments later, the discussion became moot. Their nemesis dropped over the ledge above them on a rope, but he was too far away for them to reach him before he'd turned a handgun on them.

"I see you've discovered you can't go anywhere but back into the cave," he remarked, using a sinister and superior curl of his lip to display his amusement at their predicament. "Come on over here. We're going back in." He jerked his pistol to hurry them along.

Standing with his back to the wall of the structure next to the kiva, he waited until Jenn and Brody had complied with his order. Then he instructed Jenn to secure Brody's hands behind him.

"How will he climb down into the kiva, with his hands bound?" Jenn objected.

"You let me worry about that, sweetheart," their captor sneered.

Swallowing her disgust at the endearment, Jenn did as she was told. As she did, she noticed the water was lapping at their feet. It had risen only an inch or two, but the significance wasn't lost on her. It was still raining upstream, and the constriction in the canyon meant the flood couldn't spread out, but would continue to rise for as long as the rain lasted.

"Now you go on up," their captor instructed. "Get inside the kiva and wait for me."

Jenn did as she was told, and then watched as the man climbed over the wall and down with her.

"Go on into the cave," he said.

"But Brody…"

"Will live if the water doesn't come any higher. Go on, now."

He waved the pistol at her.

Jenn sobbed as she understood. Brody was left to drown if the water got high enough. With his hands bound behind him, he stood no chance in the flood. And what awaited her was as bad or worse. She'd rather die than endure this vile man's hands on her.

She stumbled into the cave, wildly seeking a defense against whatever he had in mind. Before she could spot a likely rock with which to brain him, much less pick one up, he was inside and had crowded her against the wall.

"Don't even think about it, sweetheart. Lucky for you, your boyfriend came through. We might even give you back to him, if he stays away from the authorities. But if you show any more initiative, you and I will have a bit of fun before we kill you. You understand?"

Jenn nodded, choking down the urge to vomit. His body curved against hers from her shoulders to her knees, with the evidence of what he meant unmistakable. At her nod, he backed away slightly.

"Will you behave, or am I going to have to tie your hands up, too?"

"I'll behave," she gasped. "You asshole."

"Now is that any way for a lady to talk?" He laughed as if they were having a flirtatious conversation. "Walk. Straight ahead."

A flashlight beam appeared, and she put one foot in front of the other, following it. He was leading her into the third tunnel, the one Brody had said led deep into the mountainside.

Jenn wondered if she'd ever see Brody, Ben, or the sun again.

# Chapter Fifty-Nine

*Inside the Russian Railway*

**S**AM CHECKED HIS watch. It was two a.m. and a little over two days since he'd boarded the old steam train and headed east along the ancient lava tunnel. Matvei appeared to be sound asleep, resting on his back along the cold steel plate in front of the coal tender. The place was narrow, but wide enough that he could almost stretch his legs all the way out.

On the side of the coal tender, Tom climbed along the outside edge — the only way to travel from the first carriage to the engine cab — and up to greet him.

"Good morning," Sam said.

Tom's eyes rolled from Matvei's snoring body, and the powerful headlights that lit the otherwise pitch-dark tunnel ahead. He smiled. "If you say so, buddy."

"How'd you sleep?"

"Like royalty." Tom smiled and handed him a pack of chips and caviar. "Here, I found these in a small refrigerator back on the second carriage."

Sam took the chips. They smelled distastefully like something left over from the fish markets. Although they were more likely to be something highly expensive, more like a delicacy. "What are they?"

"No idea. The package is in Russian."

Sam took a couple and dipped them in the caviar. "Not bad. I've eaten worse in first class before."

Tom asked, "How's our guest?"

"He's all right. Loves his train."

"Did he tell you anything about who he works for and where this trains going?"

"Not a word."

Sam fed some more coal into the fire chamber and the two men carefully went through the process of balancing the fire mass. Tom had a better knack for it, but both were starting to develop the finer details of its maintenance.

Sam asked, "Have you heard from Billie since she came back from the Amazon?"

"Once. I called her. We didn't speak long. Not that that means anything. She was never a big one for long conversations or talking about her emotions."

"How's she doing?"

"Since she was abducted by an ancient race, drugged, and forced to work for the Master Builders?" Tom shrugged. "Better than you would expect, but not good."

"What's she doing?" Sam asked, knowing that it was unlikely Billie would ever be the one to ask for help.

"She says she keeps having recurrent dreams about her time in the Amazon. She feels like she was supposed to do something vitally important, but no matter what she does, she has the feeling like she's forgetting something."

Sam nodded. "The neurologist said it might take months for her brain to readjust after the trauma she went through."

"Sure. But Billie keeps telling me this is different. She says she feels fine about what happened. Better than fine. She feels good. As though it was the closest she'd ever come to reaching her life's ambition to prove current existence of the genetically blessed descendants of the Master Builder race."

"So, what's the problem?"

"She feels like she's forgetting the most important memory she's ever had."

"Like what?"

"I have no idea."

"But she did ask me a question that's stirred my sixth senses."

"What was the question?"

Tom swallowed hard. "What if the Master Builders wanted to release her so that she would return to normal civilization for a very specific purpose?"

"What was that purpose?"

Tom took a breath. "That's just it. Billie's certain it's somehow scarred into her brain and she just can't work it out yet."

# Chapter Sixty

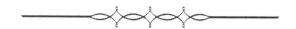

*Inside the Colorado Cave System*

J ENN HAD LOST all sense of the time that had passed and the distance or direction she'd traveled before her captor called a halt. She'd been stumbling along in the dark, but ahead there seemed to be a faint glow. Unable to see, she'd been afraid to fumble for the only weapon she had and maybe drop it. Now she had a chance, as her eyes adjusted to the faint light and she saw her captor remove his night-vision goggles.

"We're about to surface. You need to follow my instructions to the letter if you want to live. *Comprende?*"

"I understand," she said. Everyone in these parts understood a little Spanish.

He shoved her forward again. "Walk behind me. Keep up. Keep your eyes and your questions to yourself, and don't make me repeat myself again."

Obediently, she fell into step behind him. Now was her chance, though she feared a tiny penknife was not going to do the job. She felt for it in her medicine pouch while she mentally reviewed her moves. Finding it, she unfolded it without missing a step. Then she glided forward silently.

At the last moment, he must have heard or felt her breath too close to him. He turned, but not fast enough. She lunged forward, grabbing him around his head and plunging the knife blade into his neck, hoping she'd hit the carotid artery. He bucked, and she got one foot and leg in front of him to make him stumble, digging the knife in. She held on as he fell to the ground with her on top of him. She could feel the blood running over her hand and making her grip on the knife slip, but she clenched it tightly until she felt him stop struggling.

It was still too dark to see for sure, but she couldn't hear him breathing. Cautiously, Jenn pried herself up to stand, and immediately felt faint. She'd butchered animals before, but never a human being. Giving little thought to what she must look like, covered in blood, she staggered to the wall and leaned against it, breathing heavily.

She had to get out of here. She didn't think to grab the night vision goggles from the dead man's hand. Instead, she moved toward the faint light. It was only a few minutes before the tunnel turned slightly and she could see the bright opening beyond. *Thank God!*

Her steps became firmer as she moved quickly toward the light, her eyes fixed firmly upon the end of the tunnel. Until she tripped over something in her way. She looked down, puzzled, at the length of steel that had tripped her. Her eyes followed it from one side to the other, into a tunnel set crosswise to the one she was following to the opening.

Still in shock over killing a man, she thought vaguely that it must be an old mine, but her mind refused to follow the thought, focused instead on leaving the cave and seeing daylight again. She stepped over the rail and across the ties to the other rail, stepped over that, and then began to run toward the entrance.

Moments later, she stumbled out of the tunnel and looked around. *Where am I? Which way is the ranch?* She'd turned almost all the way around when she spotted something coming toward her fast. She squinted against the light, her eyes not quite adjusted after hours in the darkness. What she saw made her blood run cold.

Several motorcycles! Their riders wearing black body armor and matching helmets, were rocketing toward her. She'd never outrun them in the open. She turned and fled back into the cave system. Desperate to get out of sight before the motorcycles followed her in, she instinctively turned into the perpendicular tunnel where the tracks led when she reached it.

Behind her, she heard the roar of the bikes echoing down the tunnel. She whipped her head around to see if they'd followed, and lost her footing. She stumbled, fell, knocked the breath out of her lungs. The shock slowed her responses, but she pushed herself to a sitting position. Looking back toward the entrance, she couldn't see the bikes or anyone following.

She kept running along the tracks until the sound of the motorcycles became little more than a distant echo. Her heart was beating so hard, and her lungs burned. Adrenaline surged through her body and she could hear the pounding of her heart in her ears. She bent forward, resting her hands on her knees, breathing deeply in an attempt to catch her breath. In the distance, she imagined the ruffled motors of the bikes chasing her. She needed to keep going, but her body refused to move.

They would be in the tunnel, any minute now.

In front of her there was nothing but darkness. She kept going, using only the railway tracks for guidance. Those tracks now started to vibrate. At first, she thought it might be the motorcycles gaining on her, but then she put her hand on the cold steel of railway tack.

A fine vibration ran through her hand. She looked behind, but there was nothing to see. Even the speck of light from the opening far behind had become nothing more than a distant speck. She turned to run again, and spotted something up ahead — a tiny shaft of light with dust swirling in it.

*No, it can't be possible!*

Motorcycles, and now a train? She couldn't escape. She

couldn't hide. And soon, someone would discover the body of her captor, if the motorcycle riders hadn't already done so. She was done for. The only thing left to do was ask the question, which she did out loud.

"Where the hell did that come from?"

# Chapter Sixty-One

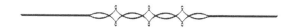

THE DEATHLY APPARITION ahead took Sam by surprise. They'd been traveling for a little over three days now without seeing anything other than the almost perfectly straight tunnel and railway tracks. Even though he and Tom had traded sleep shifts, the hours in the darkness of the railway tunnel, lit only by the old train's headlights had taken their toll on Sam's grasp of reality.

This section of the track had a slightly upward gradient to it, forcing them to travel only a little faster than a walking pace.

Matvei asked, "What is that…?"

The elderly driver's voice was creaky from disuse, as he'd refused to talk about his masters and they'd run out of things to talk about otherwise. He hadn't spoken for hours. He was looking in the direction of what Sam had seen, however.

Sam said, "You saw it too?"

"I saw something," the driver answered.

Sam pulled the throttle to the right, bleeding the steam and removing energy from the pistons. A moment later, he pulled the airbrake and the wheels of the train screeched to a halt. Despite their already slow movement, the train took every foot of track between it and the person to come up to a stop.

He leaned out of the locomotive and peered down the tracks. There! Sitting slumped beside the tracks, a human form.

"Hey! Are you all right?" he called. He ducked back into the cab of the locomotive and grabbed his shotgun, then stepped down. His weapon was trained on the figure. It stood.

"I surrender," a soft, female voice answered. "I'm unarmed. Please don't shoot."

Sam's mouth dropped open. He lowered the shotgun, but kept it clutched in his hands. Behind him, he heard Tom.

"What's going on? Why are we stopped?"

"There's a woman on the tracks up ahead," Sam said. Even to him it sounded strange. Where could she have come from? Who was she? She'd raised her hands over her head and begun walking toward them.

"Be careful, Sam," Tom warned.

"Says she's unarmed."

"That doesn't mean she's telling the truth." Tom stepped out from behind him, his shotgun leveled at the approaching figure.

They waited until they could see her clearly in the yellow light of the train's headlights. She was clearly unarmed. She wore jeans and a short-sleeved plaid shirt, a pair of hiking boots, and something around her neck that Sam couldn't identify. But it was too small to hold a weapon. Her eyes were wide, as if she was in shock, her dark hair pulled back but strands escaping from whatever held them. And she was covered in what looked like… blood. She was about ten feet away when her legs suddenly folded and she fell to her knees.

Sam handed his shotgun to Tom and ran toward the woman. "Are you hurt? What happened to you?"

She looked up at him with huge brown eyes. "No. I… I escaped. I'm tired. Kill me if you have to, but I'm done running and I don't want to be taken hostage anymore."

Sam drew back, startled. "Kill you? Why would I do that?"

His voice held genuine curiosity.

"I killed your friend. I know you'll kill me for that. Just get it over with."

"Lady, my friend is alive and well and standing back there a few yards. Want to tell me what this is all about?"

Up ahead, a roar sounded. Sam looked up. "What the hell is that?"

"Motorcycles," she answered. "I thought you were with them."

Sam's eyes darted farther up the track, at the motorcycles approaching fast. "All right, everyone back on the train!"

# Chapter Sixty-Two

S AM CLIMBED INTO the train's engine cab. His intelligent blue eyes determined, and his jaw set firm. He released the two engine brakes on the left-hand side of the control panel and opened the throttle to full. There wasn't a lot of steam available to send to the pistons, but it was enough to start the forward movement. He opened the damper and switched on the blower to increase steam generation.

Matvei looked up. "What's going on?"

"We've got company. A number of motorcycles."

Matvei's eyes narrowed. "Really?"

Tom pointed the shotgun down range and fired three rounds. The train started to creep forward at a slow walking pace. It wasn't much, but still no one was going to want to get in the way of it, and there wasn't a lot of room in the tunnel.

Sam looked at the woman he'd just met. Her brown eyes were wide, but her face was full of defiance. "You might want to take cover over here in the engine bay."

The woman moved quickly, but said nothing.

"I'm sorry, I didn't catch your name. I'm Sam and this is Tom."

"Jenn." She smiled at him and her eyes darted toward the

prisoner, with his wrists bound sitting next to the coal tender. "Who's that?"

"That's the train driver. Right now, he's our prisoner." Sam took aim with his shotgun and fired once down the line. "It's a long story and I'd love to tell you all about it, but right now we're a little busy."

"I can see that." She glanced at his weapon. "Got another one of those?"

"Can you shoot?"

"You bet I can."

He handed her the shotgun and picked up the Kalashnikov machine gun that Tom had secured in the engine house earlier on.

Extensive gunfire erupted from farther down the tunnel. The riders were pelting the steam engine with maintained bursts of machine gun fire. Sam ducked down and Tom stood up toward the left side of the engine cab and released several shots down the railway tunnel. To the right of him, Jenn started to shoot.

The incoming shots slowed and the riders appeared to back off. Sam leaned to the right side of the engine house, spotted two riders turning in somewhere to the right. He fired a quick burst of machine gun fire with his Kalashnikov.

When he released the trigger, the tunnel went quiet.

And the train continued to move forward at a walking pace.

"Where'd they go?" Sam asked.

"There's a crossroad another hundred feet up ahead. The tunnel to the right leads to the surface and the one to the left, deeper in the cave system."

The headlights of the bikes suddenly went out, as the riders must have turned to speed out of the tunnel rather than be run down by the train. Sam saw one go down and disappear from view as the train reached their spot. Another's motorcycle fell over as the rider took a shot in the back and flew off. Moments later, the train crushed the bike under its monster wheels. He'd counted five to begin with, but only by their headlights. Was that all of them?

"How many were there?" he shouted over the noise of the slowly moving train.

"Five," Jenn called back. "I think there were five."

"Two down," Tom said, calmly reloading again. "But they're faster than we are. I spotted two head to the right tunnel and one to the left. What do you want to do?"

Sam looked at the crossroad slowly approaching. "Jenn and I will take out the single rider to the left tunnel as we go past."

Tom grinned. "Sure. The two of you against one rider and I'll take out two riders on the right myself."

"You got it." Sam matched his grin. "Only, I think you should race back to the trailing carriage and take a seat in the machine gun turret. That way, once we're past the crossroads, you'll be able to hold off against anyone else who comes down this tunnel."

"Now I like your plan."

Sam watched Tom start to make his way quickly to the trailing carriages.

He loaded another magazine into the Kalashnikov and looked at Jenn. "Are you ready?"

She fired two shots down the tunnel, sending a spread of shotgun pellets toward the crossroads. It would be enough incentive to make any of the riders think twice before doubling back to attack them. "I'm ready."

"Good."

Matvei said, "I can't believe what you're doing to my girl!"

"Hey, I'm not the one shooting at her!"

A moment later, the front wheels of the steam train reached the crossroads and machine gun bullets began to spray the smokebox. Steam whistled at a crisp pitch as from the holes. Jenn emptied the remaining twenty odd rounds from her shotgun as they reached the crossroad.

The three motorcycles were arrayed in the cross-tunnel, two on one side of the track, and one on the other. Bullets flew through the locomotive's windows as they entered the crossfire, but the momentum of the locomotive carried them into the mouth of the other side of their own tunnel. Sam squeezed the trigger, and held a sustained burst from his machine gun, killing the rider down the left-hand side tunnel.

Sam pulled back on the throttle and let the train coast. They couldn't afford to just keep going and leave those guys on their tail. They'd have to run back through the other cars and finish the fight.

A moan from the driver caught his attention.

Sam glanced at him. "What happened?"

Matvei coughed. Blood frothed at his mouth. His breathing was labored, and Sam saw he'd been shot multiple times in the chest. Sam cut the old man's bindings and pressed his hands to the wound.

"It's no good," the driver wheezed. "I'm dying. Listen... important. The Stone. It will... will answer. When... time comes... train will lead you. To salvation."

# Chapter Sixty-Three

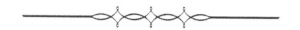

TOM RAN THROUGH each of the carriages, racing against the speed of the train. With his shotgun over his right shoulder, he held a flashlight in his right hand, it's powerful beam reflecting off the narrow carriageway and the glassy volcanic stone of the outside tunnel.

Gunfire sprayed the front of the train behind him as it passed the crossroad. The sound quickly became intermingled and lost with Sam's machine gun fire and Jenn's shotgun blasts. He reached the third carriage, squeezing between the stockpile of weapons and the Death Stone. At the very end, he jumped across the coupling, onto the fourth carriage, containing the machine gun turret.

It took him two more steps to reach and climb inside. The machine gun turret appeared to have been appropriated from the tail-gunner's compartment of a disused B52 Stratofortress Bomber and specifically modified to rotate in a 270-degree arc at the end of the rail-cart. It was one of the original versions used, utilizing a Browning M2 quad .50 caliber machine gun, not the electronically remote controlled M61 Vulcan used on the later models. Tom sat down, flicked on the power switch for the rotating turret, and gripped the two sets of triggers.

Tom shoved his foot on the left pedal and the heavy

machinery whined like something out of Star Wars as it rotated to the left in an instant. He lifted his foot again, and the guns locked into place, now perpendicular with the railway track. Perfectly set up to fire down the tunnel leading to the surface, he relaxed and adjusted his grip on the two-firing hand holds, until the quad .50 caliber machine guns became extensions of his hands.

The turret carriage slowly rolled into place and the view of the tunnel to the surface opened up. Tom jammed his thumbs on the twin-firing triggers. The electric-boost, mechanically fed ammunition belt whirred into life.

Flame erupted from the four barrels.

And from the cold, dark steel of the four muzzles, .50 caliber M33 shot left at a speed of 2910 feet per second. Tom held his thumbs on the firing trigger, and the lethal barrage continued at a rate of 1200 rounds per minute.

Seconds passed, and it was over.

The train rolled by the tunnel and he released the triggers. Smoke vented from the heated barrels. Tom could no longer see into the tunnel, but he knew that anyone who'd been there was now dead. He pressed his foot on the right peddle until the machine gun turret once again faced the railway tracks directly behind the carriage.

Two motorcycles sped across the railway track at the crossroads.

Tom squeezed the triggers and the machine of war fired again. He held them for a few seconds and let go. There was no sign of the riders on the track. Which meant he reacted too late and they'd cleared the tracks.

Tom lifted himself up out of the turret and jumped off the back of the slow-moving train. He bolted to the crossroad twenty feet away. Shining his flashlight to the right, he spotted the dead rider that Sam or Jen must have killed earlier, lying in a pool of blood next to his bike.

Confident he wasn't going to be shot from behind, Tom turned his focus to the tunnel leading to the surface. There were two riders racing out. He pointed the shotgun down the tunnel and squeezed the trigger multiple times until the last round was finally emptied.

He stared at the smoke-filled tunnel. The weapon was lethal at close range, but lacked power and accuracy from such a distance. As the dust cleared, he watched the two riders disappear at the end of the tunnel.

# Chapter Sixty-Four

THE ENCLOSED SPACE held an acrid bite of propellant that was rapidly dissipating with a fresh breeze blowing in from the opening a few yards beyond.

Sam looked at the four bodies, three one side of the track and three on the other, and said, "I thought we counted five."

Tom shook his head. "There were another two. They must have been searching for Jenn farther down this side of the tunnel, deeper into the cave system. When they heard the gunfight, they must have returned and made a B-line for the surface. I saw the taillights disappearing around the outside of the opening. At least one got a way."

"That was bad luck." Sam said, without heat.

"Yeah." Jen cast her eyes over the dead bodies. "Now they know we're in here, there'll be more coming. We need to get out."

Sam nodded, deep in thought and turned to Jenn. "Are you from around here?"

Jenn smiled. There was a youthful honesty in it. "I don't know where *here* is. But yeah, I walked through this tunnel, so we can't be too far from my home. If we can reach the surface, I'll be able to figure it out."

"Tom, go with her and cover her while she looks outside. I think we're going to have to abandon this old train."

"Aw, and I was just getting fond of it." Tom's eyes glanced toward the engine cab. "What about Matvei?"

"He took a few bullets in his chest. I'm afraid his own men killed him."

"Tough break." Tom climbed back onto the train and grabbed another twenty-eight-round magazine for his shotgun. "All right. Let's go see where this strange portal has taken us."

Tom jumped down from the train and chivalrously held out his hand to help Jenn. She took it and sprang lightly from the carriage, then strode off with Tom following.

Sam considered his options. If the riders were out there preparing to come in and attack again, it wouldn't work. But at this point, a way out seemed like the right time to offload the Humvee, get the stone, and disappear.

He started by deploying the ramp. Before he'd finished, Tom was back.

"There's nothing around here for miles. Just mostly flat sand and sandstone, with some taller mesas in the distance. Jenn thinks she knows where we are, and she thinks she can find a road to take us back to the ranch she's from."

"Good to know. Help me get the Humvee off here, and then we'll back up and load the stone onto her."

Tom backed the Humvee down the ramp into the relatively large area of the crossroads, the wide track of the vehicle straddling the rails. He steered it toward the opening to the outside and bumped it over the track. He came to a stop just beyond. Sam backed the locomotive up, with Tom signaling him to stop when the stone was next to the Humvee. By the time Sam climbed out of the locomotive and made it back, Tom had the forklift started.

Working like the team they'd always been, the pair still took nearly an hour to get the stone situated on the Humvee and tied down, though if something bad happened, the tie-downs wouldn't be adequate to prevent it from rolling and either crushing them or falling to the ground, potentially breaking.

Jenn had come back in about twenty minutes before they finished and asked when they'd be ready to go. Sam watched her eyes widen when she saw what they were doing.

"What the heck is that?" she asked. "And why are you taking it? Those guys could be on their way back right now."

"That's why we're taking it," Sam answered.

When everything was ready, Tom gallantly handed Jenn into the front passenger seat, while he took the jump seat most recently occupied by the unfortunate Gallagher. At least the blood was dry now.

"Everybody ready?" Sam asked cheerfully.

"More than," Jenn muttered.

"Giddy-up," Tom offered.

Sam put the big vehicle in gear and cautiously edged its nose out the tunnel opening. "Okay, Jenn. You're the navigator. Which way do we go?"

"That way, I think." She pointed to the right.

Sam turned slowly, getting the feel of the truck with the four-ton stone on the back. He picked up speed as he got more comfortable with the stone's stability.

"Better keep it slow until we cut the road," Jenn cautioned. "Some of these mesas, you can't see the fissures and canyons until you're right on top of them."

Sam immediately slowed, and flicked his eyes at her. She wasn't grinning. "You're serious."

"Yep," she said.

"I think it's time to hear your story, Jenn. Who are you? Where did you come from? And why don't you know whether there's a canyon between us and the road?"

"Thanks for saving me. I think," she started. She quickly told them what she'd been through, ending with running back into the tunnel to escape the motorcyclists, whom she'd taken to be cartel members come to meet her and the man she'd killed.

"Is that his blood all over you?" Sam asked. He was impressed in spite of himself. That story was worthy of Genevieve or Elise. She was a simple, honest-working, ranch woman, but damned resourceful if she'd killed her captor with a penknife as she'd claimed.

"I guess so. It isn't mine."

Sam threw his head back and guffawed. Priceless answer. The woman — Jenn — was looking at him as if he'd lost his mind.

"Well," he said. "One way or another, we've got to get to civilization. Where do you *think* we're headed?"

"Pretty sure we're headed south," she answered. "If I'm right, there's an old dirt track up ahead that will lead us west to my boss's ranch. I should be able to see landmarks in the distance soon. I'm just not as familiar with this side of it, because of that deep canyon that cuts it. I've lost track of time, but it can't be more than a day or so since I entered the other end of that tunnel."

"What makes you say that?" Sam asked.

"We walked the whole time," she said. "I'd be done in if it was more than a day. And I'm hungry, but not starving."

Her remark woke Sam's own hunger. The train hadn't been stocked with much food. It had been maybe forty-eight hours since he and Tom had eaten. His stomach growled in response to the thought.

"And you've never known of that cave system, or tunnel, whatever it was, before now?" he asked. It didn't seem possible. But then, looking around as he drove with one eye on the ground a few yards ahead, maybe it was. The surrounding terrain was an expanse of reddish-colored, sandy soil, dotted with lone bushes and scrubby-looking trees.

Here and there, lumps of sandstone and blacker stones that could have been lava intrusions rose at random from the ground. Some as large as the locomotive he'd just left, some smaller than the Humvee. The latter he drove around. The former, he tried to skirt without going too far off a straight line.

"Before today, or maybe it was yesterday or day before, I never knew about any of this," she answered. "But I can tell you what I do know. This tunnel system is used by drug dealers."

Sam gave Tom a significant look over his shoulder. Drugs for weapons? Weapons for drugs? It made sense. Jenn's fight was probably their fight.

"Okay, so where's your ranch?"

"Don't know that either, until I can get my bearings. But I think it's to our west."

Sam worried that they were leaving a clear track in the sandy soil for the motorcyclists to follow. He worried that they were somehow going in a different direction than Jenn thought, though the sun seemed to confirm her claim. And he worried that they'd never find the road she thought was up ahead, and were driving into a trackless waste where they'd eventually run out of gas, and out of time. But he drove on.

The sun was clearly sinking to their right when Sam spotted tracks crossing their path. He slowed, and then came to a stop with the front wheels of the Humvee atop the tracks he'd seen. "Where do you suppose these go?"

Jenn must have fallen asleep, but was drowsily coming to when he stopped. She stretched, yawned, and then said, "Why did we stop?"

"Tracks," Sam explained. "Right below us, going east and west. Where do you think they go?" Inside he was seething. If they'd missed their turn because she wasn't alert… But then, he hadn't noticed her falling asleep, either. He was desperately in need of some food, some sleep, and some answers.

Jenn leaned out of the vehicle. "This is it!" she cried, suddenly sounding excited. "This is the road I told you about."

Sam leaned out of his side. Below the truck, tracks disappeared beneath the undercarriage. Maybe five or six tracks made by smaller vehicles, if he had to guess. "This is a road?" he asked, incredulous.

"Well, not a road, but yeah, it's the four-wheel trail I told you about." She sat up, then climbed out of the vehicle and turned, looking into the distance. "There it is." She pointed.

Sam couldn't see anything that looked different from what he'd been driving through for the past three hours. "Where? What?"

Tom opened the door and rolled out of his jump seat, rubbing his butt. "Man, they didn't build this thing for comfort," he grumbled.

"Church rock," Jenn said, mysteriously.

"Church what?"

"Church rock. I know that formation. Come on, it's going to be dark soon, and we've got about twenty miles to go." She climbed back in and sat as though she hadn't just dumbfounded Sam again.

"Ma'am, I don't see anything that looks like a church."

"You will. And it's Jenn, please."

It was only a few minutes when Sam spotted it for himself. A round dome of sandstone, with a smaller sandstone cap that looked like a bell tower. As they drew near, he could see what looked like an arched opening carved a few feet into the south side of the rock.

"I'll be damned."

"This is what people come to see out here," Jenn explained.

"Both from Durango and from down in New Mexico. We shouldn't be far from a main road, now, but there's a back way onto the ranch that comes off this trail, about three miles up the road. From there, we're on my boss's land, and it's fifteen to the ranch house."

Relief swept over Sam like a warm shower, which he also needed. He urged Jenn to tie up some loose ends in her story. "By the way, if you didn't know anything about that cave system before, what were you and your brother doing when you found it?"

"Oh, I guess I didn't start at the beginning. Well, he found it, actually. Terrible thing." She recounted the story of Malcolm's hat being swept away and then the man himself being drawn into the cave by a strange wind."

Sam turned around and looked at Tom, whose mouth was wide open. He turned back to watch the track for a turnoff. "Stetson hat?" he asked.

"Yeah. How'd you guess?"

"You're not going to believe this," he began.

# Chapter Sixty-Five

I T WAS ALMOST another hour on the rough track leading to the ranch house before Sam could see it in the distance. He wasn't surprised when Jenn spotted it first. She'd already proven her eyes were sharper than his, or more attuned to the landscape where she lived. He preferred to think the latter.

She'd been in a brown study since he'd told her of the fate of the hat, and probable fate of poor Malcolm, whom he suspected to be the former owner of the body he'd found wedged in the lava tube. No wonder the man had looked almost boneless, with contusions from head to toe and his clothes in shreds. What he must have gone through, helpless in the wind on that journey. Sam could only hope he'd been dead for most of it.

Jenn suddenly sat straighter and said, "What's that?" She was pointing at the sky ahead.

Sam, who was taller, had to duck to see what she meant. A thrill of fear shook him as he recognized three black helicopters, though he couldn't make out their insignia.

"Choppers," he said sharply. "Tom."

"I see them. What do you think?"

"I think they're about to land at the ranch house we're heading for." Tom glanced, casually upward. "Unless they're the bad guys out hunting us."

His first prediction proved to be true as they watched. They were still too far away to make out who the people were who got out of them, but their moves weren't suspicious. Sam decided to continue to the compound. "Is there somewhere I can hide this vehicle before we get to the ranch house?" he asked Jenn. "Maybe a barn or something?"

"Sure," she said. "You can't see it from here. It's behind the house. Just swing wide right now, and we can approach it from the other side."

He followed her directions, skirting wide around the back of the ranch house. With luck, the occupants were busy with their company, and not looking out the back, where they might see the plume of dust the Humvee kicked up. Before long, he'd pulled the vehicle into the back door of the barn. It wouldn't stay hidden for long, since Jenn told him there were normally about a dozen horses stalled there, rather than the three she identified as hers, her boss's, and the unfortunate Malcolm's ranch-owned mount. The hands were probably all out doing whatever ranch hands did.

"Well, Jenn. Shall we go let your boss know you're safe?"

Jenn's eyes were troubled. "Yes, of course. I have to find out if my brother is safe as well."

"What are you going to tell him about us?"

"I'll just say you rescued me. What you tell him is up to you. I owe you."

Sam nodded, satisfied. "Then let's do it." He walked beside Jenn out the front door of the barn and up to the house, with Tom following only a step behind. He spared a glance at the three helicopters dominating the front lawn, if it could be called a lawn. They bore the insignia of someone he knew well. This was an interesting turn of events.

As they entered the front door, a Native American man and

woman with striking red hair pulled up in a crisp bun and emerald eyes, looked up at him. The woman wore the sour expression of disgruntlement, as though her time had been needlessly wasted.

Sam spoke as her face betrayed recognition. "Good afternoon, Madam Secretary."

# Chapter Sixty-Six

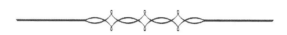

S AM HAD NEVER seen the Secretary of Defense at a loss for words.

Today was no different. She composed her face and answered coolly. "Good afternoon, Sam. I was told I might find you loitering in these parts."

"Really?" It was Sam's turn to be surprised.

"I figured it would take more than half a million tons of rocks to dent that thick head of yours." Her eyes glanced at Tom. "Besides, you were with Tom, so I figured he'd keep you from doing anything too stupid. So, I asked Elise to work out where the lava tube was likely to resurface."

Sam's lips, curled into an incredulous, wry smile. "And her first suggestion was an old cowboy ranch in Colorado?"

"The first one she bothered to bring to me. There was an article in the paper about a report of a cowboy from New York being mysteriously sucked into a sipapu. There was a photo of the man."

"She matched it with the image of the cowboy we'd found in the tunnel on Big Diomede island?"

"Exactly."

Sam glanced at Jenn, waiting silently. "I'm sorry. This is Jenn, she helped guide us out of the tunnel."

The Secretary of Defense shook her hand politely. "Pleased to meet you."

He then turned to the Native American man and offered his hand. "Sam Reilly and this is Tom Bower. You must be the owner?"

"Ben Whitecloud," the man nodded as he took Sam's hand. "Thanks for helping get Jenn out."

Jenn turned to face Ben, as though the words reminded her of something vitally important. "Did Brody get out? Is he safe?"

Ben shook his head. "I'm sorry. We haven't heard from him since we left the sipapu. He must still be out there."

That made Sam think of the riders. "On that note, there were a number of motorcycle riders who attacked us in the tunnel. Some of them got away. I believe they're linked with same group who attacked us on Big Diomede Island."

"Where are they now?" The Secretary of Defense asked.

"I couldn't tell you." Sam spoke truthfully, although he suspected the riders may have regrouped and returned to the train. "Somewhere out there along the mesa most likely."

"All right," she said, with authority.

Sam smiled. "All right, what?"

"Let's go get them."

Sam, Tom and the Secretary headed outside toward the helicopters.

"Tom, you can take the co-pilot's seat in the lead and navigate for the pilot."

"Yes, Ma'am."

The Secretary then looked at Sam. "And you can come with me. There's more I still need to discuss."

Sam followed her into the middle helicopter. Assigned to the elite Army 12th Aviation Battalion, it had been fitted with a rich and luxurious interior, appropriate to the daily commuting needs of the powerhouses from Congress and global dignitaries. While the other two were armed, and ready for war.

The three Black Hawks, filled with Marines, took off in unison. They flew in formation in the direction of the mesa and tunnel leading to the steam train.

The Secretary looked him directly in the eye. "Well? Do you have it?"

"No. I'm afraid the *Gordoye Dostizheniye* was buried under half a mile of rubble."

She stared at him, her eyes questioning him. "You never found it?"

"No. We found it, but the explosion caused a secondary cave in and everything was buried in the process."

"Some things can be dug out."

"Not this."

Through pursed lips, she leaned forward and said, "I told you to protect it with your life."

He shrugged. "Maybe if you'd told me what *it* was I was protecting, I could have removed it earlier?"

"It wouldn't have changed a thing. I just wished you'd done your job." She took a breath. "You'd better pray one of these riders have the answers I'm looking for."

Sam raised his eyebrows. "Aren't you the least bit curious how I turned up three thousand miles from where I entered the ancient lava tube?"

Her response was predictably curt. "No. I just care about the contents of shipping container 404."

# Chapter Sixty-Seven

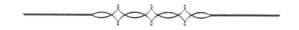

**T**OM DIRECTED THE pilot to follow the tire tracks made by the Humvee.

He said, "Follow this trail for about three clicks. Keep your eyes out for a second one that breaks off and swings north. That's where we came from. Watch for it... we were breaking trail before that, so it won't be as clear."

"Check."

Flight time was a lot less than driving time, and despite the vibrations of the aircraft, a lot more comfortable, too. Tom watched the tracks intently. If they missed the place where the Humvee had crossed the four-wheeler trail, they'd be miles off-course.

He had some time to decide what to do when they got to the mouth of the tunnel where they'd exited. From memory, the motorcycle tracks had been plentiful there, and had led north, in the direction he'd seen the taillights disappear. But how far, and whether the terrain would let them follow, was another question. He'd just have to play it by ear.

The pilot asked, "Do you live around here, Mister–?"

"Tom Bower."

The pilot smiled, recognition in his voice. "I've heard that name. You work for that crazy bastard, Sam Reilly, don't you?"

Tom grinned. "That I do. That's our turn." He pointed ahead, where he could clearly see the Humvee tracks crossing the 4-wheeler trail, then backing up for a three-point turn.

The pilot swung north as directed, and dropped a few feet so they could see the fainter tracks more clearly. He didn't speak again until the Humvee tracks led back into an escarpment.

"You came from there?"

"Inside a cave system, yes. Keep going. We're looking for those." He nodded his head in the direction where multiple motorcycle tracks crisscrossed each other, leaving a more visible mark on the landscape.

"Bad guys on motorcycles?"

"Yeah."

"How many?"

"We don't know."

Five minutes later, they located the riders. Seven of them. Their headlights flickered as they rode straight toward the chopper.

The pilot said, "If they're the bad guys, why are they riding straight toward us?"

"I have no idea." Tom stared at the riders. "Maybe they were expecting to be met by someone else, and are about to be shocked when they see who we are."

He spotted the flashes first.

Then the sound of bullets raking the side of the Black Hawk's tail.

"Shit!" the pilot yelled. He banked away and then climbed. "You didn't tell me they were armed!"

"I told you they were bad guys!" Tom said. "What did you expect?"

The pilot ignored him and circled around, speaking into his headphones he said, "Black Hawk squadron Alpha One. We're taking fire from multiple bogies on the ground. On my lead, commence attack formation Delta Three."

Tom heard the pilots of the trailing helicopters acknowledge the command.

A moment later, the pilot circled inward and dropped the nose.

The UH-60 Black Hawks were equipped with twin M60D machine guns on their M144 Armament Subsystem — one on each side of the helicopter. The pilot lined up the nose with the ground of riders, and depressed the firing button.

And the Gatling-style miniguns began to fire.

At converging angles, the other two helicopters targeted on the riders. Tom felt the vibrations of the twin machine guns working through more than a thousand rounds per minute. The electronically fed ammunition belts whirred, and below them the thick sand was churned into a cloud of dust.

"Stop, stop!" Tom yelled. "The Secretary of Defense wants someone alive."

The pilot took his thumb off the firing trigger. "Alpha One, cease fire."

Tom stared at the decimated ground below and wondered if he'd spoken up too late. Was everyone already dead? Then two riders took off.

The pilot dropped their altitude until they were following from only twenty feet above. The two riders followed the line along the top of the mesa, racing from ledge to ledge like professional stuntmen.

The Black Hawk banked to the right of the riders, the downdraft of its rotary blades forcing the riders closer to the edge of the mesa and its 500-foot drop.

The riders had to lean to their right to stop their bikes being blown off the edge.

About five hundred feet ahead, two dark scars in the mesa suggested another large opening to a cave system. If the riders reached them, it would mean they'd have to go after them on foot—not a good option.

Tom said to the pilot, "Don't let them reach the caves."

"I'm on it."

The pilot increased his speed, and banked into a large circular arc, coming to a hover a few feet off the ground in front of the openings to the caves and facing the riders directly. The two following Black Hawks moved in, with one to the side of the riders and another directly behind.

Red dust and debris rained down on the riders. The one in the lead looked like he'd been momentarily blinded. His bike hit a rock and started to fall toward the helicopter to his side. The Secretary of Defense's pilot—concerned that the rider would be killed—banked to the right and gave him more room.

The instant the helicopter's downdraft disappeared, the rider, no longer having to lean to the right to correct his balance, started to fall. He corrected it quickly, but in the process, he'd overcorrected and a split second later, his bike was heading straight off the mesa.

Tom swallowed as he watched the bike and rider fall into the darkness below.

The remaining rider slowed his motorcycle. He circled around, with his tire spinning heavily in the sandy red soil. Each of the three Black Hawks was now facing him. The rider's helmet darted from each helicopter back to the 500-foot drop behind him, as he searched for an escape.

"I'll be damned," Tom said. "But I think he's seriously contemplating suicide!"

The pilot said, "The Secretary of Defense is going to be pissed."

Tom felt the bile churn in his stomach. He'd already seen her in a bad mood today, the last thing they needed was for this bastard to take his own life.

The rider started to rev his engine. His helmet darting between the helicopter Tom was in and cliff to their right.

"I'm going to have to take him out if he comes at us," the pilot said.

"I know."

A moment later, the rider stopped. He stepped off his bike, letting it fall to the ground next to him and took off his helmet. His hands lifted in the air in surrender.

# Chapter Sixty-Eight

**T**HE PILOT PUT the helicopter down on the mesa.

The other two Black Hawks didn't have any room to land, but Sam and the Secretary of Defense had been hot-dropped and were now making their way along the mesa to meet the rider who'd surrendered. Sam still carried his Kalashnikov and the Secretary was unarmed.

Tom swore. The rider was a trapped animal. His response would be unpredictable. Getting this close to the Secretary, he might just be willing to sacrifice his own life to attack her. Tom turned to the pilot. "Can I borrow your handgun?"

"It's serviced issued. I'm not supposed to lend it to…"

"I get it. You're also not supposed to let your Secretary of Defense get herself killed."

The pilot handed him the pistol.

Tom took it. He glanced at the weapon, a Glock 17. Its box-magazine was full. Being a Glock, there was no safety to remove. "Thanks."

He stepped out of the helicopter. The rotor blades spun slowly in silence above. He ducked and moved toward the rider. Taking a firing position, he aimed the Glock at the rider.

The Secretary spoke loudly. "Don't move!"

The rider placed his hands on his head. "I don't want any trouble. I'll come with you willingly. But you have to promise me that you will protect me from my boss."

"All right." The Secretary smiled as she approached. "We'll protect you, but we're going to need answers."

"What do you want to know?" the rider asked.

"Everything," the Secretary answered.

The man's voice was gentle and relaxed, as though he'd been relieved that it was now all over. "All right..."

A second later the rider fidgeted with his hands.

Tom fired three shots in an instant.

The 9x19 mm parabellum left the barrel at the speed of 1230 feet per second. One nicked the edge of the rider's face, while the other two struck him just above his left eyebrow. The bullets ripped through his skull, rearranging the soft and vulnerable tissue of his cerebellum, before departing in a large exit wound to the back of his head.

The Secretary turned to face him. She didn't need to check the body. It was obvious before the man hit the ground that he was dead.

"Tom Bower!" she snarled. "What the hell did you do that for? Did I not make myself clear that I needed to take one of the riders alive? I need answers, and you just killed my only source. What do you have to say for yourself?"

"You're welcome."

"What did you say?"

Sam bent down and rolled the man over. Still clenched in the rider's right hand was a Russian Makarov pistol. The rider must have had it stored behind his head somehow, and was in the process of drawing the weapon to shoot her.

Tom smiled. "I said, you're welcome, ma'am."

"Thanks, Mr. Bower, for saving my life." The slightest

upward curl formed on the Secretary's lips. Her eyes were defiant. "But I do wish you hadn't quite killed him."

Ten minutes later all three of the Black Hawks were back in the air. They flew west, rising over the escarpment and heading toward the coordinates for the ranch house. As they flew over the broken land, Tom noted a narrow canyon running north and south that looked as though it had been swept clean by a massive river.

"Look at that," he remarked. "Wonder where the water went?"

They flew on. A few minutes later, Tom spotted something in the distance—a man walking along, out in the middle of nowhere. He was limping slightly. As they flew closer, he turned to look at the helicopter, raised his hands in the air and waved them up and down to his sides.

"He's in trouble," the pilot said. "Should we land?"

"I don't see a weapon. Sure, take us down there," Tom answered.

Moments later, they were on the ground. The man faced them. His clothes looked disheveled and his face bore the signs of more than a few days of hardship and suffering.

Tom looked at the man and grinned. "Brody Frost?"

"Yeah. How did you know?"

"There's a woman named Jenn who's worried sick about you."

# Chapter Sixty-Nine

S AM AND TOM rejected the Secretary's offer to fly them to a major airport, telling her that Ben Whitecloud had graciously offered them a meal and a place to sleep for the night. They were in need of a rest and the old ranch seemed like as good a place as any to achieve it.

As they pulled out their bedrolls, Tom looked at Sam. "What a day."

"Yeah."

Tom grinned. "I told you the Secretary would be pissed about the stone."

Sam nodded. "You want to read the note again to ease your conscious for lying to her?"

He pulled out the note and read it again.

> *If you want the human race to survive, you need to convince the Secretary of Defense that this container was empty. The Death Stone needs to be removed in secret and examined by an Astronomer who has no connection with the U.S. Government. He or she will be able to work out what the stone means and what needs to be done.*
>
> *THEY are watching the Secretary of Defense.*

*What she did twenty years ago must be kept secret if you want her to live.*

*If you want anyone to live, you need to look to the stone for guidance. It has all the answers. Particularly the greatest one of all, for which THEY have killed to hide — how to save the human race from extinction.*

"All right," Tom said. "We continue with the plan."

Over the course of the next two days Elise found them a retired professor of astronomy. The man, Douglas Capel, had once led the astrophysical research team at Mount Graham International Observatory, the largest land-based telescope in the states. He'd once gone up against Congress over the Strategic Defense Initiative known as Star Wars, during the Reagan administration — arguing that space should not be militarized, which suggested he couldn't be bought by the government. He was retired, and as far as Elise could tell, had never received any government grants for his own research projects. Upon retiring, Capel had remained in Arizona, where he could still visit his precious observatory.

Sam contacted Capel, and the man had agreed to examine the stone. Over the course of the next two nights he and Tom drove the Humvee and the Death Stone the eleven-hour trip to Arizona, keeping off the well-traveled roads, by traveling via the backroads of several Indian reservations.

A total of five days after leaving the steam train behind on Cloud Ranch, Sam finally handed over the Death Stone and the note left by the dying man on board the *Gordoye Dostizheniye*. Capel was an older man of approximately seventy-five, with a warm and gregarious smile, and the unkempt, casual appearance of a man who knew that it was his intellect that people required, and his appearance made no difference. Despite his age, the man had clearly maintained a sharp edge, keeping up with the progress of the highly digital age.

Sam gave him money to hire a laboratory room at the

University of Arizona and hundreds of hours on the submillimeter telescope and main binocular telescope at the MGIO site. The man warned him it might take months to have definitive answers, but he was confident he would find them.

They left Capel delighted to have a new project to work on and caught a commercial flight to Anchorage, Alaska, where the Maria Helena was refueling and taking on additional supplies. Back on board the Maria Helena, Sam set Elise the task of finding where the railway system they'd dubbed the Aleutian Portal eventually came out upon the Siberian Peninsula side of the Bering Strait.

Matthew walked into Elise's office, took one glance at Sam's hardened expression, fixed over the multiple array of computer screens displaying old railway trains, and said, "I guess the Queen Elizabeth Islands and polar ice caps are going to have to wait?"

Sam said, "Afraid so. Something's come up." He then turned to Elise. "The driver we met in the tunnel made a comment about his master owning the train before they'd discovered the Aleutian portal. Any chance we could find the train and the owner?"

"Sure. Do you have a photo of the train?"

"Yeah." He took out his smartphone and emailed her a few photos. "The lighting's pretty bad, but you can still make out the main shapes and there's an image of the detailed coachwork inside what appeared to be the owner's cabin."

"Okay, let's see what we can do with it."

Elise opened the image Sam had emailed her of the front of the steam train they'd crossed the Aleutian Portal in. It could have been any late nineteenth century steam train, but then again, the carriages were clearly built for royalty.

She copied the image and set the search engine finding any matching shapes. These days the internet had so many images it could take days to scroll through all of them. Google came up with no precise matches, but her Boolean search on her own search engine that entered the Dark Net, returned one single article.

On the first page of the article, was a single red railway steam engine. Sam said, "That's it!"

The article was written in Russian.

Sam said. "Can your computer translate that for us?"

Elise shook her head. "Only the basics. It's nowhere near accurate enough to translate the oddities and nuances of the Russian language."

"All right. I'll go find Genevieve."

He returned a couple minutes later with Genevieve and Tom.

Genevieve read the article, translating it to English as she went. "The train was originally made for Prince Aleksandr Baryatinsky in 1872. There's little information about what the train was used for over the course of the next hundred years. There's a side note that it was used during the Great War to mobilize people and armaments to the Eastern Front and the latter, during World War II it was used to cart prisoners to the Gulag camps in Siberia."

"Anything more recent?" Sam asked.

"In 1992 a wealthy businessman named Leo Botkin purchased the train and spent a fortune returning her to her former glory. Like many of the other oligarchs, his rapid accumulation of wealth occurred during the era of Russian privatization in the aftermath of the dissolution of the Soviet Union in the 1990s. He went on to become one of the richest men in Russia."

"What did he do?"

"Not much by the looks of things. He owns real estate around the world and enough shares to command voting rights in some of the world's biggest companies. He was one of the most powerful men in Russia until the early 2000s."

"What happened then?" Sam asked.

"Nothing. There's no note about his death. Instead it looks like he simply went into hiding, although from what, I can't say. He owns a castle in the outskirts of Moscow, but hasn't been seen there for nearly twenty years."

"What about his train?"

Genevieve shrugged. "It says the train hasn't been seen in Moscow for twenty years, but there's stories of mysterious sightings throughout the Siberian Peninsula. But none of those can be confirmed. They're mostly local people who have spoken about a mysterious steam train, with heavy smoke billowing from its boiler, seen making its way across the country tracks."

Sam stared at the image of the train. It was definitely the same one. His eyes then fixed on the image of Leo Botkin. This was the man who had answers. Find him, and we'll find out the secret to the Aleutian portal and why a gang of arms and drug traffickers were so focused on stealing the Death Stone.

# Chapter Seventy

*Washington, DC*

I T HAD BEEN almost twenty years since she'd seen Leo Botkin.

Today they met at the West Potomac Park, overlooking the Jefferson Memorial. Japanese cherry trees lined the water, their foliage long past their April bloom. She chose the location, but the mere fact he accepted such a conspicuous meeting place in Washington showed how confident he'd become. People would almost certainly recognize him, but they too would be in his pocket.

He approached the park bench she'd been sitting on and pretended to admire the Jefferson Memorial.

"Madam Secretary," he turned to face her. "May I please share this seat with you?"

"No, you may not." Her voice was firm and pugnacious. "You can remain standing. I don't intend to keep you here any longer than I have to."

"As you wish, Margaret."

It had been a long time since he'd called her that, too. She was surprised to see that the years had been so kind to him. Time had done little to diminish his intelligent good looks. Over his intense blue eyes, he now wore glasses, but they seemed only to add to his allure. His hair now showed minor graying around the sides, but had maintained its thickness from his youth. The arrogance was still there, too.

"So, the colony's hiring mercenaries now, are they?"

"A necessary precaution, I'm afraid." Botkin shrugged. "We are dealing with the ending of the world. It would be foolish to think those who weren't invited would simply stay out of our way."

She ignored his narcissistic response. "New evidence suggests the Death Stone might hold the solution to the extinction of the human race."

"We already have the solution."

Her piercing green eyes focused on the monument ahead, and she wondered what Jefferson would think if he saw the great leaders of today. "One that doesn't involve the death of all but a handful of the elite."

He shrugged. "The Death Stone's already been destroyed. You made sure of that twenty years ago, didn't you?"

"You know damned well I never went through with it!" Her jaw was set hard, and her voice full of accusation as she spoke.

"Really?" She could hear the contempt in his voice. "You don't say?"

"Instead I chose to have it stored away, hidden in a secret vault in the barren Siberian Peninsula. When Sam Reilly told me about a megalithic stone once found in Göbekli Tepe depicting a future comet that was predicted to end the human race, I put it all together. I ordered Ryan Balmain to return the stone so it can be properly examined." She smiled. "That's why you sent your pack of wild dogs to come after it once the *Gordoye Dostizheniye* sunk."

"And now its buried under a mountain of stone debris." He spoke with the indifference of a man who'd lost at a social game of cards. "Margaret. The colony has never forgotten what you've done for us. There will always be a place inside for you when the time comes. Why don't you simply accept fate, and return to us?"

"I said it twenty years ago, and I'll say it again now. I have no interest joining the last survivors of the human race. What possible benefit would I offer in the new world? All I know how to do is conduct war. I pray that if the human race does get a second chance, the first thing the survivors do isn't prepare for war."

"So, you're not with us?"

"If the Master Builders knew about this cataclysmic event and had a solution, I'm willing to bet we'll find the solution."

"The Master Builders are dead. They died out more than a thousand years ago. Poor genetics, you see. They lived long lives, but it was a double-edged sword. The genetic trait that allowed them to live extraordinary long lives, rendered them close to infertile."

"And yet there are some descendants who have made it." She gritted her teeth. "When we find them, we'll solve this puzzle, with or without the Death Stone to guide us."

"The colony put you where you are today, and we can take it from you."

"Don't you dare threaten me. This is Washington D.C. You might have helped put me here, but I've made damned certain no one gets to throw me out. I made a mistake twenty years ago. But I'm sure as hell going to do my best to rectify it."

"Then why did you even bother to bring me here today?"

She smiled, as though she was taking pleasure in his reaction. "Because I wanted to tell you in person that you've lost."

"I'm sorry, but with the exception of many of my handpicked friends and specialists, the human race is about to become extinct." His voice was charming in its perversity. "So, you must be somewhat more explicit when you tell me that I've lost."

"You're right. How very remiss of me. Although I'm not

usually one to gloat, with you I'll make an exception. I fired your puppet and my Deputy today. Sam Reilly discovered the Aleutian Portal, and your arms and drug trafficking system just became a whole lot harder."

He turned to face her. A curious and wry expression on his lips, as though it weren't particularly concerning for him. He had control over more than a dozen global enterprises, so the loss of the secret tunnel wasn't going to faze him.

Botkin laughed. "I never really liked your Deputy anyway. Some people just aren't worth the effort. You on the other hand. You the colony would be willing to make sacrifice for."

He was egging her on.

"Oh, one more thing."

"Yes?"

"When my people were combing the surveillance footage of the attack on the Big Diomede Island, you'd never guess whose face came up."

"Go on."

"Your golden-haired man, Ilya Yezhov."

Botkin shrugged. "What about him?"

"I just thought I'd mention that every one of your men were killed inside the Aleutian Portal."

She watched his face pale. Botkin was the king of the world right now. A leader and master in the shadows that few realized even existed. A puppet-master, who controlled the greatest leaders on the planet.

There had been predictions about a future where the world was governed by one system. A type of one-world leadership. What most people didn't realize was that Leo Botkin had already formed that system, by putting his own people in positions of power in countries throughout the world. He had no desire to lose that power. But the colony would be different. There, money no longer mattered. Power had to be wrested from others through sheer might. Ilya Yezhov, she expected, was supposed to be that might. His most loyal servant, and most dangerous of men.

His turned to face her. "I believe we're done, here. I promise you this is the last time you will ever see me."

The Secretary watched him leave. Her eyes returning to the Jefferson Memorial. She had no doubt she'd see him in hell, sooner or later.

# Chapter Seventy-One

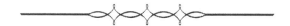

*On-board the Maria Helena — Anchorage, Alaska*

S AM PICKED UP his cell phone on the third ring.

"Hello, Mr. Reilly?" It was Douglas Capel, the astronomer who he'd left the Death Stone with.

"Yes, speaking." Sam took a breath in and held it. "Mr. Capel, did you make any progress with the stone?"

"Yes. I found your asteroid."

"Really? That was quick." Sam swallowed. "What did you find?"

"I have some good news for you. The asteroid going to get close, but no matter what model of trajectory I put into the simulator, the thing's going to miss Earth. It's a narrow gap, but a gap nonetheless."

"Are you certain?"

"Yes, I'm certain. I've spent my life studying astronomy. I've led the knowledge base on the topic for nearly forty years. So yes, I'm damned certain of my math."

"All right. Thank you so much for this good news."

Capel said, "There's one more thing you're gonna want to know about."

"Shoot."

"We ran the stone through an MRI machine."

"And?"

"There's four secret chambers inside."

"Are the chambers empty?"

"No." Sam could hear the man sighing on over the phone. "I didn't want to open them until you're here, but I have an image of each stone that was found inside — and given the suspected age of the Death Stone, it's creepy as all shit."

"Really. What's the image?"

"There's four separate ones, actually."

"Of what?"

"I won't know for certain until the mortar has been cracked and the ancient stones removed."

"But?"

"We used ground penetrating ultrasound, it appears to be the Four Horsemen of the Apocalypse. Beneath which, there are letters of the Greek alphabet — *Thita, Sigma, Phi,* and *Omega.*"

"All right. Can you email me those images, please?"

"Yes, of course."

"Thanks for everything." Sam paused. "Just one more thing."

"Go for it."

"Can you tell me when the asteroid will come close to earth?"

"Not specifically. Only a rough date range."

"And?"

"Soon."

"How soon?" Sam persisted.

"Within our current calendar year."

Sam swallowed. "Do you have any idea what sort of effect it might have on earth as it passes by?"

"Well, I'd have to speak with some of my colleagues, but

depending on the size of the asteroid, its magnetic pull could wreak havoc."

"How so?" Sam asked.

"Best case scenario, tides will become more volatile." Capel clicked his lips as though he was trying to calculate the cost of a burger or something trivial. "Worst case though, the magnetic poles might rapidly and catastrophically flip. My goodness, if that were to happen, there would be massive subsequent shifts in earth's tectonic plates. Volcanoes would erupt, the ocean's thermohaline circulation would change direction, most likely resulting in an ice-age. Something like that, I doubt very much the human race would survive."

# Chapter Seventy-Two

S AM ENDED THE phone call and immediately dialed another.

He spoke as soon as the phone was answered. "Billie. I need your help."

"I'm doing fine, Sam, thanks for asking," she said, speaking with the dedicated hard-ass bitchiness Sam had come to expect from his conversations with her over the years.

"What?"

"In case you forgot, I spent nearly two years drugged and enslaved to an ancient race. But I'm doing fine, despite not even getting a phone call since I was let out of hospital."

"I've been busy." The excuse sounded weak, even to himself. "Besides, did you want to talk to me?"

"No, not really." Billie asked directly, "What do you want Sam?"

"I'm going to forward you an image of something…"

"And?"

"I need you to tell me if you saw it in the pyramid inside the Amazon jungle."

"Didn't you hear? I can't remember a thing from my experience in the Amazon."

"I know. But the neurologist said there was a chance that certain things, important things, might still be buried somewhere deep in your subconscious."

"Whatever. Just send the image."

Sam added the image to his cell phone message, without any words, and clicked send.

A moment later, he heard Billie's cell make the customary beeping sound associated with a new message. He heard her open the message up.

And then she swore.

"What is it?" Sam asked.

"I have to go back."

"Where?"

"To the pyramid in the Amazon, of course!"

"Why?"

"Because I've seen that image before! It was at the pyramid. What's more, I don't think Elise was the only person responsible for getting me out of the jungle. I think it was them — the Master Builders — they wanted to release me."

"Why?"

"So that I could come back and complete my part in the prophecy."

# Chapter Seventy-Three

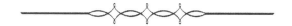

*Volcanic Dome, Inside the Aleutian Portal*

LYA YEZHOV WAITED in complete darkness. He was lying down, trying to conserve his energy. His head rested on the now unusable railway track inside the great volcanic dome. A week ago, he'd nearly lost his life fighting three crazy men in a Hummer. He was pretty certain he killed one of them, while the other two got away, but not before first destroying his motorcycle.

His flashlight had become flooded and it had taken him an entire day to wade through the warm, shallow waters of the Cathedral Grotto, to reach the volcanic dome in total darkness. By the time he had, Botkin's stupid old steam train had already left. Judging by the two dead guards he felt with his hands — both carrying old Soviet issued machine guns — he could only imagine that the two men in the Humvee had taken the train.

Confronted by the choice of waiting or attempting to walk over three thousand miles through the underground tunnel without food or water, he'd decided to wait. He was certain they would come for him.

Now, a week later, he regretted that decision. But what choice had he had? Even if he'd made the three-thousand-mile underground journey in the dark, then what? He would have climbed out of the Aleutian portal into the Colorado desert, still without food or water.

No. He'd made the only decision available to him.

The railway beneath his head vibrated. It was fine, but after a week in total darkness and seclusion the change was instantly noticeable.

He stood up. His eyes fixated on the darkness toward the east. There was still a possibility the distant vibrations originated from the return of the steam train. If that was the case, there was always the risk that on it would be a specialist force from the FBI or CIA's drug and weapons trafficking department.

Turning to the west, his heart began to race. One way or another, his life was about to change. He had a fifty-fifty chance who was coming for him. If they came from the east, he was going to prison, if they came from the west, he was going to be king.

Nothing changed.

He placed his hand tentatively on the cold, hard, steel of the old railway track. The distant vibrations were gone. Had he imagined the entire thing? There was always that possibility, as he became more and more starved. Had his blood sugar fallen so dramatically he was now starting to hallucinate?

Turning around, he searched for answers. In the total darkness he switched from east to west and back again more times than he could remember. Now he had no idea whether he was facing east or west.

He gripped the handle of his Kalashnikov for comfort. Then, up ahead, in front of him — he spotted a light. At first just a faint glow, but gradually it became brighter.

The question was, which way was he now facing?

His finger rested firmly on the trigger and held his breath. The light increased and started to flicker in ripples. He expelled his breath in a silent wave of relief, as he watched the miniature submarine surface above the railway tracks. He moved closer to meet it.

The main hatch opened. A man looked at him, his eyes scrutinizing him, as though judging what could possibly make him so valuable to Leo Botkin.

"Ilya Yezhov?"

"Yes?"

"Climb in. It's time. There's a lot of work to be done."

## The End

*Want more?*

Join my email list and get a FREE and EXCLUSIVE Sam Reilly story that's not available anywhere else!

**Join here** ~ www.bit.ly/ChristopherCartwright

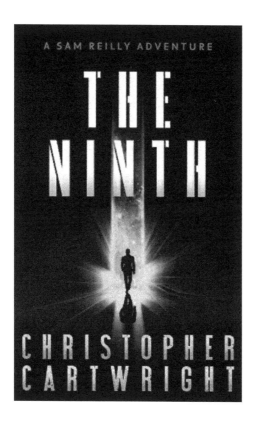

F
CAR
SR#8

**10178962**

**Cartwright, Christopher,**
**The aleutian portal**

43471071R00181

Made in the USA
Lexington, KY
28 June 2019